LYING TOGETHER

D. M. Thomas is the author of seven previous novels, a memoir, and six collections of poetry. He has translated works by Akhmatova, Pushkin, Yevtushenko, and other poets. He lives in England, where he conducts writing workshops and apprenticeships.

L·Y·I·N·G
T·O·G·E·T·H·E·R

D. M. Thomas

PENGUIN BOOKS

PENGUIN BOOKS
Published by the Penguin Group
Viking Penguin, a division of Penguin Books USA Inc.,
375 Hudson Street, New York, New York 10014, U.S.A.
Penguin Books Ltd, 27 Wrights Lane,
London W8 5TZ, England
Penguin Books Australia Ltd, Ringwood,
Victoria, Australia
Penguin Books Canada Ltd, 2801 John Street,
Markham, Ontario, Canada L3R 1B4
Penguin Books (N.Z.) Ltd, 182–190 Wairau Road,
Auckland 10, New Zealand

Penguin Books Ltd, Registered Offices:
Harmondsworth, Middlesex, England

First published in the United States of America by
Viking Penguin, a division of Penguin Books USA Inc., 1990
Published in Penguin Books 1991

1   3   5   7   9   10   8   6   4   2

PUBLISHER'S NOTE
This is a work of fiction. Names, characters, places, and incidents either are the
product of the author's imagination or are used fictitiously, and any resemblance to
actual persons, living or dead, events, or locales is entirely coincidental.

THE LIBRARY OF CONGRESS HAS CATALOGUED THE HARDCOVER AS FOLLOWS:
Thomas, D. M.
Lying together / D. M. Thomas
p.   cm.
ISBN 0-670-83218-9 (hc.)
ISBN 0 14 01.3284 8 (pbk.)
I. Title
PR6070.H58L9   1990
823'.914—dc20   89–40670

Printed in the United States of America

· AUTHOR'S NOTE ·

Lying Together concludes a quintet, *Russian Nights*. The preceding novels are *Ararat* (1983), *Swallow* (1984), *Sphinx* (1986) and *Summit* (1987).

Quotations from Russian poetry are in the author's translation. The Quintet is in homage to Alexander Pushkin.

I wish to thank Andrew and Margaret Hewson, my literary agents, for their unfailing support and their honest and constructive criticism throughout the writing of this sequence; and also Sylvia Kantaris, who read *Lying Together* while it was in progress and offered excellent suggestions. I am grateful to my editors at Viking Penguin, New York, and Victor Gollancz Ltd., London, Amanda Vaill and Joanna Goldsworthy, for their patience and understanding as I kept changing my mind about whether the work was finished. I should have realised that an author does not decide this; the work itself decides, by suddenly letting go—as it has now done.

Finally, now that glasnost has arrived, I am happy to acknowledge the collaborative assistance throughout of my Soviet friends Sergei Rozanov, Victor Surkov and Masha Barash. I extend greetings to them and all the authors present at the 1988 Writers Internationale in London, where this novel was conceived.

L·Y·I·N·G T·O·G·E·T·H·E·R

· I ·

I slipped a bookmark into *Psychological Correspondences*. Paddington Station: it always creates a disturbance in me. It's the point where home and the great world intersect. I remember the tired yet excited feeling when, as a youth studying Russian at Cambridge during my military service, I escaped on occasional weekends, taking the train to King's Cross, and then the tube to Paddington. The midnight train to Cornwall, silently waiting.

But on this day, an unusually cloudless Sunday late in October, I had travelled *from* Cornwall; the train was two hours late, and I rushed, humping my case, past the mute crowds gazing up at the information board, towards the taxi rank. There was a long queue; before me, an Asian couple stood with a trolley piled ludicrously with shabby luggage. I lit a cigarette. Three cigarettes later, the Asians had struggled aboard and I was directing a cabbie to the Hyde Park Regis.

I kept looking at my watch as we drew through twilit streets. I was late for the reception. I didn't know why I'd agreed to attend this Festival. The invitation had arrived only three weeks ago; clearly I was an afterthought. Well, yes, I did know; it was because my Russian friends would be there. And I had unfinished business with Masha.

I hate hotels where a uniformed porter leaps to open your door and grab your luggage. It signals an affluence I can't live up to. The lobby opened onto a bar-area where men in dark suits and ladies in cocktail dresses sipped before-dinner drinks. They took this luxury in their stride. I wanted to spring an automatic rifle from my case and fire off a few shots, making them shriek and cower. You could say it is envy, and indeed that is partly true. And I won't pretend that a factor in one's accepting such an invitation is not the thought of spending a week in a grand hotel. On this occasion, as an added piquancy, the Festival promised to have a distinctly radical flavour.

I signed in; took the lift with a bored porter to my room, which was twin-bedded, overlooking the park. I declined to tip the porter, who left with a surly expression. I splashed water over my face, slicked unruly grey hair into a more reasonable disorder, and headed down to the lobby again.

Following a sign saying 'Writers Internationale, Queen Mary Suite', I mounted broad marble stairs. To the right, open double-doors hinted at shadowy figures. Entering, I took a glass of white wine from an offered tray, and found for myself a space near a table laden with an unappetising buffet. My heart sank as I looked around. It wasn't a welcoming scene.

I couldn't spot my Russian friends, nor any writer whom I recognised. That wasn't surprising, given the denseness of the throng. What was dismaying, however, was the sedateness of the gathering, the low voices, the dark suits and ties (I was conscious of standing out in my baggy white suit and light-blue open-necked shirt), and above all the absence of women. I could spot only four or five, grey-haired and staid-looking, dressed in muted, somewhat old-fashioned, frocks. Surkov, I thought, would be particularly devastated by the absence of nubile young women.

This was like no gathering of writers I had ever attended. By now, with the reception well under way, there should have been a roar of tipsy conversation and laughter. There should be men in dinner jackets and others in stained gardening-clothes; women gaudy as parakeets and others indistinguishable from the men. I pushed into the polite ranks, with no improvement. Okay, Bellow, I knew, was not due to arrive till the end of the week; but where the hell were Márquez, Lessing, Gordimer? And where were my friends from Moscow? Either their flight had been delayed, or they had taken one look at this sober crew and retired aghast.

Then I spotted Rozanov, leather-jacketed in a huddle of dark suits and tight white collars. His appearance shocked me. I had seen newspaper photos of him since his release from the *psikhushka*, but they hadn't prepared me for his gauntness, pallor, baldness. I rushed up. His eyes glassy with boredom, he greeted me like a drowning man clutching at a lifebelt. He had only just arrived; hadn't even booked in. He didn't know where Victor and Masha were; they had separated at Heathrow, some Amnesty guys had taken him off for a boozy lunch.

Our greetings over, he introduced me to the hovering writers. 'This is Brown. And this is Bramble—'

'—Bromley,' corrected the flabby-faced elderly Englishman.

'And I'm John Davenport,' said the third tight-white-collar, offering his hand.

'We were just saying,' murmured Bromley, 'that we didn't expect any foreigners here.'

'And I was saying,' Rozanov growled, 'I expected it will be truly international.'

'Well, it's very good,' Davenport murmured. 'These affairs can be dull. Useful, of course, but dull. It will be wonderful to have some Russians.'

Brown, thirtyish yet elderly: 'One can always learn from how it's done elsewhere.'

'That's right,' agreed Bromley. 'I don't suppose the changes we hear about in your country, what's it called, this gas—'

'Glasnost?' Rozanov offered.

'Yes. I don't suppose it's made much difference to you—in our line of business?'

His voice trembling with anger at the English writer's ignorance, Rozanov said, 'It's making a huge difference. At last I can work in relative freedom.'

'Gosh! You mean you couldn't before? But you didn't suffer any restrictions, did you?'

'I spent two years in a *psikhushka*,' he replied curtly. 'A madhouse punishment block. To stop me to work.'

'How ghastly!' Brown exclaimed.

I saw one of the dowdy ladies gliding up; she touched his arm, and he turned. On close inspection her rather stern, dark-complexioned face was striking. The patterning of fine wrinkles reminded me of an aerial photo of Easter Island. Her black eyes, penetrating still, must once have been beautiful. 'Aren't you Sergei Rozanov?' she enquired in a soft, diffident voice.

'That's right.'

'I'm so glad to meet you! I recognised you from your photographs. It was terrible, what happened to you. I'm Maria Sanchez, from Bolivia.'

'Delighted to meet you!'

Her eyes turned politely towards me. 'I'm Don Thomas,' I said. Her handshake was warm and firm. It was a relief to meet a genuine writer, a woman whose face was etched with a record of suffering and sensibility. Those eyes still burned with a reflection of the fires of youth. From Rozanov's expression, it was clear he felt the same. Brown, Bromley and Davenport introduced themselves.

'I feel rather lost,' she said. 'It's my first time in England, my English is not good, and I don't know anyone.'

'We're in the same ship,' Rozanov said. 'It's my first time in England also.'

'Well! It's certainly much more international than we expected,' said Bromley. 'Are you particularly interested in any of the topics?' He glanced from Russian to Bolivian.

Rozanov said he didn't know what they were. With a shy smile the elderly Bolivian lady, prompting him, said, 'Shamanism?'

It was well known—except apparently to Bromley, Brown and Davenport, who looked hopelessly puzzled—that Rozanov had survived his ordeal in a *psikhushka* partly by developing shamanistic powers. Shamanism, he explained patiently for the three idiot Brits, was a primitive practice of self-denial so that one could travel in the land of the dead and return unscathed. But he rather doubted, he said, glancing around mordantly, that shamanistic powers would be of any interest to such a gathering.

'I'm sure you're wrong,' said the elderly woman fervently.

'It would be fascinating,' I said, and the others nodded.

'Well, yes,' the Russian murmured, 'it certainly should be— what's the word?—relevant. After all, as Pasternak said, we are people who meditate upon death and thereby create new life.'

Bromley considered this, frowning, sipping orange juice. 'I've always thought our most important job is to comfort the bereaved.'

Brown nodded. 'The journey to the cemetery. It can be depressing or consoling; and that's largely up to us.' Rozanov's false teeth—he had lost all his natural ones in the *psikhushka*—flashed in appreciation of the metaphor. Brown continued: 'I imagine cremation is obligatory in your country?'

Rozanov said he didn't understand. Taken aback myself, I was about to translate for him, but Brown added in explanation: 'The burning of corpses is—essential—in Russia.'

Rozanov's puzzlement cleared; fervently he replied, 'Ah, yes! You're dead right! And there are many, many corpses to burn.'

'There must be. It's a vast country.'

The Bolivian poet excused herself, vanishing in the direction of the toilets. Davenport spoke of the paper he was to read, on the New Cosmetics. Doubtless, I thought, it would be a defence of solid workmanship in the novel rather than gimmickry and flashiness.

'Nowadays,' observed Bromley, 'one can make a corpse look almost alive.'

Bromley would be one of those writers who produce corpses. 'Realistic' novels, full of fine and lifeless observations. You could tell it just by looking at his flabby features. And so would Brown who, busy demolishing a sausage roll, observed through flaky lips: 'But it's not necessarily what the relatives want.'

Rozanov frowned again at this incomprehensible remark. At that moment Maria Sanchez, her face embarrassed and alarmed, glided up to us and asked if she could have a word in private. We excused ourselves. I guessed what she was going to say before she opened her mouth. We beat a retreat from the Queen Victoria Suite and climbed the stairs towards the second floor. A comforting hum of loud conversation descended to meet us. As we climbed, I asked after Rozanov's wife, Sonia, and Sasha his son. They were fine. Sasha had played a draw with Kasparov, and was centre-forward for the Dynamo Komsomol team.

'That's amazing, Sergei!' I remembered the pale, shy little boy. And I remembered Nina, his mother, with her long straight blonde hair. But all things change.

We pushed into the peacock-coloured gathering, deafened by the babble in various languages. There was Sontag, Márquez. . . . Everyone seemed to have found an old friend to talk to. Maria Sanchez, with a nod and a pleasant smile, took her leave of us. We accepted drinks.

I saw Masha gliding through towards us: that unmistakable froth of brown hair, the exuberant, doll-like face; and behind her, over-topping her, the bleak, dark face of Victor Surkov, his hair not grey as it had been when we last met, some six years ago, but a brilliant yellow, spreading down over his shoulders. I barely had time to notice that Masha was wearing Circassian trousers before she was in my arms, kissing my cheeks; and Surkov was pumping my hand warmly. My brain adjusted slowly to the Russian language and to Victor's hair. 'Where have you been?' Masha asked. We explained about the conference of funeral directors, and Surkov, glancing around, said we might well find this crew equally tedious. I told him I liked his hair.

He grinned. 'It makes me look young, huh?'

'Incredibly young!'

'Well, I'm fifty-six next month. No, my God!—fifty-seven. It's awful.'

'And I've reached the grim forties,' said Masha, pouting her lush red lips.

'I can't believe it, Masha! You never seem to look any older! You're exactly as you were on the day we met!'

That frigid November of '81—or was it '82?—warmed by the smile and energy of my Intourist guide, Comrade Barash. Who proved to be not merely a lively guide but a brilliant physicist and a secret poet. Those nights of passionate improvisation, after she'd introduced me to her two friends from Peredelkino, the writers' village. It was almost literally true that she looked no older. Yet straightway I knew that something had changed, since that distant Moscow meeting and our encounter three years ago in Switzerland: for some reason I no longer felt desire stirring for her. It could not be just the billowing Circassian trousers, though it is true I find trousers on women an anaphrodisiac.

'*You* look older, my friend,' Surkov said, fixing me with a compassionate gaze.

'I feel older,' I confessed.

'Victor's had some wonderful news!' said Masha. 'Show them the letter!'

His face glowing with pride, Surkov extracted an already creased letter from a trouser pocket. 'My American agent,

Dave Abramsohn, dropped in. He's in London doing some talent-spotting. He gave me this.' Sergei and I read the letter together.

> Dear Comrade Surkov, You are warmly invited to do me the honor of attending my forthcoming Inauguration in Washington, D.C., on 20 January 1989, as 41st President of the United States, and to read your famous poem of international accord, *Friendship*. Cordially yours, Michael Dukakis.

'That's wonderful!' said Rozanov.

'It is!' I agreed. 'The only problem is that Bush is sure to win.'

Surkov shook his head. 'Dave has inside information. He's on Dukakis's team, and knows the confidential polls. Dukakis will be elected. I shall be the first writer at an Inaugural since Frost at John Kennedy's. It honours all Soviet writers, of course, not me personally.'

The noise was stilled as a voice came over a loudspeaker. It belonged to an editor from the *Guardian*, the main sponsor of Writers Internationale. He welcomed all the authors, promised a splendid week. Then he announced the winner of the Lloyd George Memorial Prize, an annual award for the best novel by a handicapped person. For the first time, he said, the winner was a mentally handicapped person. There was loud applause as the young man was led up to receive his award.

Then we were requested to assemble in the lobby, ready to be taken to the Riverside Theatre for the opening public event. We joined the surge out through the doors and down the marble stairs. We were driven through dark and quiet Sunday streets. Pressed against Masha's raincoated buxomness, I wondered at how unaccountably desire had all but vanished—though I had dreamed often of our reunion.

The coach drew in outside the Thameside theatre and disgorged us. We were late; only a few stragglers, eyeing us curiously, queued at the box office.

The auditorium was comfortably full, and predominantly female. The chattering hushed as we filed into the front rows, which allowed easy access to the stage. Tonight was a free-for-all on the topic Woman and Writing. As it got under way, it began to develop (understandably, I felt) into a tirade in favour of abortion. Author after author denounced Bush, the likely (except to Surkov and his agent) President of the United States, who disapproved of abortion. Stalking onto the stage with the proud air of a Red Indian chief, Surkov was the only dissenting speaker. 'I didn't come a thousand miles,' he muttered into the microphone, 'to kill babies, or to support their killing. I came to talk about literature, and to hear some good readings. I don't like killing even a fly, so I sure as hell don't like killing babies. It's a very difficult moral question, and it does no good to talk as if it was a simple black-and-white issue.'

The response was coldly polite. Though disagreeing with the line he had taken, I patted him on the back when he sat down. It had been courageous. An author sitting off to our right, a man in black tie, grey suit and polished black shoes, stalked up to the microphone and said, 'John Holcraft, Guildford. I'm puzzled. There are no funerals for aborted fetuses.' He stepped down. The laconic demolition of the Russian's argument was rapturously applauded. A novelist from Ghana stood up and demanded to know why Surkov had used the expression 'black-and-white'.

We were driven back through the nearly empty streets. There was little conversation.

The writers ate a late dinner at three separate, long tables in the hotel dining-room; the Russians and I conversed among ourselves, feeling vaguely ostracised. It didn't surprise me that the other four male English writers who had been invited had changed their minds and stayed away. I regretted their absence. Not that, probably, I would have found much in common with Kington Aimes, the humorous novelist, or Douglas Parkin, the Northern poet, or the two left-wing critics, but the dearth of English tones left me feeling even more culturally isolated than usual. Holcraft, having discovered his mistake while chatting to Sontag during the ride back to the hotel, had hurried off to find the other funeral directors. I resolved to cling to my Soviet friends, as if this were Moscow or Leningrad; my rusty Russian soon became relatively fluent again, helped by alcohol. Afterwards we grabbed a few bottles and headed for my room.

With still more glasses of Beaujolais in them, my friends became animated. We weren't going to get much literature at this Festival, it seemed, so let's show the bastards. Let's improvise something, as we'd done on those remarkable nights, six years ago. Let's celebrate our reunion appropriately.

'Could it work again?' I asked. It was a long time. I had tried since, alone and with others, and I'd been tongue-tied.

I hadn't been tongue-tied in Switzerland, with Masha, Rozanov pointed out. I needed them; and they, me. For some reason we sparked each other off.

'Okay, we can see how it goes.'

'Excellent!'

'Shall we tell him?' Surkov asked, glancing at his comrades. They looked uncertain; I said, 'Tell me what?'

'We've decided to reveal our part in the sequence. There's no reason to disguise it anymore, now that glasnost is upon us. The truth can come out at last.' He plucked some grapes from my complimentary fruit-bowl.

'We'd like our friends to know we weren't entirely inactive these past few years,' said Masha with a smile. 'Are you pleased?'

Actually I felt acutely alarmed. I tried to show pleasure at their decision and at the same time annoyance that our contract simply wouldn't permit it. I felt grateful to my publishers for their insistence that we guard against any change of mind by my secret collaborators—unlikely as that had seemed in the frigid era of Brezhnev.

'The contract is that strict?' Rozanov enquired.

'I'm afraid so.'

Surkov gave a shrug. 'Well, we tried.'

It didn't matter, Masha said. They had done it for the joy of creating, without having to look over their shoulder at the censor. Well, and also for a little foreign currency, which would be handy this week. It had been very worthwhile.

Her comrades nodded agreement and my alarm subsided. We each of us scribbled a theme on a piece of hotel notepaper—I wrote down, rather predictably, Glasnost. Lacking a porcelain vase—the womblike container used in Pushkin's *Egyptian Nights*, our major inspiration—we dropped the crunched-up papers into a glass. Masha, shutting her eyes, drew one out and unfolded it. '*Lying Together*,' she announced. Then we drew lots to decide the order in which we should improvise, night by night. Surkov was to go first. I took my Sony from a drawer, slotted a tape in, and pressed the Record button. Victor concentrated; asked for the lamp to be turned down low. His cigarette glowed and faded and glowed again.

He sat forward in his chair, and began to invent.

After my friends had left quietly, some two hours later, I undressed and tumbled into bed. I fell instantly asleep. Then I was in a tram, rushing across a snowy wilderness. The tramcar was full of Russian authors. Everyone was merry and laughing, drinking beer. Lermontov left his seat at the back to go and neck with Tsvetaeva, and Solzhenitsyn gave up his place at the front to go back and chat to Gogol and Pushkin. I felt a trifle sad that no one wanted to talk to me. A motorway ran alongside the tram-like-a-train; English cars sped along it. I caught sight of Forster driving a Mini.

When I awoke, I stretched for my cigarettes and the tape recorder. I ran the tape back, wanting to listen again to some of Surkov's improvisation; but when I pressed to start it there was only a crackling silence.

· 2 ·

'If I'd been in your shoes I'd have walked right out on him.'

'I could hardly do that, Sergei: we were in my room!'

Rozanov and I, on another extraordinarily fine autumn morning, perched on stools in a grimy Soho café.

'I was more embarrassed for Masha's sake,' I continued. 'She was clearly my mistress in the Swiss hotel, though he didn't name her. Whereas in reality it was all very respectable. We ski'd by day, and the rest of the time we explored our idea for *Summit*.'

It had been an unexpected meeting with her, brought about by the Geneva Summit of 1985. I was to write about it for *Cosmopolitan*, she for *Trud*; it was the first time she had been outside the Soviet bloc. Afterwards we had spent a few stolen days at the ski resort of Grindelwald, in the shadow of the Eiger North Face.

'Well,' I confessed, 'it wasn't only that. She happened to have a period for most of that week. It wouldn't have bothered me, but it bothered her. I'm not saying I wouldn't have enjoyed some torrid love-making.' I swallowed bitter coffee dregs and the last mouthful of chocolate cake. 'It was superbly done, though—didn't you think?—imagining the Eiger looking through a telescope into our bedroom. I don't blame Victor for being angry: I simply don't know what happened to my tape recorder; I've never fouled it up before.'

'Oh, you didn't foul it up,' he said, mumbling through a mouthful of jammy doughnut; 'I found it unpleasant, his needling you both like that, so I wiped the tape.'

I stared at him, bewildered. 'How?'

He shrugged. 'My friend, if you'd spent two years burning up with sulphur injections, or shaking from haloperidol, you too might develop certain uncanny abilities. . . . It was a very unfair portrayal of you. I don't think you're in the least manipulative.'

I said I thought Surkov felt resentful because the novels hadn't made more money.

'That's true. And he thinks you and Masha ought to have consulted us on *Summit*.'

'But we did!'

'At a late stage, when you couldn't change very much. Maybe he thinks we might have improved it a little, even turned it into a bestseller. I don't agree with him; I think you did a good job. Anyway, don't worry about it, Don.' He patted me on the shoulder. 'Victor's fiction has vanished. Like the buried Armenian books. Like Mardian's balls. Oh, we could have consigned it to memory if we'd set our minds to it—but we didn't. Tonight it's my turn; he'll expect me to take up the story where he left off, but I've no intention of doing that. I shall move it some other direction. The Devil knows where.'

I paid our bill and we went out into the cold-blue day. Sergei, in a rumpled navy suit, attracted stares. Bald, and with an attenuated El Greco face, he looked like a victim of chemotherapy—but also of a Transylvanian vampire, for his chin and neck were covered with what seemed to be bite marks. He had left his electric shaver behind, he explained, and had had trouble with the disposable Gillettes he had bought at the hotel shop.

He wanted to visit Collet's, the Russian bookshop. There were portraits of Gorbachev and Mandela, glinting with red, in the window. Inside, I was gripped, as I always was, by the intense atmosphere of revolutionary zeal. Posters commanded us to remember Chile, Nicaragua, South Africa, the nurses, CND, the NHS, the wrongs of women. Unidentifiable Russian music was playing.

Rozanov, too, was gripped by a kind of excitement. 'I feel it's 1917 and anything can happen! Even justice!'

He bought a paperback Henry Miller. As we left he said, 'We shall know glasnost has arrived when we have a capitalistic bookshop in the middle of Moscow.'

He gazed at the slim, stilted legs of typists and shop assistants, hurrying to their low-calorie lunches. 'London is wonderful!'

Then he took me aback by saying, 'It's lucky to be still here.'

'What do you mean?'

'Victor told us a very grim story on the plane. Apparently in the summer the captain of one of our nuclear submarines went crazy. He was going to unleash a warhead on London. One of the other subs had to wipe them out. He and his crew, and a lot of radioactive material, are at the bottom of the Baltic.'

I swore; then asked if it was believable. He replied that this was one anecdote of Surkov's which had seemed to carry conviction.

We strolled on. He had a preoccupied air. It was not, somehow, the air of a man contemplating nuclear catastrophe, but a more pleasant dream. I suspected the image of a woman lurking behind his bloodshot eyes. Whoever she was—if she existed at all—she went with us through the mild, cleaned-up sordor of Soho side-streets.

We browsed through a desolate pornographic bookshop wearing a Monday morning hangover, then entered a crowded pub. We managed to find a corner. Someone had left a copy of the *Sun*, and Sergei grabbed it, saying, 'Ah, your free press!' I shouldered my way to the bar.

Sipping lager, we gazed at the front-page face of a dour middle-aged nurse who had been sacked for making porno movies on hospital premises. Rozanov lamented her undeserved misfortune—nurses needed a little recreation—but enthused over the lurid story, so much more interesting and poetic than, say, the American or Israeli elections. This was the stuff of life.

He admired a big-breasted girl.

'The hard feminists want it banned: the page-three nude—there's one every day.'

'But why?'

'Presumably because breasts are obscene.'

'Well, that's true. We are pornographers in the cradle. . . . It's a strange world. . . . Tomorrow you take us to Freud's house, h'mm?'

I promised to do that. A jukebox started up. We stared at a girl in a too-short red T-shirt, the writhing, glistening flesh in the pit of her back exposed. Sergei got us another drink. He began to scribble verses on the blank inside cover of his Henry Miller. I regarded with distaste a group of sleek young yuppies in city-suits, guffawing. How healthy, in comparison, seemed the orgiastic nurse. I sipped my lager quietly while Sergei scribbled.

Shutting the book he said suddenly, 'So you didn't fuck Masha because she was having a period.'

Surprised, I nodded.

'Menstrual blood can be magical,' he said. 'I used to find with Nina and Sonia that they would often menstruate at the same time; and various telepathic events and coincidences would occur.' He folded his arms, leaned back in his chair, sighed, devoured with his sad, sunken eyes the writing girl. 'Should I buy this word processor? What do you think?'

We had spent an hour in an office equipment shop. I said I thought he should buy it, he wouldn't regret it.

'But have you found there's a Muse in yours?'

'I think so, though she's very shy.'

There had to be a Muse, he said, if he was to buy it. But what would happen, probably, was that his spirit-wife would take over the computer, just as she took over almost everything. Her name was Avavnuk; she had been an Eskimo in her life. She came to him maybe two or three times a week: sometimes in the form of an animal, sometimes disguised as a live, normal woman. She was mischievous, aggressive, and totally immoral. He wasn't enough for her; she slept with many others.

His face was completely serious, even slightly mournful.

'Does Sonia know about her?'

'Of course. I explained the situation, after she found me jerking about on the bed one afternoon. She knows I can't refuse a spirit-wife, and on balance she prefers that I fuck Avavnuk rather than have affairs with ordinary women. Well, maybe she hopes I'm just imagining it.'

Back at the hotel, the Festival organiser, a wiry Scot dressed in a Superman outfit, accosted Rozanov. He bore a message for him. Extracting a crumpled note from a breast pocket, he gave it to Rozanov, who scanned it. 'Ah, yes! A couple of Russian exiles; I haven't seen them for ten years. They want tickets for my performance next Sunday. Is it possible, Jock?'

'I think we can scrape up a couple. But with you and Bellow and Finn on the programme, it's a sell-out already. We could have sold twice as many.'

'How are the sales going for Wednesday?' I asked.

His face clouded. 'They're coming along nicely.'

As Sergei went off to call his old friends, I turned into the lounge-area where tea was being served, and found Surkov and Masha there. They had accompanied Maria Sanchez to a Mass at Westminster Cathedral; the long and, compared with an Orthodox Mass, rather colourless service had drained them: in contrast the elderly Bolivian lady had seemed energised by Christ's body. 'She needs her fix every day,' said Surkov.

Relaxing in the comfortable chairs, we surveyed the plushness of the chandeliered hotel and its sleek well-dressed patrons. Again I wondered what I was doing here. This wasn't the Dorchester or the Ritz, but it had their ineffable air of serene affluence. These people, I remarked, could pull out of their pockets, thoughtlessly, as much money for a round of drinks as most single parents have to live on for a week; could pay as much for a few hours' sleep as a Third World peasant and his family had to live, or die, on for a year. Masha nodded, saying that for the first time since Geneva she could feel the attraction of Communism.

Apart from one lone Nigerian sipping tea, we saw no one else from the Festival. The Regis was so vast it absorbed the Writers Internationale just as it absorbed the British Congress of Funeral Directors. Except in the Press Room and Hospitality Suite, on the fifteenth floor, the Festival only really existed during the twice-daily theatre events and at dinner. The hotel bookshop went on displaying Archer and Sheldon and Forsythe, happily oblivious to the world-famous authors who flitted in from time to time to paw the paperbacks.

Surkov signed the bill for our teas, and it was time to board the coach to take us to the late-afternoon theatrical performance. We considered giving it a miss, but decided it would look rude. With one liberal white and two coloured Africans reading, it proved to be an impassioned attack on apartheid.

'I'm against apartheid too,' growled Surkov, 'but I don't want it thrust down my throat like this.' Rozanov spent the whole performance scribbling in a notebook, and did so again at the evening performance. He paused in his writing only to listen to a rather attractive Finnish poetess reading a sequence about her husband's alcoholism. I recalled he had struck up an intimate conversation with her in the lobby after breakfast. Could hers be the image he carried?

It was Hallowe'en, but the rows of suburban semis near

the theatre as we drove back in the coach looked profoundly unmagical.

We watched the late-night news in Masha's bedroom. Surkov and I sprawled on the twin beds; Rozanov sat on the floor, his back against the drawn curtains; Masha, in a comfortable chair, kicked off her high-heels and drew her legs under her flower-patterned skirt. A mother and her three babies had been killed in an attack on a bus in Israel. Happening almost on the eve of the Israeli elections, the attack would, it was agreed, wreck Labour's chances of victory and let in the hard-line Likud. We stared gloomily at the screen. There would be no peace conference; the crime against the Palestinians would become even blacker. 'It wouldn't surprise me,' Masha said, 'if Likud carried out the massacre.'

'Against its own people?'

We heard a male duet of drunken voices, and a body lurched against the door in passing.

'Why not? What's a woman and three babies? The ends justify the means.'

'Now we improvise,' said Surkov, tossing me a cigarette. 'Fuck this crazy planet. We should try to lay the groundwork for another novel this week—you agree?'

Sergei and Masha nodded, and glanced at me queryingly. I shrugged: 'Okay.'

'Just make sure you press the Record switch tonight,' Surkov growled. 'But I take it you'll have no problem remembering my fiction?' His glance swept all three of us challengingly: as if one could possibly forget a Surkov improvisation!

'So it's my turn,' mused Rozanov. 'Remind me of your last line, Victor.'

Taken aback, he stammered. He couldn't recall it precisely. It was something about the lovers skiing across the Alpine mountainslope, vanishing into the mist. He glanced swiftly from Masha to me.

Masha: 'Weren't they on a ski lift, rushing across pine trees?'

'That was earlier,' I objected. 'But they weren't skiing either.'

We found ourselves lost—just as Masha and I had been when a sudden mist had descended on the lower slopes of the Wetterhorn. Surkov growled his irritation, but Rozanov seemed to enjoy our floundering.

'It's not meant to be,' he said, rubbing his stubbly chin, staring into space. 'We shouldn't fight it. Let's imagine . . . Let's imagine—'

· 3 ·

It was a mild night late in May. Anna Charsky awoke in the
bedroom of her pleasant flat overlooking an historic river.
She kicked away the heavy limbs of the man who was sharing
her bed, at the same time dislodging a grey cat from the bed's
foot. Half-asleep still, she stumbled from the room and across
the hall to the bathroom. Hoisting her night-dress she squatted. Then she ran her hands under the tap and dried them.

She returned to bed. The man's hairy arm had strayed
across into her space, and she had to move it in order to lie
down. She turned on her side away from him and closed her
eyes.

Images of her dream still flashed vaguely before her. 'I
wonder what it meant,' she asked herself sleepily. 'I had an
English lover, we were in Switzerland, on the ski slopes.
. . . And then we were rushing across pines . . .'

She felt the sudden weight on her legs which told her the
cat had leapt up again. She parted her feet to make a hollow
for her.

The man's arm, in his sleep, fell around her shoulder.

Her vague thoughts drifted to him. How strange it was,
when you thought about it, that she was lying in a bed with

this particular man. It might have been anyone in Russia—or indeed, the world.

The man started to make a whistling sound through his teeth. He wrenched his arm away and turned over, away from her.

She touched her groin, her stomach. Perhaps her erotic dream had something to do with her condition.

Anna Charsky, native of Leningrad, relaxed her mind and was soon asleep again.

Meanwhile her husband, Dmitri, was not too far away. He was standing on an improvised stage near the statue of the Bronze Horseman. Late though it was, the sky was still clear. Around the stage a large crowd, mostly of young people, sat on foldable chairs and stools; others stood in a semi-circle behind. The low, expectant chatter of the audience was muted further by the soaring granite walls of the city, the rushing Neva, and the sky which somehow seems more vast in Russia.

A performance by Charsky—a gauntly handsome man in his early thirties—was a rare event. He had the gift of improvising verses at will to any given theme. Since unguarded and uncensored words have usually been anathema in Russia, he mostly limited his performances to select private gatherings. That this performance was completely open to all comers signalled unequivocally that the Gorbachevian renaissance was a reality.

His performance was intended as a celebration of that renaissance, and also of the prospects for world peace: for in Moscow, Comrade Gorbachev and President Reagan were holding a summit meeting which promised to bear fruit in disarmament. Celebratory events were taking place all over the Soviet Union; but none was more extraordinary, in its modest way, than Charsky's promised to be.

Squatting, tossing back his black curly locks from time to time, he was chatting to his elderly accompanist:

'I think we should have the Bach.'

'Are you sure the Bach wouldn't be more suitable, Dmitri?' replied the cellist, who was hard of hearing.

'Bach will be fine.'

A slim fair-haired girl in a long black dress was threading between the ranks of spectators, holding open a bag into which people dropped folded-up pieces of paper. Having reached the most distant onlookers, a young couple pushing up and down a baby in a pram, the girl drew tight the neck of the bag and strolled with it to the stage. Charsky, rising, reached down a hand to assist her in mounting the stage. He fumbled with the microphone while the girl sat down at the rear, the bag in her lap. The crowd-noise hushed. The cellist took up his bow, and drew across his instrument a few subdued notes of Bach. Charsky spoke into the microphone:

'Well, my friends, we'll begin. Bella?' He glanced over his shoulder at his assistant. She opened the bag, dipped in a hand and pulled out a slip of paper. Unfolding it she read aloud in a clear voice: '*The Veteran.*'

Grief seized Charsky's heart. His father, a brain-damaged veteran of the Great Patriotic War, had recently died. Charsky gazed around the hushed audience, hoping to catch sight of a friend whose kind smile might give him strength. But there was no one. If only Anna had been able to attend; she had told him she would try to come, and her nonappearance added to the depression caused by the theme. Even the weather did not help. Cumulus had drifted into the sky.

He stepped back from the microphone and lowered his gaze, lost in painful emotion. It occurred to him that—

· 4 ·

I had not yet escaped the strangeness of being with people who, over the years, had become largely fictional to me. The voices of Surkov and Rozanov on tape, played over and over in my study in the first year or so after our meeting, had brought their living presence to me; but later, as those tapes were discarded in favour of overscrawled typewritten pages, Surkov and Rozanov increasingly became characters under my control, their improvisations almost lost under the refinements of a thousand and one nights (and days) of my own labour.

Yet here they were, as large as life—Surkov with his long yellow hair and Rozanov with his attenuated face and his baldness—clearly the living people with whom I had boozed and improvised in Moscow, so long ago. It was disconcerting. Only gradually was I learning to adjust; learning to take some pleasure in their two-fold existence—in their own consciousness and between the covers of novels bearing my name, somewhat inaccurately, as author.

Surkov, in a Yale T-shirt, was sitting alone at a table when I went down to a late breakfast. He didn't know where the others were, but he could guess. Sergei's bed hadn't been slept in; presumably he'd been to bed with Masha. That seemed highly unlikely, I said, taken aback—also, possibly, a shade put out. Surely she was too much in love with Liubov? An image of Liubov Charents, that tall, leonine Georgian soprano, flashed before my eyes. I might have added that Masha once told me she didn't know what women saw in her two ageing friends.

'Oh, I don't think she's entirely lost to healthy sex. But what do you think?—you ought to know!' He leered across the table.

'That's where you're wrong. We've never slept together.'

His fork, dripping scrambled egg, paused in midair. 'Really? I'm astonished. We all assumed you had an affair in Moscow.'

'An affair of the heart.'

'Good God!'

Chewing slowly, he shook his head in disbelief. 'An affair of the heart . . . astonishing!'

Yet it had not been especially noble of me. By the time I had reached Moscow I had exhausted myself physically in a purely sensual relationship with my Leningrad guide, Natasha. For Masha I'd had nothing left but the heart.

'But what about your Swiss encounter? You shared a bedroom, didn't you?'

I nodded. 'But we didn't lie together—except in the creative sense.'

'Then my improvisation on Sunday night was pure fantasy. I'm sorry, my friend. I assumed too much. But after all,' he added, in self-excuse, 'you fantasised quite a lot of things about Sergei and me, in the novels.'

'They were mostly what you and he had improvised,' I pointed out.

'Well, okay, but you expanded a lot. I—' He broke off while I ordered rolls and coffee. '—I was being true to our principle, in creating a Swiss love affair for you: real people— ourselves included—but a mixture of fact and fiction. I thought it was time you got involved in it too, my friend: a few memories of your adolescence, in *Swallow*, was pretty safe territory.'

I admitted that was true. I couldn't have exposed myself as he and Sergei had done.

'Well, Sergei and I are kind of symbols.' He waved his arms expressively. 'We stand for what's good in our country, so we have to be brave and reveal ourselves. But even Masha, who's very reticent, confessed her desire for Liubov—which was remarkable considering our country's attitude to homosexuality. Oh, admittedly the novels aren't available there, but people got to know about it, and wondered how she had the nerve to reveal it. Because they assume you were writing from knowledge. But you—you kept out of trouble.' He sneered a smile over his coffee cup. 'You were the discreet narrator.'

I accepted his just criticism in the manner of Shostakovich, and concentrated for a while on eating. Then he launched an assault on his Moscow neighbour: Sergei's improvisation had been crap. The pretence that his, Surkov's, opening had been merely a dream was a pathetic cliche: there had already been too much of it in our novels. And poems in a novel simply didn't work; they'd been crap poems anyway. They weren't even genuine improvisations: he'd been scribbling verses all day.

'I thought one or two of them were good,' I said. 'The poem about Charsky's dead father, for example, was terrific.'

'I can't remember any lines from it. It wasn't memorable. No, my friend, it's probably a good thing the tape ran out.'

I felt myself blush. My own stupidity, rather than Rozanov's shamanistic powers, had once again wrecked a recording. I'd slotted in, by mistake, a tape on which I'd recorded some Sixties pop music for a party, and which I'd never run back. When we'd checked the recording we'd heard Sinatra singing 'My Way.' Only a fraction of Rozanov's wonderful improvisations of improvisations had been captured, at the end of the tape. He had been remarkably forgiving. It was fate, he said: the poems of Charsky on the Neva bank were not meant to survive.

Surkov offered me a Marlboro. 'Tonight,' he said, clicking his lighter for me, 'why don't you try to get back to the Swiss hotel room? Masha won't mind. Actually I didn't say it was she—you could invent a different woman if you like—ah, here's the happy couple.'

Masha entered, holding a rolled-up magazine, followed by Rozanov, a newspaper under his arm. They seemed faintly embarrassed.

'We've been walking,' said Masha, rather red in the cheeks. With her bouffant hair, her crimson lips, her plump raincoated figure hourglassed by a tight belt, she looked more than ever like a *Matryoshka*, a Russian doll.

'Neither of us could sleep,' said her companion, falling heavily onto a seat. 'I went to the hospitality lounge for a cup of tea at about seven, and found Masha there before me.'

She flushed a deeper red, as if the lie was too transparent. As she slid out of her raincoat, revealing her plump, red-sweatered breasts, I had a moment of irrational jealousy of Rozanov.

'You were fucking good last night, Sergei,' said Surkov, putting an arm round his shoulder. 'Who's the guy who slept with Anna? It was a nice touch when she came running along the embankment, late, fresh from her lover's embraces!' He chuckled.

The latecomers ordered breakfast. Rozanov removed his parka, then hid his face behind the *Guardian*. I read the head-lines: 'DEGREE BY VOUCHER' PUT ON ICE . . . DUKAKIS BOARDS THE PEOPLE'S TRAIN . . . It all sounded terribly boring. The sheer weight of boring events sometimes overwhelmed me. I wondered what the *Guardian* headlines would be on the day of the Second Coming. Almost certainly it would lead with welfare cuts, while the *Sun*—or maybe *Sunday Sport*, if He came on the sabbath—would get the scoop.

November 1. So it was All Souls' Day. Though I am not

particularly a Christian, I thought with sadness of my beloved dead.

Masha was glancing at *Newsweek*. Surkov caught sight of a smiling photo of Raisa Gorbachev with her husband. 'Ah, our beautiful queen!' he exclaimed. 'She was terrific in bed!'

'So you've told us, many times,' said Rozanov, not looking up.

'I fucked you once; perhaps I fuck you still,' murmured Masha, misquoting Pushkin. Rozanov and I chuckled. 'Didn't you also fuck Thatcher, Victor, when she was in Moscow?'

'No, but I got pretty close.'

'Ah!' Rozanov said. 'I see that all men are potential child abusers!' His eyes rapidly scanned the article. 'Some society of angry women has been formed. Child sexual abuse is a product of patriarchy, it will continue as long as men regard women as ultimately existing to meet male needs. . . . I don't see the logic of that—boys get abused too. . . . If you foster a child you must not hug her. You must not tell her she has a nice bottom, because that's sexist.'

Surkov grabbed the paper from him. 'Jesus Christ!' he muttered, his glance trailing up and down the columns of print.

'What an insult!' said Rozanov. 'If this is freedom of expression, I don't want it. How can they get away with saying such things?'

Masha: 'Maybe it's true.'

'Oh, in a philosophical sense,' Rozanov countered, 'we are all capable of everything. But most of us don't *do* it. It's like saying all women are potential whores or baby-batterers. Like, in the Middle Ages, they were all witches, potentially. You can imagine what an outcry there'd be from women if we made some such generalisation about them; but we men are supposed to take this shit!'

It was because we felt guilty, I suggested. Men *had* screwed things up; so we were like Western liberals tiptoeing round Stalin's Russia, anxious to find it good, afraid to find fault.

We were like that about women's lib. That was a stupid analogy, Masha said, at the same time as Surkov was pointing out that Katya had always glowed when he'd praised her nice bottom and tits.

'But sexual abuse occurs, on a wide scale,' Masha insisted, pale, her glass of juice gripped between her hands.

'I know that, Masha. But it shouldn't make people scared of touching each other. Is there really much harm in a father or stepfather fondling a girl? I'm not talking about shoving a prick up a five-year-old, which is beastly, or years of sexual dominance, but just a little playing around?'

He rubbed her thigh affectionately under the table.

'You bloody men, you know nothing!' she snarled. Tears springing to her eyes, she pushed her chair back, rose, and ran out of the dining-room.

'What have I said?' Surkov asked.

'Masha was abused by an uncle,' murmured Rozanov. 'I'd forgotten that. She told me once.'

'Oh, shit!' His hand went to his eyes. 'It obviously is damaging. But why? Why should eroticism be so disturbing? Girls love their fathers, fathers love their daughters. Caresses are expressions of love. What is this incest taboo? Why should a father stroking his daughter's tits create enormous problems?' He glanced from Rozanov to me, probingly, seriously puzzled. 'My poor old mother used to caress my little cock when bathing or undressing me. I guess she was frustrated, living alone. Well, I thought it was kind of nice, it didn't ruin my life.'

'We're all fucked up,' Rozanov said with a deep sigh, spreading strawberry jam on a croissant. He had sensed, he said, a kind of antisexual hysteria in the audience at the pro-abortion meeting. A secret, unconscious hostility to life and tenderness and the flesh. They'd argued like blackshirts.

Surkov: 'Discussion with rifles, as Lenin expressed it.'

'Oh, come on!' I said, exasperated. 'They were vehement, it's true; but you can understand it. What does Bush know about having a baby? What right have men to tell them what to do?'

Surkov stared at his plate thoughtfully, then slowly lifted his face. 'There's a poem by the American, Simpson . . .'

'Louis Simpson?'

'That's right. I've heard him read it. It's very short. It's about a firing squad. And it says that wherever we see a firing squad, we are always on the side of the man tied to the post. That's how I feel about abortion. I am on the side of the one who's going to be killed.'

'Well, it's not so simple.'

'Maybe not.'

'And sexual abuse is a big problem. In this country, anyway. You should apologise to Masha.'

'I'll do it right away.'

A couple of hours later Masha, placated, was standing with us in the workroom of Sigmund Freud in Hampstead. During our journey on the Northern Line I'd sketched in the background to his coming to England in '38, fleeing the Nazis. I had only visited the house—now a museum—once before. It seemed strange, walking over brown leaves to a very English suburban house in Maresfield Gardens, to visit the great mid-European.

The Sphinx of Gizeh gazed down at the red velvet couch. Oedipus, in another part of the spacious room, asked his question of the Theban Sphinx. Rank upon rank of classical, Egyptian and Oriental statuettes brooded upon the stillness. There stood falcon-headed Horus, and bronze Osiris whom Seth brought back to life by fellation. There stood the wise old Chinaman whom the wise old Moravian would greet every morning when he entered. An Egyptian long-boat continued to row into eternity.

The stones seemed not to weigh the room towards the earth but to be ready to lift it into the sky.

The mysteriousness of sexuality lay all around. We gazed in silence, like the four or five other visitors. I wondered if they too felt the presence of Freud's serene wisdom, his lucid intelligence. I wanted to lay on him the burden of our fractured present.

Masha seemed oppressed. She kept glancing at her watch. It was simply tiredness, she explained, she needed a couple of hours' sleep.

'Yes, Freud was there,' Sergei said when we had emerged into the unnaturally brilliant November day.

'He was stroking that American girl's bottom,' said Victor with a chuckle; but his weak joke fell hollowly.

I took them into the Underground. Rushed along through the dark, their faces soon settled to the same blank, tranced appearance as everyone else's. I was almost nodding off when Victor, sitting beside me, spoke, the noise of the train turning his voice into a whisper:

'So it's your turn tonight.'

'Yes. I'm dreading it.'

'Will it be in English or Russian?'

'I'll try it in Russian.'

'Good! That's brave.' He added that I must not be intimidated by his and Rozanov's fluency; I was really quite good.

I didn't feel annoyed. I knew I couldn't begin to match them.

'It would be really great if we could lay the foundations for a novel.'

I nodded.

'It's not too late, despite our problems with the machine. I'm sure you'll get it right tonight, when it's your turn.'

I nodded again.

'We have, I would guess, about two pages of narrative so far, and it's already Tuesday. Still, never mind . . . You were foolish, my friend, to say our work was concluded as a quartet.'

'I know that.'

'You remember,' he said, 'how we predicted, on our very first night together, that it might turn into one book, or a trio, or a quintet—but certainly not a duet or quartet?'

'Ah, that's right! We did say that! I'd forgotten.'

Memories of that particular evening, at Rozanov's dacha, came flooding back. I'd met Masha's husband earlier in the day, and he'd improvised for me. Shimon Barash was a fine *improvisatore*—though his gift has apparently faded since he defected to Australia. I, of course, had no experience of the impromptu tradition, and the others had had little more practice. But that night, inspired by talk of Pushkin and Akhmatova, we decided to try. Nina Rozanov, tired, had gone off to bed. Vera Surkov had left, to relieve their baby-sitter. In the midnight stillness, Rozanov pointed out that we were three men and a woman—as in Pushkin's story about improvisation, *Egyptian Nights*.

We could either take on Masha, Surkov said drunkenly, and pay the penalty at dawn—or else improvise. 'We'll improvise,' said Masha.

And so it had begun . . .

At the Chalk Farm stop an attractive, freckled schoolgirl, about sixteen, in a smart navy uniform and white blouse, had got on and sat a few seats away. She had a satchel by her feet and a violin case in her lap. She stared blankly at the adverts. 'That bitch . . .', said Surkov softly, and I knew at once he was referring to Imogen. Hampstead had already brought her sharply into his mind—that had been obvious when the name had leapt into view on our arrival. Imogen had lived in Hampstead, and had been just such an attractive sixth-former when he had met her on a trip to the States. He/I had described their meeting in earlier novels.

'She's trying to take me for everything I've got, my friend,' he said. 'She ruined everything. I had a pretty good marriage going with Vera. We're still friends. It's not her fault Petya won't speak to me; it's just that he turned against me when I divorced his mother. I can't blame him. Jesus, what gets into me? Why this constant need to change, to try something new, to search for paradise? It doesn't exist. I certainly didn't find it with that fucking bitch. . . .' He laughed sardonically.

'Women survive better than men. Look at Masha—she has a seraphic look on her face. She's either thinking of Liubov or tonight's screw with Sergei. Shimon is clean out of her mind, he might never have existed, he's far further away from her than Australia. . . .'

When we arrived at the Regis, Masha rushed straight for the lifts. I had some tea with the others, then also went to my room. I was nervous, I wanted to prepare. I planned roughly the direction of my 'impromptu'. Unlike Pushkin's *impro-visatore*, for whom there was 'no toil, no dearth, nor that unrest which is the prelude to inspiration', I had to prepare the way. I missed dinner, and the theatre readings after.

My phone rang just after eleven, so startling I broke my pencil on my notepad. It was Masha. 'We're going up to Hospitality for a while—we're out of drink, we need to steal some. You care to join us?'

I stowed my notes in my pocket, and headed for the lifts. There were about a dozen writers in Hospitality, most of them busy knocking back the hard stuff. My friends were chatting to Sean Murphy, his beady eyes and Guinness-fringed lips at a level with Rozanov's chest. A green shirt beer-bulged over a low-slung belt. Edging in, I apologised to Murphy for missing his reading. 'Oh, there's no need, there's no need at all!'

'Mr Murphy read us a terrific piece about the IRA hunger-strikers,' said Surkov, gulping vodka.

'I'm sorry I missed it. Was there a good crowd?'

'Sure, it was nearly a full house,' Murphy said: turning, at that moment, to be grappled by Helmutt Hauptmann, a bear of a man with thick spectacles, blond beard and broad, humped shoulders draped by an even broader mauve jacket. Hauptmann drew the tubby red-haired Irishman away.

'There was almost no one in the gallery,' Surkov growled. 'And they sold hardly any books. You were right to give it a miss, my friend. Before the IRA we had liberation theology and Greenpeace.'

'Everything but literature,' said Rozanov.

'Murphy is obviously a political conspirator,' Masha remarked, 'but what about Hauptmann?'

I glanced in his direction. 'A brigand of the wood.'

'Correct,' said Rozanov. 'Sheer marauding ego. But I don't agree with you on Murphy. He's a charlatan trading in elixirs and arsenic.'

No one unfamiliar with Pushkin's *Egyptian Nights* would have understood our conversation. In his story, a scruffy Neopolitan *improvisatore* breaks in on a Petersburg gentleman-poet in his study. The Russian poet mistakes him at first for a brigand of the woods, a political conspirator, or a charlatan trading in elixirs and arsenic. It doesn't occur to him that he is his creative spirit.

'And what is Cita?' I asked.

Cita Lemminkaïnen, the tall, rather attractive Finn, half-hidden by the white overalls of Judith Steinway, was sipping a juice. She wrote poems about her husband's alcoholism.

Rozanov glanced towards her appreciatively. 'I'm not sure. I think she may be a genuine *improvisatrice*.'

'And which are we?' asked Masha.

Before we could consider the question, we were distracted by the arrival of Geraldine Porter. Her weird, rather witchlike appearance always drew eyes; who could ignore that bony frame in its tent of an ethnic dress, those rimless spectacles and thin bloodless lips under spikes of white hair radiating all round her head?

'This is a true political conspirator,' said Rozanov.

We nodded. The New Zealand–born playwright's attacks

on Thatcher and Thatcherism at dinner were audible wherever one sat, and unmistakably virulent. Surkov always had
to hold on to his temper.

Porter was carrying a large, floppy-covered book; she went
straight up to an African writer, N'dosi, showed him the
book, held open, and offered him a biro. I saw the book was
a very popular mail-order catalogue. I was stunned. And the
polite, formally suited African was writing something on a
sheet of paper, to her instructions. Porter was obtaining or-
ders! She was a mail-order agent! It was as staggeringly out
of character as the Pope reading *Playboy*.

And now she was heading for us, the biro between her
teeth, the light of battle glinting behind her frameless glasses.
'Hi! I'd like you to sign our petition.'

'What petition?' enquired Masha.

Opening the catalogue, a gnarled and beringed hand
pointed to a slim dark-skinned young woman modelling a
trouser-suit. 'You may have read about her in the *Guardian*.
They wanted her to model dresses for next year's catalogue,
and she refused. She's a Muslim. She doesn't want to show
her legs. So the bastards sacked her! And the appeal tribunal
backed them. So we think the Writers Internationale should
stand up for her rights.'

The Russians courteously declined, saying they couldn't
get mixed up in an issue that didn't concern them. Porter
offered me the biro. 'I'm sorry,' I said, 'if she's a model she
has to expect to model dresses.'

She stared at me furiously.

'In any case, I don't see what the Writers Internationale has
to do with it—as a body.'

'Because we're *writers*, for Christ's sake!' she hissed. 'We're
the goddamn intelligentsia!'

I shook my head, and with a toss of her spiky white hair
she veered away towards Murphy and Hauptmann.

Rozanov sighed. 'The ego of writers!'

'Let's get the fuck out of here,' said Surkov. His eyes darted around before he slipped a couple of bottles under his coat.

A few minutes later he was uncorking a fine claret in Masha's room, saying he had something to celebrate: he'd been invited to breakfast at Downing Street, helping to brief Maggie for her trip to Poland. 'I guess she's missed me,' he boasted.

I sought Masha's face; she rolled her eyes.

Glasses foamed. Surkov said to me, 'Now to the serious part of the evening. Take our story on, my friend . . .'

The bedside lamp was dimmed, the tape recorder set going. Quelling panic, I took out my notes and glanced through them hastily. 'This Charsky,' I murmured, addressing Rozanov: 'we've met him before. In *Swallow*. You improvised a poem about him.'

Masha said, 'Oh, that's right! It was one of the performances at the Olympiad in Finland.'

'That was Konstantin Charsky,' said Rozanov. 'This is Dmitri. It could be a brother. . . .'

I felt somewhat thrown by this information, having assumed Sergei had simply made a mistake in the Christian name. I would have to change certain things I'd planned. As I concentrated my thoughts I saw Surkov move his hand in a downward curve. I guessed he was trying to imitate the movements of a skier. He was saying, in effect, get back to Eiger and the hotel room; fantasise sexually—reveal yourself!

I had no intention of doing that. Nor did I have the urge to linger on the Neva embankment with Charsky. There was a very simple, if rather banal, way of spinning off from Surkov's lost story and Rozanov's all-but-lost one; and I would take it.

· 5 ·

Anna was bending over him, holding out a mug of coffee. Grunting, he flopped over onto his side. She had put the mug by his bed and gone to the window to let in the light. Returning, she surveyed in a dispassionate way her husband of twenty years: the incipient double chin, the receded hairline, the hairy chest—constricted by his sideways turn—pouched almost in a female way. She wondered again, as she had in the night, why fate had sent this particular man to her.

Yet she had no doubt she was lucky; he still moved her with his intelligence, his charm, his sensitivity. None of which was apparent in the overweight figure coming slowly alive in their bed.

Opening his eyes, he groaned, and blocked out the strong morning light with his arm.

He mumbled a thanks for the coffee.

He heard, as he lay gathering his thoughts together, a monotonous voice coming faintly from the kitchen. It was the news-reader. Then he heard, softer, more expressive, in American English, Reagan's tones. Charsky raised himself on an elbow and picked up the mug of coffee, while Anna slipped off her dressing-gown and climbed into bed. 'How's the Summit going?' he asked.

'Reagan's talking quite a lot about human rights, which probably suits Gorbachev.'

'Good. What's the time?'

'Eight.'

'What time did we get to bed, do you think?'

'Three?'

That was the only trouble with the white nights—you never wanted to go to bed. And after last night's performance of *Hamlet*, some of his friends from the theatre had come back with him for an informal reading of their next play.

'But it was enjoyable,' he said. 'It's a damn good play. And you read Hedda beautifully—I bet Lydia won't do it any better.'

Lydia was the Arts Theatre's star actress. Currently she was Gertrude to Charsky's Claudius.

'That's rubbish, you know it is.'

'No, no!' he protested.

'I can read not badly, but I wouldn't be any good onstage.'

'You could learn stagecraft easily. You're a natural. It's a crime you never took it up, darling. This coffee is weak; is it Nescafé?'

'No, we've run out.'

He grunted in disappointment. Every time he went abroad with the Company he came back loaded up with Western goods.

A slim example of Western luxury nestled at this moment in Anna's vagina.

She stroked his thinning dome. 'You'll need a good wig if you're to be Hedda's long-haired poet.'

'That's strange,' said Charsky, sipping the coffee; 'I dreamt I was a poet. I was slim and young and improvising verses to an audience on the embankment. Doing it damn well. The trouble is, I can't remember a single line!'

He stared out at the dappled sky, trying to remember. 'Of course we both know it's wish-fulfillment. I envy you, envy my brother.' He pecked her a kiss. 'Apart from the actual poems it was a very vivid dream. Is it because—has your period started?'

She nodded. 'It started in the night.'

'Ah! Splendid! So that's the reason! What did you dream?'

'Nothing that I can remember.'

'That's a shame!'

He had come to believe that a period affected dreams—and not only Anna's but his too. And down-to-earth though she was, she had to admit there were often some weird parallels. There had to be some sort of telepathy at work. They guessed it was an emotional response to another womb-death; though, heaven knew, they would hardly have wanted a child, in their mid-forties, even if Charsky's infertility could be miraculously cured. They had long ago come to terms with that sorrow.

'Oh, I remember now,' she said: 'I did have one dream, just as I was waking up. It was about an old boyfriend—before you, my dear—when I was fat and lacking confidence. Well, you know how I was. This man was a real cultural snob who quite destroyed me. He played me a record of some Stockhausen, whom I'd never heard of.'

He pressed her to remember details, and she found a few; none of them matched anything in his vivid dream, which disappointed him. But there was still their 'experiment' to try.

He touched her thigh over the sheet, and gave her a smile full of meaning. 'I should really get dressed,' she responded. 'The lounge is in a mess.'

'I'll do it later.'

'I'm hungry. I'll make breakfast.'

'Don't worry, I'll do it. Scrambled eggs?' He leapt out of bed, grabbed his bathrobe and scampered from the room. The bathroom door slammed. Anna put down her coffee mug, stubbed her cigarette, lit another, then stretched to pick up a book from her bedside table. Straightening, she opened the book at a page marked with a tram ticket.

The book, published in France, was called *Psychological Correspondences*. Recently she and Dmitri had developed an interest in Freud and psychoanalysis. It was mainly thanks to Kurminksy, director of the *Hamlet* production, who had suggested his actors read Freud. A few battered English paperbacks had gone the rounds, and Anna had read them too. Now the Charskys were scraping together, mostly from abroad, as many books on the subject as they could get. Anna thought Freud was probably wrong a lot of the time, but he was beautifully, illuminatingly wrong.

She'd found *Psychological Correspondences* among her brother-in-law's books. Konstantin Charsky was a poet like herself, but much better known, and he had been able to gather quite a few Western books. He confessed he had never read this one, given to him by a Parisian admirer. French was tough going for Anna, but she had ploughed through the correspondence of Rilke and Lou Andreas-Salomé, and Freud and Lawrence of Arabia. She enjoyed reading people's letters. Now she began to tackle the section called 'Krafft-Ebing & Sophie Arandt.' She was still struggling with the short introduction when her husband entered, bearing a breakfast-tray.

She took it from him while he climbed in. 'It smells good!' She saw there were some letters. 'Any for me?'

The post was usually for him. He received lots of fan mail.

'Yes, there's one.'

She found it; handed the others to him.

They attacked the eggs. When they had eaten a couple of mouthfuls they started to open their mail.

'Sergei and Sonia send their condolences,' he said.

'Ah. That's nice.'

Charsky picked less hungrily at his scrambled egg. The sympathetic letter had reminded him he was grieving. The worst moment, apart from his father's collapse while being helped to the toilet, had been going on stage on the night of his death, and hearing Lydia Dorinskaya say, 'All that lives must die, / Passing through Nature to eternity.'

Anna let out a cry of disbelief and joy.

'What is it?'

'*Novy Mir*'s taken two of my poems!'

'That's wonderful, darling! Terrific! It's high time—you're a marvellous poet!' He leaned and gave her a smacking kiss on the cheek. 'Which ones?'

'*Varvara* and *Violence and Beauty*.'

'Have I read *Varvara*? I don't recall it.'

'Haven't you read it?' she replied vaguely. 'I really don't know.'

'*Violence and Beauty* is one of your best.'

'You think so? I'm not sure. I've written some much better poems and they threw them back. Now, here . . . And *Violence and Beauty* comes out against *all* violence in South Africa, including black violence. . . . They don't mention taking any lines out! It's amazing!'

Innocuous though most of her poems were, she had been driven by the stupidity and cowardice of the censorship to publish in samizdat. Officially, Anna Charsky did not exist. She had not even attracted any positive repression, nor been significant enough to affect her husband's career. She had had fewer than a dozen poems published in magazines—usually small, regional magazines—during the twenty-five years she had been writing. No one ever invited her to read in factories or schools. Yet now—the very best literary magazine!

'Tonight we'll celebrate; we'll go out for a meal after the performance,' said her husband, slitting open the last of his letters. The next moment he let out a cry, of disbelief and joy, similar to hers. 'It's from Bella Kropotkin!'

It took Anna a moment to identify the name. 'The blind film director?'

'Yes! She says she's to be in Leningrad for a day or two—she's on location at Lake Baikal—to meet Mrs Reagan on her flying visit to the Hermitage. That's tomorrow—good God! . . . But more particularly to see me on stage—tonight! She's got permission to film *Doctor Zhivago*—isn't that incredible, darling?—and she has me in mind for the part of Komarovsky!' Charsky's voice was on a rising graph of excitement. 'She hopes I can meet her at her hotel after the performance, so we can talk! She's going to ring me to confirm!'

Charsky leaned back against the pillows and raised his eyes to the ceiling as if thanking the Almighty. Then he breathed out: 'Phew!' He handed her the letter. She scanned it.

'It's a major part, Anna! I wonder who they'll choose for Lara. And Zhivago. Well, no matter. It would be wonderful.'

His wife smiled. 'Another adulterer!'

He was jumping out of bed, rushing towards the door.

She shouted after him: 'Claudius, Lövborg, Komarovsky!' He rushed back, clutching a copy of *Moda*, an Italian magazine, leapt into bed, and flicked through the pages. Unable to read the text, he had brought the magazine home from Naples because of its glamorous art work. 'There she is!'

The large photo showed a handsome blonde-haired woman wearing dark glasses. Charsky could decipher that she was filming an ecological documentary of Lake Baikal. As always, she 'saw' through the eyes of her faithful assistant; but the final, unmistakable imprint of all her films was Kropotkin. She was a remarkable genius. Only in the Soviet Union could a blind woman have risen to her eminence in cinematography.

'She's very attractive,' Anna commented.

'I guess so. You see, we *are* getting some luck! Our *carezza* works!' He lifted the tray from her lap and, stretching, set it down by the bed. He took her in his arms and kissed her. Sensing a lack of response, he said, 'Aren't you pleased for me?'

'Of course. Of course!' And she pressed her lips to his.

He untied the girdle of her dressing-gown.

'Take out your . . . ,' he said, touching her lightly between the thighs.

They began to engage in a ritual practice of the Caucasian gypsies.

It was his mother, Yevdoxia, who without meaning to had given him the idea. On the night of her husband's funeral she had overcome her usual reticence and talked about their married life. In the early days, when they still slept together, he had insisted on taking her during a period: remaining perfectly motionless in her, on her—sometimes for hours. He had learned it from his father, a full gypsy; it was supposed to bring good fortune and happiness, something magical to do with blood.

Yevdoxia, who had grown up with the belief that sex was disgusting even at normal times, had refused to take any more of it, ever.

This is what the gaunt, red-eyed old lady had told them; and of course Charsky, needing to draw close in some way to his dead father, wanted to try it out. This was their second experiment, the second month. Anna didn't mind indulging him in his grief. They didn't believe in the magic spell literally, of course, but they had had their experiences of telepathic closeness at that time of the month. The Caucasian gypsies must have known about it too.

She lay on her side, turned away from him, still. His right thigh was between hers, and his face was buried in the pillow and strands of her hair. The position provided a tight and comfortable union. Even if the man drifted close to sleep, which the stillness encouraged, the union remained unbroken.

In some parts of the world, Anna had discovered, this mystical form of intercourse was known as *carezza*.

They were almost asleep now, bathed in warm light, half-hearing Scriabin on the kitchen radio. The shrill notes of the telephone, on Anna's bedside table, shocked them awake. She moved her torso without breaking the union, and stretched her arm to pick up the phone.

It was Zoya, a friend from work, asking Anna if she'd managed to get soap. Yes, said Anna, she would bring it. And Zoya said she had got hold of the toilet rolls, and would bring them for Anna. Zoya rattled on about the appalling queue, and some interesting gossip she'd picked up there, but Anna cut her short, saying she was busy and would see her later. The lovers drifted again; again the phone rang, and Charsky cursed.

'Yes, he's right here.'

She handed the phone awkwardly to Dmitri. It was so close to her head she could hear Bella Kropotkin's husky, languid voice. 'Yes, I've just had your letter,' said Charsky. 'I'm very interested . . . It would certainly be possible, I'd like that . . . The Leningrad, right. Say about eleven thirty? . . . Okay, I'll see you. Thank you for ringing.'

Anna twisted to take the phone back, and replaced it on its base. 'Would it be *possible* to speak to Comrade Charsky?' she said mockingly in Kropotkin's husky, languid, somewhat condescending tones. Charsky stroked her shoulder, kissed her nape. 'I think you'd better come up to my room,' she mimicked again.

'Don't tell me you're jealous?'

'Of course not. But she obviously intends to seduce you.'

'Rubbish!'

'Why else should she invite you to her room? It would be easier to meet you in the bar. She'll have to bribe the *dezhurnaya* to let you visit her at that time.'

He flecked her shoulder with kisses. 'The bar would be noisy. Besides, she's famous, and I'm not totally unknown myself. We would attract attention.'

'I think you're being very naïve.'

'Well, she won't cause us any trouble.'

'Go on!' she exclaimed more lightly, chuckling. 'Of course

you'll sleep with her! I know you sleep with dozens of women; and I really don't mind, only I wish you'd be honest. Have you ever had a beautiful blind woman?'

'How can I convince you I've never slept with anyone but you? I know that's very boring of me, but it just happens to be true, my dear. I don't want anyone else. I'm a very lucky man, and I'd never risk losing you. How could anything match this?' He ran his hand softly over her thigh; his tone became bantering: 'I'm not so sure about *you*, my darling!'

'Now you're being stupid.'

'What about Ivan?'

'Ivan?'

'Sakulin.'

'You can't seriously imagine there was anything in that. We're friends.'

'Why do you say "*was* anything in that" and then "we're friends"? Has your relationship changed? *Was* there something?'

'Of course not. I only said *was* because I hardly ever see him anymore. Perhaps he spends more time with his wife when he's ashore these days.'

He slid his arm around her, cupping her breast. 'I know there's nothing between you,' he murmured. 'I was just trying to show you *you're* being silly. Do you know, I can't tell where I end and you begin. I feel as if my skin has dissolved down there, and it's a part of you. Or that *I've* got a vagina! I'm drifting . . . It's so beautiful.'

'Yes. Yes.' Over his cupping hand she placed her own.

'I shouldn't say this, with Father just gone, but I don't think I've ever felt so happy, Anna. I don't simply love you, I'm still in love with you, after twenty years! Isn't it amazing! And our work is going well—it's thrilling about your poems—and we're healthy. . . . There's a little more freedom and decency; we don't have to talk about getting out of Russia anymore.' He sighed with happiness, burying his face in her hair.

They fell silent. The light at the window grew stronger, but their eyes were closed.

She awoke from a light drowse to the distant strains of Tchaikovsky's Violin Concerto, the lyrical theme of the first movement.

From his inertness and his light breathing she could tell that Dmitri was asleep. He was still inside her, but softened and withdrawn, and she could not have said honestly that the experience was an exciting one. She stretched to pick up her cigarettes and matches. Balancing awkwardly on her elbows, she lit up. Then she picked up the book of 'psychological correspondences' again and began with difficulty to read the letters . . .

Frankfurt

Dear Professor,

I do not know if this will find you. I just wanted to tell you that I glanced at your book while cleaning my master's study (he is a doctor) and it has had a terrible effect on me. I can't sleep at nights from thinking of those dreadful things you describe. I know I am just an ignorant servant-girl, aged 17, but I do know some Latin. The governess here, Miss Lambert, has kindly taught me a little. Well, I am shocked that such things can be published, I do not think it is right. I am sure you are well meaning, but I wanted you to know how I feel.

Perhaps you can advise me how I can stop thinking about that horrible book.

Sincerely yours,
Sophie Arandt

Vienna

Dear Fräulein Arandt,

I am very sorry to learn that my book has had such a distressing effect on you. I can only tell you that it is intended to be read by a very limited circle of people in the medical profession. I would be distressed to hear of any ladies reading it, let alone a girl of your tender years and experience. I am sorry. Your master should really have kept the book under lock and key. Forget you ever saw it.

Sincerely yours,
(Prof.) Richard von Krafft-Ebing

Anna felt touched by the simple letter of a girl dead, no doubt, these fifty years. Her thoughts drifted to when she herself had been seventeen. So terribly serious and ignorant, and rather prudish like Sophie. So insecure about her sexuality that she'd eaten too much and got fat. She didn't know what Dmitri had seen in her.

The poetry reading at the Institute. Akhmatova, elderly, swollen up with thyroid, yet still majestic. Konstantin was there, the rake of her class; with him, his younger brother. Dmitri. Gentler, shy too. Relaxed her. The first sweet, shy kisses; the first fumbling passion . . . Freezing in her white dress, posing under the Bronze Horseman . . . Ecstasy of the honeymoon . . . But why does everything have to fade, drift away like the leaves, grow sober? . . .

I was interrupted by the phone's ringing. It brought me back too precipitately into the small, dimly lit world of the hotel bedroom. Masha reached to answer it. We heard her say, 'Yes?' in English, then, in her own language: 'Shimon? What a nice surprise! How did you know I was here?'

I got to my feet and stretched. The others did the same, and yawned. I glanced at my watch: one thirty.

'What time is it in Australia? . . . Is it very hot? . . . Wonderful weather: blue skies, and very mild. Well, compared with Moscow . . . No, I wasn't asleep; we're improvising. The Festival's pretty awful, so we're entertaining each other . . .'

I went to the bathroom; when I came out, she was murmuring sympathetic noises down the phone. Surkov silently offered me more claret but I indicated a bottle of Perrier.

'Don't worry, she'll be back; she's left you before . . .' Clearly her ex-husband's Australian girlfriend had decamped. 'You shouldn't have played around; she's not as soft as I used to be . . . I wouldn't go to her straightaway, if I were you: give her space for a couple of days, then send a big bunch of roses . . .' And so on—sympathetically, yet also with the indefinable remoteness of a woman speaking to someone, once close, who has faded out of her life.

'I'm sure it will be okay; good-bye, my dear.'

She put the phone down. 'He sends his regards,' she said.

Surkov asked how he'd known she was in London. He'd rung Liubov, she replied. He was very upset; and still, after five years, he turned to her for comfort and advice; still like a child, *her* child. And she didn't want it.

We sipped our drinks quietly. I felt tired. 'Do you want to call it a night?' asked Surkov, perhaps hopefully.

'Soon. But I'd like to finish it off.'

Rozanov said he must have a pee. I reflected on the next phase; and when he returned, sitting on the floor and resting his back on Masha's bed, I plunged in again . . .

· 6 ·

In the disputed territory, the Karelia or Sudetenland, between waking and sleeping, Charsky heard the distant screech of a violin and, close to him, a rustle of pages. These sounds blended into one, then fell into oblivion. A different drama was being enacted in his mind . . .

He was climbing. He was climbing the Eiger North Face. No one had ever climbed it, or even attempted it. It was unclimbable. Yet Charsky was not merely attempting it, but doing it solo! It was foolhardly.

After more days and nights than he cared to remember, he was perched on a ledge, perhaps halfway up, unable to move up or down. The first hint of dawn was touching the valley. In the villages of Grindelwald and Kleine Scheidegg, tourists were breakfasting and getting ready to rush out and stare through telescopes or binoculars at the sinister face. Its poised, out-thrust head gave it the appearance of a cobra, a white cobra.

The weather had been kind, but now cloud was closing in. Charsky heard a strange rustling sound beneath him. Unknown to him, two German climbers were also attempting the face. The lead climber, Sedlmayer, caught sight of a possible bivouac ledge, and simultaneously a man's face, looming up out of the icy fog—the German was so startled by the sight he almost slipped and tumbled back. The face was covered in stubble and the eyes stared in numb exhaustion. Hands tugged at the German and helped him up onto the narrow ledge. Then the two men hauled Mehringer up. The Germans, panting for breath, sank back against the ice.

'Who the hell are you?' asked Sedlmayer at last.

'Charsky. I'm glad to see you. I couldn't have gone any further. I was waiting for death.'

The Germans introduced themselves.

Over some bread and sausage, the two Germans engaged the Russian in chat, trying to keep him awake. This was their second night; he could rope-up with them, and they'd reach the top for sure tomorrow. Yes, the face was tough work; but they were working men, they'd be working almost as hard if they were at home in Munich.

'What do you think of Hitler?' asked Charsky.

'He's a tough guy. He makes our trains run on time. We need him.'

'He'll attack us Russians.'

They cracked their frozen lips in grins. 'Not very likely!'

'Twenty million of us will die. The Jews will be wiped out in gas-chambers.'

Tired cackles came from Mehringer and Sedlmayer. Exposure on the North Face had unhinged the Russian climber.

Roped perilously to the ice-face, the German pair drowsed through the night. When they awoke, the Russian was gone. Evidently he had fallen.

Those who stared through telescopes or fieldglasses saw how drastically the two climbers had slowed on the third day. Sometimes they would hang motionless for twenty minutes. This icefield was steeper than the first, and twice as high. Boulders constantly swept down on either side of them. The watchers saw how hopeless it was.

That night a storm blew up. The face was veiled in cloud;

thunder and lightning raged. No sight of the climbers as a day passed that was like night. But towards noon of the next day the clouds parted for a moment. Two tiny shapes climbing towards the Flatiron. The lead climber looked strong still, but his partner often slumped in his ropes. The storm closed in once more.

Mehringer was slumped in the rope when his partner, above, saw what seemed a huge sheet of glass cascading down. Sedlmayer shouted a warning but his friend was too weary to move. He was carried away down, the rope snapping. Sedlmayer turned again to the mountain, hacking out another footstep, and another. Then he crouched against the ice, and stayed there. He grew one with the ice. It looked as if he were copulating with the ice. You couldn't distinguish German from ice.

He was groaning and clawing at the pillow. She wondered if she should wake him, but his breathing became easier and she relaxed.

She returned to her book.

Frankfurt

Dear Professor,

It was kind of you to write, and unexpected. I never dreamt of a reply from such a distinguished person.

All the same, I can't forget what I saw, what I read. Those dreadful, ghastly images have stayed in front of my eyes every moment of the past five months. I even see them in my nightmares, and have often woken up screaming. Tell me there are a few men, somewhere, who do not think such dreadful thoughts, do not commit such unspeakable deeds. Tell me that, so I may hope still to find, one day, a man of pure heart. I have more than once thought of doing away with myself.

But no, you have spent enough time writing to a poor

ignorant serving-girl. Thank you again for your kind letter. Forget me.

Sincerely yours,
Sophie Arandt

Anna liked and sympathised with the girl who had written this letter. And yet letters are very enigmatic, she thought. Maybe she is naturally melodramatic.

She pictured Richard von Krafft-Ebing slitting open the letter in his office. It would be a very neat, slightly stuffy office. Nothing would suggest the man who had collected the material for *Psychopathia Sexualis*. She could imagine what kind of material was in that book, and her nape prickled. She wanted to read it. But even if one of her husband's Western friends sent it, it would never reach them.

Vienna

Dear Fräulein,

On no account must you think of suicide! I urge you to take your master into your confidence, explaining that you glanced at my book by chance while cleaning his study, and that you have been greatly disturbed by it. As a doctor, he will understand and help you.

I ought to have explained in my letter—as is made clear in my book—that the case studies are those of pathologically disturbed men (and some women); people locked-away in asylums or prisons, or who have paid for their vile perversions with their lives. What you chanced to read has no connection with the feelings and desires of normal men: have no fear on that score. Pure-hearted men are all around you. You will one day find such a man and marry him, I am certain.

Yours sincerely,
(Prof.) Richard von Krafft-Ebing

How can he be certain of that? thought Anna indignantly. The girl is obviously fairly intelligent, and so will find it hard to find a man worthy of her among the servant classes; and how will she meet anyone else? She probably has one half-day free per week, and then she will have to visit her parents, no doubt. In any case she'll be too exhausted to do much with her half-day.

The sensation in her vulva was quite pleasurable, but not to be compared with the quiet delight of teasing people's thoughts and feelings out of an unfamiliar language.

Frankfurt

Dear Professor,

How very kind of you to write again. I wish with all my heart I could believe what you say. I continue to be very depressed, and last night I took a kitchen-knife to my bedroom and drew blood from my wrist. But I thought of you, your concern for me, and how it might trouble your conscience (not that you would ever hear of it), so I stopped. Dreadful nightmares, when I finally got off to sleep, of men attacking me—like that man who had to cut women on their arms before he could find them desirable. I have to look after two dear little boys, but these days I can only see them growing up to behave so cruelly towards women. So I don't feel the same towards them anymore.

I couldn't possibly tell Dr Grossman what I did. I shouldn't have been in his study in the first place. I was not supposed to clean there, it's just that I love reading and sometimes I feel starved. He is very strict, and would dismiss me if he found out I'd been interfering with his books. Can you tell me a way to get these dreadful pictures out of my head? I see blood before my eyes, and am often dizzy. My hand is shaking as I write. Please excuse my handwriting.

Yours sincerely,
Sophie Arandt

Vienna

Fräulein,

   Consult another doctor, who is bound to keep your confidence. I wish you well.

Prof. von Krafft-Ebing

Anna smouldered with indignation on poor Sophie's behalf. What possible justification could there be for such coldness? All right, he is very busy, one could understand a degree of impatience; but this girl is in a bad way, she has taken a knife to her room, she sees blood before her eyes. It was typical male selfishness and cruelty.

She had to light a cigarette to calm herself a little. Angry with Dmitri, who obviously lied about his affairs with adoring women, she felt like pulling out from the *carezza*; however, it might wake him, and she would be unable to continue reading the intriguing correspondence.

Frankfurt

Dear Professor,

   Thank you for your curt note. I could not possibly go to another doctor. He would be a man—therefore probably a beast. If you cannot help me, there is only one way out.

Yours sincerely,
Sophie Arandt

Charsky was in trouble. He was pressed against almost sheer ice, clinging on by his fingers. Somewhere not too far below him were the wooden doors of the Gallery Window of the Jungfraujoch railway; defeated in his climb, he had been descending, heading for the Window, hoping he could hammer on it and attract someone's attention. But ice and spindrift made it impossible to see where he was going; and now he was trapped.

Suddenly through the howling gale he heard a yodel from below. Thank God! Some railwayman must have opened the doors, perhaps sensing he was in trouble. Charsky tried to call for help, but his voice was frail; then, to his amazement, he heard a strong voice from somewhere to his left shout: 'We're on our way down! We're okay!'

At that moment the mist parted, and Charsky caught sight of four dim figures, not twenty yards away from him. He recognised Kurz and Hinterstoisser, he'd seen them at the hotel; strikingly handsome fellows, especially Kurz, an officer of the Wehrmacht, blue-eyed, blond-haired. Kurz had been boasting that they would be the first to climb the face, thus adding to the triumph of the Berlin Olympics.

One of the other figures seemed to be injured. His three comrades were bringing him down.

Charsky summoned all his weak strength to shout: 'Help me!'

Hinterstoisser, startled in the act of untying his climbing rope, missed his footing and plunged. The movement of the rope pulled the injured climber from his stance, he fell, a rope coil whipped around his neck and he strangled. He hung some fifteen feet below Kurz, on the same rope; and their joint weight thrust their remaining comrade against a piton. Charsky watched him freeze to death before his eyes.

The Russian wanted to say, 'I'm sorry, it was all my fault,' but just then his left foot felt a ledge and he was able to take the weight off his fingers. The ledge, he found, was quite broad, and from it there was a reasonable climb up. But he crouched, he would wait, he would wait to see what happened to Kurz. The German was hanging helpless on his rope. Half an hour passed; nightfall blanked out the mist and spindrift. Charsky heard a voice float up: 'Are you all right?'

'No!' cried Kurz in a weak voice. 'The others are all dead. I'm the only one alive. Please help me!'

'I'll be right back!'

An endless time, then a babble of voices. They were asking Kurz if he could lower a rope so that they could attach some supplies to it. He cried that he had no rope. He had also lost his left mitten. He couldn't feel his left arm.

'We'll be back at daybreak. Stick it out.'

'No! No! I'll freeze to death here! Don't leave me!'

'You can do it!'

Then there was only the shrill, relentless voice of the gale.

Relatively comfortable himself, Charsky suffered every moment of the long night with Kurz. It seemed to him that he *was* Kurz, in some strange way. He was forever on the verge of falling into sweet, endless sleep, but somehow he forced himself to stay awake. And at last he heard: 'We're here! Are you all right?'

Kurz uttered a weak cry, between yes and no.

'Good man! Now here's what you must do . . .'

What they were asking was impossible, but he would try. Using his one good hand, he inched down to Angerer and with his ice-axe cut him loose. The body in its shroud of ice stayed fixed to the rock-face. Then he climbed inch by inch up to Rainer. Anchoring himself to a piton, he cut the climbing rope and started to unravel its strands, working with the nearly frozen fingers of one hand. Then he tied one strand to another. It took him six hours to make a long, thin rope, but he had lost all sense of time.

He tied a stone to the makeshift rope and lowered it. He felt a tug, and drew the rope up. Attached to its end was a climbing rope, a hammer, pitons and carabiners.

'Wait!' the shout came up. 'The rope's not going to be quite long enough. Lower your rope again and we'll tie a length on.'

Kurz did as he was asked.

Now, somehow holding a piton with his useless hand, he had to hammer it into the rock with the other. He threaded the rope through the spike's eye. Then he set out to rappel down the cliff, jerk after jerk as his feet hit the rock.

'You're doing fine!' they shouted. 'We'll soon have you!'

Suddenly he could go no further.

'What's wrong?'

The rescuer's voice was not far beneath him.

'The knot! It's jammed in the link. The knot tying the ropes together.'

'Force it through! Come on, man, you can do it!'

He bent to the carabiner at his waist, and tried to chew at the knot, to make it more supple. It was no good. He felt something touch his boots; heard a gasp: 'It's no good! Bring me down.'

Kurz cried out. 'What?' they called back.

'I'm finished . . .'

His head slumped forward as he gave up the ghost. His body tilted to horizontal, legs and arms hanging, like a spider from a strand.

Charsky came back into himself; he sobbed for the brave Bavarian. Then, cautiously, inch by inch, he started climbing again.

Frankfurt

Dear Professor,

So this is how much you care about me! I plead for help, to you who caused my suffering, and you do not even bother to reply! I could have been dead, for all you knew or cared. Your indifference is cruel. Well, I will not bother you ever again.

Sophie Arandt

Frankfurt

Dear Professor,

Forgive me, forgive me, for thinking you didn't care! I didn't know you were away from home. When my master summoned me and told me you had written to him, at first I was angry with you for betraying my confidence. But then I realised it was a sign of your caring, and I blessed you.

There is one good man in the world. I tried to remember that, when my master punished me. He made me expose my bottom to him and he whipped me. I feel horrible, degraded. If I had anywhere else to go I would leave this house. But please, please don't write to him again!

Sincerely yours,
Sophie Arandt

Vienna

Dear Fräulein,

You are a contemptible girl to tell such mischievous lies about a master who has shown every care towards you. I wash my hands of you.

Sincerely yours,
R. von Krafft-Ebing

Frankfurt

Dear Professor,

I deserve it. That belittling word *Du*, after you have addressed me as *Sie* so respectfully, showed me what you think of me, and affected me even more than contemptible. I did not tell you lies but I do deserve your contempt.

I would not bother you again, only I have a last request. You can't refuse a condemned girl her last request, can you? It is, that you will sell me a copy of your book. You see, I think I was in such a state after glancing at those few pages simply because I didn't read any more. My master, Dr Grossman, says it isn't at all a dirty book if you read all of it. When I asked him if I could borrow his copy he said I wouldn't understand it, which is true, I suppose. I think I could understand enough, however, to be able to put my experience into perspective.

Please won't you do me this favour? Please send me

the book, letting me know how much it is. I don't go out very much to spend my money, so I have some saved up. Please do this for me and then forget about

> Your humble servant,
> Sophie Arandt

Charsky stood on a narrow ledge above the Spider Snowfield. Below and above him were overhangs; he had lost all his equipment; the few inches of rock beneath his feet threatened to crumble away; a blizzard tore at him constantly; his situation was entirely hopeless.

True, there was a mixed Italian and German team climbing not far away, heading for the Traverse of the Gods; he could see them, but for some reason they couldn't see him. He tried to shout for help, but was too weak to raise even the feeblest of cries.

He could see that Longhi, the lowest on the rope, was in a bad way; his hands kept slipping. It was no surprise to the Russian when an anguished cry rang out: 'Falling! Hold me!' Despite the gale, Charsky heard the whiplash of the rope snaking through the second Italian, Corti's, gloves, as he struggled to hold his partner. He would have burn marks on his hands. Somehow he managed to brake the fall. Longhi was hanging in midair.

'Lower me about six feet!' shouted Longhi. 'There's a ledge.'

'Okay, Stefano!'

Charsky watched him being lowered onto a ledge, a little wider than his own.

'Can you climb up?' Corti shouted.

'Impossible. My hands are frozen stiff. That's why I fell.'

'We'll try to pull you up: hold on . . . It's no good, Stefano. We'll climb on up and get help to you. Tomorrow we'll be back and pull you up. Courage, old friend!'

'Yes, pull me up,' cried Longhi, not understanding.

'Good-bye, Stefano. Courage!'

'Good-bye.'

The Russian's eyes followed Corti's climb, in the wake of the two Germans. By late afternoon they were more than halfway up the Exit Cracks. Then he saw a stone fall, glance off a crag, and hit Corti on the head. He tumbled sixty feet before he was brought up short with a jolt. He was hanging head down; blood fell into the snow. The Germans climbed down to him, packed snow into the head wound, then dragged him to a ledge. With cords and pitons they anchored him to the rock. Then they set off climbing.

Night fell. Charsky, who had no idea how many nights he had spent on the face, tried to keep himself awake by recalling all he knew of Russian history, from the founding of Kiev Rus to the death of Stalin and the suppression of Hungary.

Sometime during the next day he saw a man in a harness being lowered by cable towards Corti; heard a shout: 'I have him!'

'Nothdurft? Mayer?' the rescuer asked the injured man.

The Italian feebly shook his head. 'Corti. Nothdurft and Mayer went on up to get help.'

'It seems they didn't make it.'

'My friend, Stefano, is down there.' Corti pointed.

'I'll come back for him later.'

Charsky tried to shout that he too was here, but couldn't utter a sound. He watched the harnessed pair being lifted up. When they came into contact with the rock-face, Corti tried to bite the snow, saying, 'Hungry'. They were lost to sight; yet Charsky heard the Italian's voice float down clearly: 'How beautiful the sun is!'

The snowswept day was turning towards darkness. Another man with a harness was being lowered. Then the cable could go no further. The man shouted, 'Longhi! Longhi!'

A weak cry: 'Come!'

'Courage! Courage!'

Then the cable was being pulled up.

Once more, before darkness covered the grim face of the White Cobra, voices were heard distantly: 'Longhi! Are you there?'

'Come! Come!'

'Just hold on, Stefano! You'll be rescued in the morning without fail!'

'Hungry! Cold!'

Then again the mountain face belonged to the wind and the snow. During the long night Charsky managed to find his voice; he called out, 'Stefano!' But Longhi did not respond, and did not speak again. When morning came, the Russian saw he had fallen from the ledge and was hanging upside-down, his ice-face and the rock-face united in a *carezza*.

· 7 ·

I collapsed back into the armchair, almost as exhausted as if I'd been climbing the *Eigernordwand*. Surkov lit me a cigarette and placed it between my lips.

This kindness was soon drowned in a torrent of criticism. 'It's completely fucked up. There's no point going on. I know you did your best but—Jesus! There's simply no unity, no consistency, no narrative thrust. All these pseudo-dreams and irrelevant letters!'

'I loved the dreams,' said Masha. 'The *Eigernordwand*! It brought it back to me!' For a moment her eyes and her smile, turned to me, conveyed a hint of past emotions.

'There was one sheer impossibility,' he growled. 'Charsky mentions Ivan Sakulin. We've heard of him before. Nadia's husband in *Sphinx*. But he had drowned. Or possibly been smuggled out of Russia by the CIA. He certainly can't be still in the Soviet Navy. Or have you resurrected him?' he sneered.

'Given the Russian setting,' said Rozanov, sprawled on a bed, his eyes closed, 'I don't accept that it's an impossibility. In the Soviet Union anything is possible, you know that.'

His eyes opened and he gave me a weak smile. I nodded gratefully. He hauled himself into a sitting position.

'The blind film director . . . ,' he mused, rubbing his scarred and stubbled chin. 'A nice touch. Did you have Olga in mind?'

'Not consciously; but now you mention it . . .' Sergei's troubles had all begun with an adulterous rendezvous in Gorky with a blind woman called Olga. We had made that frantic and tragic episode the central pillar of *Ararat*, our first volume.

I asked if he knew what had happened to her. Pulling himself wearily to his feet, he walked to the window, drew aside the curtain and gazed out at the blackness. 'Well, it's a very strange story. She was married to a Jew, a history professor. We made him blind too, if you remember, but in reality he's sighted. Soon after the Gorky fiasco they sought permission to emigrate to Israel. They were refused, of course, and suffered the consequences. *You* know all about that, Masha.'

'*Da.*' Masha had suffered when her husband had applied for a visa.

Rozanov let the curtain drop and took a pace or two up and down.

'She's kept in touch with me. Last year they were given permission to go to Israel. In the transit lounge at Vienna Airport, Professor Kubik bought a German paperback. It was a translation of our novel *Ararat*: his specialism is Armenian history, you see.'

'Shit!'

'He started to read it as the plane took off for Haifa. After the first few sentences he became bewildered, agitated, thunderstruck. This was Olga—even to her skinny legs! Thinking back, he recalled her distance, agitation and depression at that time; her deep involvement with my poetry; even a night she spent, unusually, away from home, with a "friend" . . . Just as Olga was fumbling with her food-tray, struggling to unseal the utensils, she was suddenly lashed by a storm of hysterical accusations. She felt unable to lie.

'The stewardess thought he was weeping for happiness at being free. But, as Olga said in her letter to me, one weeps more often because one is *not* free. He wasn't free from stupid jealousy, over a one-night fling six years before.'

He sat back down on the bed. I felt lost for words; had difficulty breathing. We ought at the very least to have changed her name. It was unforgivable of us—of me in particular.

'He divorced her. Well, she had never been happy with him, so she was relieved. She can now go wherever she wants, read whatever she wants. . . . And something quite miraculous happened: surgeons were able to restore her sight with a brilliant new surgical technique. How clever these Jews are! But she tells me she still does not feel free. She tells me the only freedom is that of the imagination. Well, I don't know.'

Surkov said, rising, 'I must be fresh for Maggie in the morning.' He slapped me on the shoulder: 'I was too rough on you. There was nothing personal about it; you gave a very smooth performance. I just don't think we're getting anywhere.'

I woke, late, to another almost-cloudless morning, and to the knowledge that it was Wednesday, half the week had gone: therefore I could begin to enjoy myself a little more.

There is a pattern to my occasional engagements away from home. In distant prospect I look forward to them greatly, as a break from the monotonous, lonely routine of writing. As they draw near, I dread them, I don't *want* to break the routine—damn it, I want to write! When the engagements are abroad, I work feverishly in the last few days and nights to create a reasonably finished piece of work—just in case we crash. If the engagement lasts several days, like this Festival, the first half drags; I find it a strain to have to talk to people again, I'm haunted by the inevitably unfinished 'finished' work at home. At the halfway stage, however, I relax, I'm a little more at ease, and I know the remaining days will pass more quickly. Then, once I am at home, I usually think the whole of it was splendid, and hate having to settle down to the monotonous, lonely life of a writer.

While I was shaving, peacefully surveying my baggy eyes, thick lips hinting at a recent coldsore, and ever-deepening wrinkles, I saw in the mirror something monstrous appear around the side of my grey hair. A gigantic house-spider. Shuddering, I flicked it off with my lathered razor. It struggled for a moment on the floor then vanished into a crevice behind a tile. Had it wandered onto me while I slept? It didn't bear thinking of, but I thought of nothing else as I prepared to go down to breakfast.

Rozanov, hunched in his crumpled navy suit, was looking at job adverts in the *Guardian*. He was thinking of settling in this land of freedom, he told me as I sat down opposite. He might become a Temporary Water Sports Development Officer. Or a Money Advice Support Unit Officer. Possibly an Assistant Race Relations Adviser. Or an Ethnic Minority Recreation Officer. Or he quite liked the idea of being an Afro-Caribbean Woman Advice Worker.

His smile, as I recounted my terrifying encounter—I am an arachnophobe—implied that there were worse things in life than having a spider wandering over one's hair.

Ordering fresh coffee from the waitress who came to take my order, he passed me the *Guardian* and picked up the *Sun*. The big news of the day, he said, though for some inexplicable reason the *Guardian* had ignored it, concerned the lovers who had bonked in a British Rail platform photo-booth. 'There's a subheading "Knickers" and it says "Passengers complained her green knickers were flying all over the place." I love that colour detail, don't you? Is that why they were complaining? Didn't they like green knickers? Or because knickers shouldn't fly? Bonking . . . bonking . . . It sounds like two pieces of wood rubbing together . . . Now what's on the problem page? I'm beginning to love Deirdre's column . . . "I Left Secret Lover Dying" . . .'

He scanned the column. 'The poor middle-aged guy had

a heart-attack during a *bonk* with his teen-aged neighbour
while his wife was out shopping. The girl ran off and left
him. He died, and now she feels guilty.'

'So what does Deirdre say?'

'She mustn't blame herself. By running off, keeping quiet,
she saved his family further distress. Even if he'd been rushed
straight to hospital they might not have been able to save
him. I like that. I'll remember her wise words if someone
ever has a heart-attack while I'm around—there's no particular
hurry.'

I nodded reflectively; sipped orange juice.

'Who needs Freud when there's Deirdre?'

I saw Victor threading an uncertain path through the
dining-room. So he had worn scruffy jeans and a Texas University T-shirt to his Downing Street breakfast. He looked
bleary-eyed, excited, disturbed. He flung himself into a chair
and drew out his Marlboros. 'What an experience!'

'Tell us.'

'Where's Masha?'

'She's having a lie-in,' said Rozanov. Then, rather guiltily,
'Well, I guess she is.'

Over a cup of Earl Grey tea, which he had tasted and
relished at Number 10, Surkov described his visit. There had
been a dozen East European 'experts' around the breakfast
table, advising Maggie on her Polish trip. Surkov had quoted
to her a poem by Zbigniew Herbert—and she'd said this
helped her to understand Poland more than anything else.
Afterwards, she had contrived a quarter of an hour alone with
him in a private office. They had kissed and caressed, but it
was deeply frustrating.

Surkov's hand trembled as he lit another cigarette. They
felt very emotional about each other, he said. She hoped to
be able to see him again, more privately, before her departure.
Maybe at night. 'It's the first time an older woman has really
stirred me.' But then, essentially she was a young girl still,
the daughter of a grocer who had ruined her with discipline;

a girl bursting with suppressed sexuality and fun. Knotted up. Fucked up. 'She says she can be herself with me, for the first time; can let herself go.'

'Is Victor a little crazy?' I asked Sergei while our friend was in the gents'.

'He's been a little crazy for some time. Maybe ever since he left Vera for Imogen—which was disastrous for him. He's a megalomaniac.'

'Do you think he breakfasted at Downing Street?'

'It's highly unlikely.'

Of course, he said, an artist dwelt on the edge of madness. I asked him about his shamanism. Well, it had come about while he'd been receiving the wet canvas treatment. I knew all about that. You were rolled up tight as a mummy in canvas, then water was poured on it. As the canvas dried, your bones cracked, you could hardly breathe. 'And I found myself floating quite calmly above my body. I could float around the ward, and even went outside into the snow. I saw the sentries in their watch-towers. I came back when they were unwrapping me.'

Since then he could travel, from time to time, to the realm of the dead, and return. You didn't have to go in for banging drums and shaking rattles to be a shaman; you had simply to have suffered tremendously, been torn apart, come close to death. Sometimes he went into a trance. It occasionally happened when he started an improvisation. Last winter, in Minsk, the voice of Alexander Blok had come through—so people told him afterwards; he had no recollection.

'Did you know,' he asked, 'when you were improvising last night, a cat sat on your lap for a while?'

My heart started to thump. 'What was it like?'

'It was small and black, with white paws and a white patch on its chest.'

'That was Thomas!' I exclaimed, my heart beating so wildly I thought I was going to have a heart-attack right there at the table. 'She died last week.'

My eyes blurred. I could see a cat, dying stoically.

'I know how you feel,' said Rozanov. 'I howled when one of mine died. We partly weep for ourselves; they are our vulnerable, helpless selves.'

'And they keep to the house and garden,' I said. 'They never go away. They are more faithful to the house than we are.'

'Wives or children may depart, but they stay.'

'And the places that knew them shall know them no more.'

He patted my shoulder. 'Well, she's okay. She's okay. She came to tell you.'

I feel hesitant about including that—it seems almost too personal. I begin to understand why it is rare for a novelist to be his own narrator. There is a good deal of self-censorship going on in these chapters about the Festival. For a start, I spent a lot of time on my own, or with non-Russian friends. It doesn't seem relevant to describe those times; but also, as the named author of this book, I am aware that a certain decorum is required. It's not that I am fearful of telling the truth, but the reader might be offended.

With a fictional character, described in the third person, there is nothing that may not be said. With a real person, like Surkov, a shade more circumspection is necessary, but not much. It's when one moves into the first person that problems occur. Generally the reader wants his narrator to be upright, decent, honest, and not prone to the lusts that plague other people—never ourselves. I might have called myself Ross Trenear: which would have allowed a little more scope—but not much.

Supposing, when Rozanov and I visited the porno bookshop, I said I'd bought a couple of hardcore videos, hired a video recorder at the hotel, and spent two afternoons watching porn in my room. It would arouse uncomfortable feelings in many readers. It would get in the way of their appreciation, if any, of the novel. I can tell you Surkov petted with Mrs Thatcher, or at least boasted of having done so; I would not feel able to confess to it myself.

Mostly, during the day, we went our separate ways. We did so on this day. After visiting the Hayward Gallery I spent a half-hour just gazing along the river-line, the historic buildings sharp in the clear, cold, sunny air. The distant traffic-noises did not seem to interrupt the silence; the reflective water gave to the Palace of Westminster the illusion of insubstantiality. Clearly the scene was beautiful, even though I do not see London as *my* city. This London belongs to the city gents with their regimental ties and their polished shoes; it belongs as little to a Celtic writer as it does to Surkov and Rozanov.

Its beauty was alien, yet effective. I imagined it all dissolving in a white heat, or swept away in an enormous wind. Surkov had repeated for my benefit his account of the submarine commander, poised to unleash destruction on London. He claimed to have heard it from the lips of Raisa, and swore its truth. The crazy guy, now at the bottom of the Baltic with his crew, had turned out to be a secret and tormented homosexual, a condition he had hidden under an apparently conventional marriage. There had been a ghastly failure of security, and heads had rolled.

But maybe it wasn't true. Surely, Masha and I had said, there were safeguards; a madman on his own simply couldn't unleash a nuclear warhead? But Surkov had insisted there were ways.

I glanced at my watch, and set off walking. It was almost time for the afternoon session at the Riverside. We were learning to treat this daily session in a casual way. Sometimes one or two of us turned up for it, sometimes no one did.

The theme today aroused my curiosity: a Celebration of Ulrike Meinhof. A few minutes late, I slipped into the half-full auditorium, spotted Sergei near the back, and sat beside him. An American novelist was reading the prison letters of the West German terrorist, whose face, blown-up, formed the backdrop to the stage. After the letters there were various tributes. I recall a few extracts . . .

Contrast the mass-murderer, Thatcher, assassin of British working-class soldiers, miners, old people and babies, with Ulrike, who chose her victims carefully from the exploiting classes, and with the aim of liberating humanity from its chains . . .

—Geraldine Porter

It takes courage to execute someone, to put a bullet through their brains, or blow them to pieces with a bomb. Ulrike had that courage. As a man, a white, a heterosexual, from a capitalist country, the country she tried to free, I have no right, you may think, to stand on this platform, but I gladly do so in order to salute her. I salute you, Ulrike, my friend! . . .

—Helmutt Hauptmann

She was a woman. A woman who fought her way to the top of a liberation movement which traditionally had been the preserve mainly of men. She is a great pioneer of feminism. Ulrike Meinhof, I ask you to accept my tears and my gratitude . . .

—Cita Lemminkaïnen

I think too of another courageous woman, fighting for Irish freedom, gunned down in Gibraltar by British terrorists with her two male comrades while strolling peacefully along. Ulrike is not alone, but she was one of the greatest . . .

—Sean Murphy

Humane terrorist! Tender assassin! Philanthropic bomber! Candleflame in the darkness of a diabolic world! . . .

—Jean-Paul Legrand

Ulrike saw the fucking military-industrial conspiracy for what it is, and she shat on it. And then they killed her! Suicide? That's crap. Ulrike loved life too much . . .
                                                        —*Judith Steinway*

Walking back to the hotel, Rozanov and I were silent for a long time. I was thinking of a little black cat gazing up at me with dim eyes; Rozanov of I know not what—possibly Ulrike Meinhof. But at length he began to speak of our improvisations, and how the nights here were better than the days. I said I could see Victor was right, I had overcomplicated the plot; I should not have introduced the letters, which were paraphrases of a correspondence I'd been reading on my journey to London. They had been a way of 'coasting' slightly, when I'd run out of steam. The Eiger-dreams, too, were a mistake.

'Yes, you probably *have* overdone them,' he agreed. 'But at least you had the sense to realise Charsky's performance on the Neva embankment was a dream, and that he was the man in bed with Anna. Victor would have got it completely wrong.'

'It sounded all too perfect.'

'Of course! It's someone who envies creativity, and wishes to be younger, handsomer. . . . You got it! And don't worry: Masha will bring us back to earth tonight. She may not be brilliant, but she tells a straightforward story. She'll set us on the right track.'

We were soon to discover that Masha might be in no condition to set us on any track. She phoned me in my room to say she had slipped in the bath and badly bruised her face. She sounded shaky. She would rest and not have dinner nor, regrettably, attend the evening performance, at which I was to read. She was very sorry; I told her not to worry. We should ring her on our return and she would see whether she felt able to perform. I wished her a good rest.

. . .

Always the coach-journey to the theatre was a silent one. We all sat hunched and unspeaking. I guessed it was because everyone felt faintly absurd. Though literary festivals could be immensely enjoyable, especially if they took you to some pleasant distant city, like Toronto or Adelaide, there was something absurd about writers gathering together in this way. We were all of us separate and self-absorbed; each one wrote what he was able to write. The absurdity became clearer if one imagined twenty or thirty writers from another era occupying the air-conditioned coach that took us from the Hyde Park Regis to the Riverside. Suppose—I reflected that evening—Stendhal, Lamartine, Poe, Jane Austen, Sir Walter Scott, De Quincey, Wordsworth, Coleridge, Keats, Percy and Mary Shelley, Ann Radcliffe, Leigh Hunt, Mickiewicz, Pushkin, Gogol, Goethe and a dozen other well-known, forgettable writers were making this journey. Well, it was unthinkable.

There was a depressingly thin crowd hovering in the foyer and bar. Tonight was a night without stars. We filed into the boxes reserved for the writers and gazed down at the acres of empty seats. Jock in his Superman outfit took the stage and welcomed the audience to Writers Internationale. Then he introduced Joshua N'dosi from Tanzania. Normally I only listen for the first couple of minutes at a reading; either I am preoccupied by having to read later myself, or some image causes me to drift away; but N'dosi had a powerful, hypnotic voice and his poetry sparkled with fresh, delightful metaphors. He was altogether too good.

And Judith Steinway's streetwise Brooklyn fiction, delivered in staccato tones, surprised me also by its quality. She also looked great—out of dungarees for the first time and into a becomingly simple black dress. She received warm applause, and during the interval respectable queues formed before her table of books, as before N'dosi's.

After she had finished signing, I approached her, clutching a drink. 'That was great!' I said. 'And I love your dress.'

'Don't be so fucking patronising,' she said, turning her back on me to continue a conversation with Geraldine Porter.

The interval bell sounded, and soon I was waiting for Jock to introduce me, and striding on. I began confidently enough, with a humorous extract; but when the first couple of jokes went by with never a chuckle from the audience, I became nervous. I dried. Reaching for a glass of water I found there was none. Nervousness turned to panic. I couldn't get my tongue around the consonants; I lisped. The rest of the reading was torture. I stumbled off to polite applause.

Jock shook my hand in passing, and introduced the last performer, Milorad Pavic. Pavic, a moustached and gentlemanly Yugoslav, was waiting in the wings with an actress, who would read all but the first page or two of the author's book in English translation. They went on. An astonishing double of Lech Walesa, the Yugoslav spoke briefly about his *Dictionary of the Khazars*, which was in two editions, one for men and one for women. The texts, he said, differed in a single paragraph. I felt envious of his brilliant idea. Yet I felt too strung up about my botched performance to listen properly. No matter—I would buy his book. There was no substitute for reading.

Afterwards, as the sparse crowd emerged blinking, Pavic and I sat at our tables piled with books. I was relieved to see a dozen or so people form up in front of me. My biro and strained smile got to work. My third or fourth customer was a man of about thirty, with the athletic, boyish, curly-haired handsomeness of David Gower, the cricketer, or Lieutenant Gonville Bromhead of *Zulu*. Opening the paperback at the title page, I glanced up and asked him should I sign it *for* someone. 'For Paul,' he said diffidently; then—'Your work means a lot to me. Could you please write something in it? You see'—his voice trembled slightly, his blue eyes became haunted, his bloom of good looks seemed to collapse inwards—'I have cancer. I'm told I have six months to live. If you could write something—anything—I'd appreciate it so much.'

'My God, that's terrible!' I said. 'And you look so well.'

'I *feel* well. But . . .' His voice trailed away.

'Of course I'll write something.' I thought desperately, and wrote. I stood up and shook his hand. 'Good luck!'

'Thank you. And thank you for this.'

He moved away, and I put on my strained smile again for the next patiently waiting customer. Out of the corner of my eye I saw the young man join Pavic's queue.

The graceful, dying face stayed before my eyes. I hoped what I had written was okay. What can one write for a man who is dying, who is going into a world where there are no books, no words?

When I had finished signing, I went to the bar. I got talking to a Faber editor I knew slightly. I told her about the tragic young man. She asked his name. His first name was Paul, I said, that was all I knew. She nodded. 'He's been at the Festival every evening, buying everyone's books, telling the same story. A couple of years ago he wrote to several of our authors, saying that he was dying, their work meant a lot to him, could they write something for him. He's a book collector. By the time he's eighty he'll have a unique collection.'

'Shit.'

'What did you write?'

'Some lines from "And Death Shall Have No Dominion." '

'That was very suitable.'

Smiling, she turned away. A slim attractive girl in jeans hovered near, her pose suggesting I could approach her; but before I could do so, Sēnora Sanchez accosted me. She congratulated me, then enquired after Masha, whose absence she had noticed at dinner. Her black eyes peered intently into mine as she nodded sympathetically. I could see, again, how striking she must once have been, when her primly drawn-back grey hair had presumably matched her eyes, 'with all

5that's fair of black and bright'. But elderly ladies make me feel uncomfortable; our small-talk petered out; I was glad when she said she must go and congratulate N'dosi, and moved away.

Surkov and Rozanov, escaping from admirers, joined me and we headed for the exit. Sitting on my own behind them on the return journey I looked straight at the innocently sensuous lips of Isabella Rossellini, advertising a perfume near traffic lights. She brought back her mother, Ingrid Bergman, and therefore the days of my youth. I slipped into reverie.

Coming back into the present, I caught the Rolls-Royce purr of central London, the purr of privilege, money, power—as far from my little cat's dying purr as it is possible to be. For a moment, until I remembered ordinary people, children, animals, fall-out, I wanted that crazed submarine commander to have succeeded. The anger went with me into the Regis.

Surkov rang Masha from the lobby and learnt that she felt better; we could come to her room. We rose with several of our colleagues, who spilled out on the fifteenth floor to attend the nightly booze-up. We continued another three floors. A dressing-gowned Masha opened the door to us. The right side of her face was badly bruised, already purple. But really, she was fine. 'How did it go?' she asked me, as Rozanov gave her an especially tender hug.

'He was *first-rate*!' enthused Surkov, using the English adjective and thereby giving his compliment an ironic tinge. 'It was just a pity there were not many people.'

We settled ourselves. Wine glugged. She declared herself fit to 'perform'. 'Make it a firm narrative line, Masha,' Surkov requested. 'No more fucking dreams and letters.'

'I'll do my best.'

· 8 ·

She thought again of waking him, for he was struggling for breath in his sleep. He reminded her of his father, who had suffered from a lung disease. That had led to his sudden and unexpected collapse, the heart giving out. It was called being dead. It had really shaken her up. . . .

On the other hand, she really wanted to go on exploring the nineteenth-century letters . . .

Vienna

Dear Fräulein,

Excuse my delay in replying—I have been very busy marking examinations, etc. It was wrong of me to write you such an angry note: please accept my apologies. As you can see, I am sending you a copy of *Psychopathia Sexualis*, as requested. I do so with much misgiving, but I do see your point. You will I hope realise that these cases are placed in the context of a diseased sexuality. You are clearly a bright girl, and will throw off this disturbance. I did not have to pay for this copy, so there is no need for you to send any money.

Sincerely yours,
R. von Krafft-Ebing

Frankfurt

My dear Professor!

Oh, you are too kind! Your book is a treasure-trove of unspeakable delights! I have only dipped into it here and there, but already I know it will displace the Tales of Grimm as my favourite book. I read one, or sometimes two, descriptions each night, curled up in bed—I cannot bear to read any more, because each one sends my brain reeling and spinning like a moth round a candle-flame.

Tonight I have read the account of the gentleman who loves ladies' pubic hair, and I understand him so well. Do you know him personally? If so, would you kindly forward to him the tiny little package? It contains a few of my pubic hairs. Tell him that a young lady who has read his story with interest and affection offers them as a gift. It's beautiful to think there's a man who spends his life going from hotel to hotel, paying chambermaids to let him look in beds slept in by women, in the hope of finding some hairs! I could unquestionably get him several different shades of hairs from this house. Would you please tell him that?

If you should wish to look inside the packet, before sending it, feel free to do so.

Thank you. Thank you!

Sincerely yours,
Sophie Arandt

Ah, how touching! thought Anna: it reminds me of Dmitri, when I was on a field trip in the Urals, that summer—oh, was it '66, '67? He wrote to me begging me to send him some cuttings of my pubic hairs, and I did! He really lusted after me in those days. . . .

Vienna

Fräulein,

Enough! I should never have sent you my book. I am about to take a long vacation. I wish you well, but do not write to me again.

R. von Krafft-Ebing

P.S. I shall burn the packet unopened.

Frankfurt

Dear Professor,

I am hurt. Also I do not understand. If you were unwilling to forward my small gift, why did you send me the gentleman's name and address? At least, I assume this card (which I am returning) concerns the man who loves collecting pubic hair—it's much too learned and technical for me to understand most of it, but there are bits of it which do seem to make it clear. Is it that you wanted to demonstrate to me how ignorant I am? I know that only too well.

I can see I have been a great burden to you. I am sorry and ashamed. You will hear no more from me. I wish you a nice vacation.

Sincerely yours,
Sophie Arandt

Vienna

Dear Fräulein Arandt,

I am deeply distressed, and also not a little irritated, by the direction events have taken in our correspondence. I returned home to find your letter of August 4, and also a more recent one from Dr Grossman. I cannot imagine how I made the mistake of putting a patient's medical card in with my last note to you. It was an unforgivable, though unintended, breach of confidence; and it is but a small consolation to know that Herr Sussmeyer thereby gained a correspondence with a young woman which he has doubtless found extremely gratifying.

I was angry with your letter (and packet), and also burdened with too many responsibilities. At the same time as I was writing some correspondence (including the note to you), I was attempting to organise the hand-over of certain severely disturbed patients to various colleagues who were to assume responsibility for them during the long vacation. Herr Sussmeyer was one such case. In my haste, and under the influence of the contents of your letter, I evidently placed Herr Sussmeyer's medical card in the wrong envelope and sent it to you. The colleague who ought to have received it received only my accompanying note.

I have apologised to your master for the regrettable error. You are owed an apology also. Though it was foolish of you to enter into correspondence with my patient, it was predictable that you would do so, in your troubled state. You must understand that, upon discovery of such an unsavoury correspondence, your master and mistress could not possibly take the risk of leaving their young children in your hands. I hope your new duties are not too disagreeable.

Your master has persuaded me that you found our correspondence helpful, and that I should resume it. You strike me as a basically good-natured and decent girl, and if I can be of assistance in putting you back on the right path, I shall be happy to oblige, so long as you do not expect too lengthy or too frequent an exchange. You cannot imagine how overwhelmed I feel with duties sometimes.

Sincerely yours,
Prof. R. von Krafft-Ebing

Frankfurt

Dear Professor,

I don't deserve your kindness. The mistake with the card was an understandable one. I am sorry you are so burdened with duties. I will try not to add to them too much.

I do not mind at all being a parlour-maid, though I do miss the company of the children. I am glad to be able to tell you I am feeling much happier and calmer. This is because I have at last discovered the key to my existence, the meaning of my life. I need to be used by men—or preferably one man. To be used in any way they see fit, even to the point of humiliation. That's why I wrote to you about Herr Sussmeyer and enclosed the pubic hair—though I didn't realise it at the time. Because I thought he could use me in his own way, and that would make me happy. But when I wrote to him it didn't work out; he was much too polite and too adoring. I don't want to be adored, I want to be used and abused, I want to be treated with contempt.

As soon as I found out the truth about myself, all my cares and worries fell away. You can't imagine the relief! I haven't been able to explain this to Dr Grossman, because he wouldn't understand, but you will understand, and I hope be happy for me. I hope you are well, and not feeling so over-burdened.

Sincerely yours,
Sophie Arandt

Stupid, stupid girl! thought Anna sadly. At the same time, there was something poetic and almost beautiful in her extremism. Didn't passion arise from a clash of extremes rather than the equal union she and Dmitri shared—and which they were expressing in this long, unmoving screw? Weren't they missing something?

Vienna

Dear Fräulein,

I hope and believe the sad condition you describe is no more than a temporary fantasy. Possibly you have been influenced by the examples of masochism in the book—a term I coined to define that particular perversion. You are very unlikely to be suffering from it, as it is almost entirely confined to males. So have no fear, it will pass; it is not, you may thank God, the real thing.

Sincerely yours,
R. von Krafft-Ebing

Frankfurt

Dear Professor,

I am sad that you do not believe me. What I said to you was nothing but the truth. I don't care what it is called, and I must admit I haven't yet read anything about masochism, as you call it, in your book. I have to take it a little at a time, it is so powerful.

I think I must have known the truth about myself, in some deep part of my mind, when I first read those few pages of your book in my master's study. I thought I was disgusted by the men who liked to stab women in the breasts, etc., with no thought for them as persons, but just out to use them for their own satisfaction. But it's very strange that I started to masturbate, night and morning, after that. I remember imagining I was going to the market to buy food, and suddenly felt this agonising pain in my bottom, and saw my skirt all ripped, and blood—I thought I was revolted, and yet it was followed by masturbation. Is it possible to know something and yet not know, if you see what I mean?

But what really brought it to light was your letter telling me I was contemptible and that you washed your hands of me! I trembled so much I broke the vase I had been dusting, and I felt a sweet fountain of delight flow up through me! I adored the way you made your feelings quite clear by calling me *Du* instead of *Sie*! Oh, it drenched me with pleasure, even more than 'contemptible'.

Well, I don't think I *quite* realised it even then. I first knew it unmistakably when Herr Sussmeyer replied to my first letter, saying he had this quest for pubic hairs because he loved and respected women so much. I remember feeling disappointed, and wondering why. Then I knew it was because I didn't want to be loved and respected, since I don't deserve to be. I am only worth being used. Yes, that's when I felt that huge surge of relief and happiness.

If you could go back to calling me *Du* you would be more honest about our relationship and oblige

Your obedient servant,
Sophie Arandt

Vienna

Dear Fräulein,

I must accept, with concern and sadness, the truth of what you have communicated to me. Unless you can overcome these perverse desires, by a great effort of will, you are on the road to shame and degradation. Fate has placed you in a situation of subservience; but in the sight of God you are the equal of an Emperor.

You should really seek professional help; yet I suppose you could not afford it. I will do what I can, if you wish, by correspondence. I cannot deny that your condition, given its rarity among women, is of interest to me. I should have to know a great deal more about you.

To answer your question about the mind. It is not possible to know and yet not to know. The mind does not play tricks with us; it holds no secret compartments. Of course, we often push uncomfortable thoughts 'to the back of our mind'. This may be what you did.

When you next write to me, please try to jot down some details about yourself which might assist me to help you. When you stop to think about it, I really know remarkably little about you.

Thank you for your enquiry. The burdens, both

professional and domestic, do not grow less onerous. Fortunately I am of good tough stock.

R. von Krafft-Ebing

From his precarious position on an icefield, Charsky gazed down at the valley, so unutterably remote. The world turned into empty space, into shrill wind. This really was, as some climber had said, the loneliest place in the world. Even your friends ceased to exist.

Why, he thought—if one can be said to think in dreams— did I ever take this on? I was quite comfortable in Leningrad, with a pleasant, interesting job and a pleasant, interesting wife.

He mused on the state of the planet. The recent Cuban Missile Crisis had reminded everyone that Earth was on the verge of extinction; it was poised as precariously as Charsky.

Close to him was a short, narrow ledge, to which someone had lashed the corpse of a young man. The Russian did not think he could have been dead for long. Presumably his companion had turned back to try to get help. Charsky, coming upon the corpse, shocking in its unexpectedness, thought he should stay with it.

Tenderly he stroked the dead man's face. He jerked his hand back as if it had received an electric shock: a cheek-nerve had quivered. He saw the mouth twist, the eyes open. 'You're not dead!'

'No. Only dying.'

'What's your name, my friend?'

'Barry. Barry Brewster.'

'Ah! English. Rescue is on its way.'

'What good would that do? I'd rather the mountain killed me than die in some hospital.'

Suddenly the young Englishman struggled with his bonds.

He seemed to have the strength of ten; he tore the ropes off him and rose to his feet, his orange windbreaker gusting in the gale like a bird's wings. The sight must have frightened the watchers at Kleine Scheidegg and Grindelwald.

He crouched like a skier and took off, shooting down the icefield and zooming off into space, turning leisurely somersaults in the great fall, bouncing off rocks like a dummy-faller in an adventure film.

The Russian crossed himself.

Cold. Cold. Anna—

As on the previous night, we were interrupted by the phone. Surkov, stretched on the bed, asked her if he should answer it. Masha nodded. He picked the phone up.

'Yes. Who is it? . . . Oh, it's you, Sonia! Hello! . . .' Rozanov stiffened. 'Yes, he's here, we're all here.' Rozanov sprang to the held-out phone.

'Sonia? What's wrong? . . . But it must be the middle of the night . . . It's probably just nerves. Why don't you take a sleeping pill? . . . I tried to ring, but the lines to Moscow were engaged. I'm okay. The Festival's boring; we're here telling a few stories . . . I'm sorry I haven't called, but I did try . . . Anyway, how's it been? . . .'

Masha withdrew to the bathroom. Surkov and I stood up and stretched. I walked around the bedroom which, unlike mine, was neat and showed few signs of its occupant: a small pile of books, with *Psychological Correspondences* on top; a pair of flesh-coloured tights drying on a radiator; some cosmetics. Sergei was saying mostly *Da* and *Nyet*, with long intervals in between. Nodding towards the bathroom, Surkov said very softly, 'It's a disaster.'

'She's doing her best. Her fall has shaken her.'

'Okay, but most of this is just memorized stuff; there's almost nothing original.'

I was about to respond that she'd added quite a lot to the

letters, but Masha came out of the bathroom. Sergei was promising to ring Sonia tomorrow. When he put the phone down he said to us, 'She has stomach pains, she can't sleep. Ever since we married there's been something wrong with her.'

'How did she get put through to my room?' asked Masha.

'I guess they transferred the call.'

He looked ashen—even more than usual. Masha said, 'You should have called her to let her know you'd arrived safely.'

'She'd have heard if our plane had crashed. She just likes to check up.'

Surkov muttered, 'It's always the same with mistresses turned wives—they know all the tricks you play, they're suspicious every moment of the day and night.'

'Shall I carry on?' asked Masha, sitting.

'If you're up to it.'

'I think so.'

I saw Rozanov glance discreetly at his watch. I wondered if he was waiting to be alone with her. Would he leave with us and then double back? Would they melt into each other's arms? Would they try *carezza*?

· 9 ·

Cold. Cold. Anna in the cradle. Her grandma trying to light some sticks. Gunfire. Somehow the child knew it was gunfire. The door, her mother coming. Swaying, skeletal, and her face like snow. Clutching something wrapped in paper. Red on her face and her coat. 'What happened, darling? Sit down, sit down!'

'It's nothing, Mama. A scratch.'

'It looks more than a scratch.'

'I got some meat.'

'What is it?'

'It'll make soup. Don't let Aniushka see it.'

Cold. Cold.

Anna shivered, returned to her book . . .

Frankfurt

Dear Professor,

Well, what can I tell you about myself? I'm of medium height, fairly well built except that my breasts are rather small. They seemed to stop growing when I was thirteen. I have brown hair, fairly curly, and blue eyes. My nose is sort of turned-up, and I have a large mouth. That is, my lips are too thick, I'm embarrassed by them. But everyone says I have a nice complexion. I used to suffer from spots, but they seem to have gone in the last year or two, I'm thankful to say.

Does that tell you enough? If not, tell me what else you want to know. I would like to be completely open with you, only please don't tell my master.

I don't want to overcome these desires. They give me very great pleasure and delight. You didn't say anything about the masturbation. Is it so very wrong? Did you feel like washing your hands of me again?

I've been thinking about what you said, that it's very rare for a woman to feel as I do. Isn't it because women are by nature inferior, and know it, so usually there is no need for them to crave to be treated as inferior? Then why am I different? I suppose I was never contented with half-measures.

I am sorry your life is so burdensome, I only wish I could help in some way. When you said you came from good tough stock it made me shiver a bit. How I wish I could find a master like you, tough and strong. By the way, do you have children? I know next to nothing about you also. I only know you are very kind and wise.

Sincerely yours,
Sophie Arandt

Vienna

Dear Fräulein Arandt,

Thank you for your letter. I am very sorry you feel no desire to overcome this condition. I shall not abandon the effort to persuade you otherwise.

When I wrote that I would need to know more about you, I wasn't thinking in terms of your physical appearance. I am particularly interested in details about your parents. Has either of them suffered from insanity? Masochism is congenital; that is to say, you must have inherited it. Not infrequently the father of a masochist can be shown to have had some abnormal development of the brain.

I cannot agree that women are the inferior of men. However, in terms of social arrangements, you are not too far off the track. In these civilized times, husbands are no longer given the right to beat their wives (and in earlier centuries, even kill them), but society, as well as biology, still places the female in a subordinate role. A man, if he needs to express masochistic impulses, must put a great deal more effort and imagination into it.

I do not wash my hands of you because of your masturbation; but it is a lowering, weakening habit and I strongly urge you to give it up.

Tell me about your parents.

Sincerely yours,
R. von Krafft-Ebing

Frankfurt

Dear Professor,

I do not feel I can talk about my parents. Somehow it doesn't seem respectful. They are just a decent, nice couple. I am sorry if I cannot fulfill your request on this point. Of course if you were my master—I don't mean like Dr Grossman but my real, still-undiscovered master—you would have a right to ask anything of me; but that cannot be.

When I got to the part of your letter about masturbation, I went to my room and masturbated! I'm sorry! Your tone was so stern and pure and preachy, it excited me. I often get excited in church. I sometimes stimulate myself under my muff. My muff under my muff! But I will try to give it up.

I didn't understand some parts of your letter. I'm a woman, or rather a girl, and not clever. How can you say women are not inferior to men? Take Frau Grossman, all she thinks about is finery and food, whereas Dr Grossman has his spectacles always in a book. I think husbands should have the right to beat their wives, because they're so often vain and stupid and silly. I do not suppose they should have the right to kill them, though I must confess the thought makes me a little excited. I really do not think we are much brighter than monkeys, and monkeys are killed in experiments.

I have had a thrilling adventure! There was a party for the servants in a neighbouring house, and a few of us were invited to it. We had rather a lot to drink, and before I knew where I was I found myself being hustled into a broom-closet by three men. They started kissing and fondling me. Of course I pretended to struggle, but I was really terribly excited.

Just the same, it wasn't wholly satisfying. They were too drunk and crude, I want one man, one master, who I can respect but who won't respect me, and who will tell me what to do. I am going to start going into town more, on my night off, and just hanging around where I'm told the prostitutes stand. Of course I shan't sell myself, but it could be thrilling just to see what happens.

Well, I must get back to work. We are busy preparing for Christmas. I wish you a Happy Christmas and remain

> Your obedient servant,
> Sophie

P.S. You didn't say if you have children.

Vienna

Dear Fräulein Arandt,

I am sorry you could not bring yourself to tell me about your parents. But much more sorry that you have behaved in such an improper and perilous way. Masturbation is undoubtedly damaging to the health. Throwing yourself at men, men of gross natures, is a still greater act of self-abuse, and I cannot warn you too strongly that you are placing yourself in the very gravest danger. Give it up before it is too late. Try and find yourself a nice, decent husband and settle down.

It is not good for a physician to confide personal details of his life to a patient. I reciprocate your seasonal greetings. Now I fear we really must stop corresponding. I just have too much on my plate.

Sincerely yours,
R. von Krafft-Ebing

Anna glanced at her watch. If she rang now she might just catch Levkovich in his morning break. Very quietly and gently she stretched, picked the phone up, and dialled the number of his school. Dmitri stirred but did not wake. She spoke in little more than a whisper: 'Is it possible to speak to Comrade Levkovich? . . . Thank you.' A few moments later she was saying: 'Hello, Alexei, this is Anna Charsky. I'm sorry to take up your time. The grill of our cooker isn't working; I wondered if you could ask your brother-in-law to . . . The thing is, I think I could get your car repaired for you; I've met someone . . . So if you could persuade your brother-in-law somehow to . . . Splendid! . . . No, I haven't a cold: Dmitri's asleep and I don't want to wake him. We'll be in touch. Good-bye!'

Replacing the phone and lifting it again, she dialled. 'Lisa, my dear! how are you? . . . Listen, I can't stay for long, but I've twisted Dmitri's arm and he can find you a couple of tickets for *Hedda*! . . . Yes, it should be very good. But I wondered if Alexei could do us a favour: a friend of ours has a problem with his car; do you think . . . ? Ah, that's great! Ask him to ring us. 'Bye!'

Stealthily again she put down the phone. Another problem solved. But what resources of energy and cunning it took, just to survive.

Dmitri mumbled out of his almost-sleep: 'Who was that?'

'Lisa.'

'Ah. The grill.' Then he was breathing gently again.

At the top of the Exit Cracks the three men stopped for a rest. They squatted down on a narrow ice-ledge. They were at the foot of the Summit Icefield: only about a hundred and fifty feet to go, and the weather reasonable.

The two Swiss in the three-man rope, Wyss and Gonda, had encountered the third, a Russian, at the base of the Exit Cracks. The solo climber was in a bad way, and they invited him to rope-up with them.

He spoke to the others now: 'So—we've almost done it!'

Wyss, nodding, said, 'It should be easy.'

'I wonder,' said Charsky, 'if you both feel as I do.'

'And how's that?' asked Gonda.

'Sad.'

'Sad?' they both exclaimed together.

'Yes. It's such a beautiful face. The White Cobra. The White Spider. Call it what you like. Beautiful, frightening and awesome. In a way you feel it shouldn't be conquered.'

'I know what you mean,' said Gonda. 'For years I studied photos and maps of it. For two weeks Uli and I have spent every daylight hour gazing up at it, seeing it in its flesh and bone, so to speak, for the first time—yet so utterly familiar and loved. . . .'

'You're right—loved,' agreed his comrade.

'It looked small, too small for a camera. Yet we could pick out every feature, as you know every pore on the face of a woman you love. The First Pillar, the Shattered Pillar, Difficult Crack, the Hinterstoisser Traverse, the Swallow's Nest . . .'

Wyss took it on: 'The Ice Hose, the Flatiron, the Waterfall Crack, the Traverse of the Gods, the Spider, Death Bivouac, the Longhi Ledge . . . Places named sometimes after the dead, which adds to its beauty . . . Yes, it's sad to be on the point of reaching the summit.'

'We should give the face a chance,' Charsky said. 'Climb the rest of the way without pitons.'

The two Swiss stared at him as if he were mad; but then a wild humour came into their ice-rimmed eyes. 'Why not?' said Wyss. 'A kind of Russian roulette!'

'I'm game,' agreed Gonda. 'The odds are in our favour.'

They stood up and, abandoning their ice-pitons, started up the last, short icefield, cutting foot-holds with their picks. They moved carefully, slowly; clouds blanketed them and then cleared; swirled around them again.

Wyss, in the lead, was only some fifty feet from the top when he saw a tiny movement in the snow ahead of them. 'Brace yourselves!' he cried. It was only a very light avalanche: this close to the summit it had no time to gather power. Just the same, Wyss found himself sliding, and sensed the others sliding back too, and nothing could stop them.

Charsky catapulted into a rocky obstruction after tumbling a thousand feet or so. He heard the clean crack of a leg-bone but did not lose consciousness.

The Swiss pair sped down over the Third Icefield, zoomed out from the sheer rock-face beneath it and landed with a crunch on the Second Icefield; then, as limbs were torn from their bodies, they launched again off the cliff, landed on the First Icefield, and again careened down the slope and zoomed out and down.

Vienna

Dear Fräulein Arandt,

It is a very long time since I heard from you. I wondered how you are getting on? Given your unusual tastes, one naturally worries.

Of course, I told you I had too much on my plate to

be able to continue our correspondence, and I hope this is the reason you stopped writing. On the other hand, similar statements of mine have never prevented you from writing back in the past. I say that in all affection.

I would like to hear from you.

Sincerely yours,
R. von Krafft-Ebing

Berlin

Dear Professor,

You will be surprised by my change of address. I was so pleased to hear from you. I am sorry I have been so long in replying but I only got your letter two days ago. Frau Grossman was rather slow in forwarding it.

I was very upset by your note saying we shouldn't write to each other anymore. I got involved with one of the servants I told you about, that had pawed me about in a cupboard. He made me do terrible things, things with animals, for instance. Well, it is too disgusting for me to be able to tell you. I was bitterly ashamed of what I was doing, or letting people do to me, but also of course I got to like it, and even crave it, in a manner of speaking. The man in question, who is a good deal older than me, had no respect for me whatever, which I liked. But the trouble was, he was so vile I couldn't respect *him*. I have to have real respect for my Master.

So to cut a long story short, in the end I managed to drag myself away from this man. I remembered what you'd said about settling down, and as it happened I met a very nice young man from Berlin, a train driver. He proposed to me and I said yes. We got married last month, and now we have a tiny flat here. I cook and wash and clean for my husband, and we are happy enough. Of course he knows nothing about my real desires. He treats me very well, which I find indescribably boring, but I don't reveal that to him. I guess you can't have everything you want in life.

Receiving your letter brought so many things back. I hope you are feeling less harassed than when you last wrote in the spring. I would love to hear from you again, if you can spare the time.

Sincerely yours,
Sophie Stolz

Vienna

Dear Frau Stolz,

Well! I can hardly believe I am addressing a married lady! My warmest congratulations. Although you do not appear to feel the ardour which might be desirable so early in a marriage, you will find it has many rewards, I am sure.

As for myself, I cannot pretend that the time since we last corresponded has been equally fruitful or pleasant. I have not felt terribly well; but no matter.

I half had it in mind to invite you to come and work for me here in Vienna. It would have made it easier to help you, and I venture the opinion that our servants feel well-treated. Our household could do with some young life. However, you have accepted a much more attractive situation! I am delighted for you.

Sincerely yours,
R. von Krafft-Ebing

Cautiously, trying not to waken him, Anna disengaged from the *carezza*. Sliding out of bed, she headed for the bathroom. She washed and dried herself between the legs and inserted a fresh tampon. When she returned to the bedroom she was carrying a flannel. His penis, still partially erect, was stained with her blood. Very gently she started to clean him. He flopped onto his back, gurgled like a sleeping infant, then opened his eyes.

'I dozed off.'

'Uh-huh. It sounded as if you were having one long nightmare. I wondered if I should wake you up.'

'Really? I don't think I was dreaming.'

Crouched over him, she wiped his balls clean then bent to kiss the tender, wrinkled skin. His eyes shut again, and he stroked her hair. 'It was wonderful, Anna!' he murmured. 'I think I like it even more than . . . than making love normally.' He drew her down to kiss her.

'Did *you* enjoy it?' he asked as they moved apart.

'Yes.'

'You don't sound too sure.'

'Oh, I am.'

'Admit it, you were reading!'

She smiled, then brushed his mouth again with hers. 'It didn't stop me enjoying it,' she said.

He yawned, closed his eyes again and turned on his side. 'I'm still so damned sleepy.'

'Well, you can sleep. But I must have a bath and get up, or I shall be late for work.'

'Just lie here for a few moments. Please.' Nestling against her, he stroked her back. 'Your body is very beautiful still, Anna. In fact I think it's becoming *more* beautiful . . .'

'Nonsense! Men don't age as we do. And look how white I am compared with you; your tan still hasn't faded completely.'

Naples. The beautiful, topless girls on the beaches.

'I like you as you are. You're a white mountain; the Eiger North Face. Here's the Swallow's Nest.' Blindly he moved his fingers to touch her between the thighs.

'You're sure it's not Death Bivouac? Or the Spider?'

'No, no: the Swallow's Nest,' he mumbled. 'And here's the Traverse of the Gods . . .'

'They're beginning to sag.' She raised a hand to her breasts; he stroked her fingers.

'Not true, not true.'

He brushed a finger over her lips and her nostrils, murmuring, 'And these are the Exit Cracks. I felt I was filling you right up, right up to your lips. There was no me and no you anymore.'

He lay quiet, his eyes closed, and she stroked his nape. Then she slid away from him, got out of bed, and padded to the bathroom. She ran the hot water. While waiting for the bath to fill, she reflected on a fragmentary dream which, thanks to Dmitri, had surfaced to her memory. She'd had a lover in Switzerland; ski slopes, snow-white sheets. The lover was an English writer, known to her only by name. He was a friend of Sergei Rozanov. She liked Sergei a lot, had fancied him like mad when they'd first met, at the house of mutual acquaintances in Moscow. Freud would probably have said the English lover was a mask for Sergei, with his deep respect for England. And by coincidence, his letter of condolence had arrived . . .

Freud might have said her emotional life was frozen, like the Alps. In a reversal of normality, the Eiger had stared through a telescope at her. Dmitri, trying to be romantic, had found the same image. It wasn't very flattering, being compared to a lifeless mountain.

· IO ·

I was roused from a deep sleep feeling dry in the mouth and hung over. It was still dark. The knocking that had woken me was repeated, and I heard Masha's voice.

Switching on the bedside light, I got out of bed and fumbled into my bathrobe. I groped with glued-up eyes towards the door. She stood, in her white dressing-gown, looking as bleared and dishevelled as I.

'I'm sorry to disturb you.'

'Come in.'

She ghosted past me, and curled up in an armchair. She couldn't sleep, she explained. She touched her cheek, wincing.

'Is it hurting?'

'Yes, a little.'

'Shall I order up some juice and coffee?'

'Not unless you want some. Water will do.'

I went to the bathroom and filled two glasses. I handed her the water and climbed back between the sheets. I lit a cigarette, gulped the water, and started to feel a little better. She picked up *Memories & Hallucinations* and idly turned the pages. I had sent her a copy of my memoir, but her noncommital letter of thanks had given no indication of whether she had read it. Now she said, 'I was sorry you didn't mention our magical week in Switzerland.'

I nodded: wary. Her eyes were bright, fixed on mine. I wondered if her presence was an invitation; I felt that if I stretched out my hand to grasp hers she would have sat by me on the bed. I evaded her eyes.

After a while she said, 'Your account of how you wrote our books was very convincing.'

I felt myself blush. 'A lot of that book is fictional. You know how it is, Masha. We live fictional lives. Except when we fall in the bath.'

I looked at her again and she smiled fleetingly. She put my book down; said for about the fourth time how sorry she was that she'd missed my reading; but she'd simply felt too shaky.

'You missed nothing. It was brave of you to improvise still—and to do it so well!'

'Victor didn't think so.'

'Screw him!'

'Well, I didn't think I was much good either. I followed you too slavishly. It's always the same with women—no confidence. Why did I have to rush out yesterday to Foyle's to buy *Psychopathia Sexualis* and *Eiger, Wall of Death*? Why did I have to borrow the *Correspondences*? Well, you roused my interest, of course; but also I panicked, felt I must follow on from you. I should have been able to say, Fuck you, I'll go my own way: as you did, as Sergei did. Why are we so timid?'

I shrugged, and waited while she sat silently, her face lowered.

'You're wondering why I've woken you up. I've been thinking about Sophie. I find her very disturbing; I just wanted some company and to talk: do you mind?'

'Of course not.'

'What made me develop her along masochistic lines? I didn't intend to do so.'

I said it was always impossible to explain our spontaneous decisions. It might mean nothing or everything.

'What does Freud say about sadism and masochism?'

I tried to clear my sleepy brain. She waited, sipping the water, her eyes fixed on me.

My memory began to clear. 'I think he says they have their roots in normal human patterns—active and passive, male and female. That's to say, it's natural for the male to be more aggressive—because he's the one who has to penetrate. And natural for the female to be more passive, because she's penetrated. Sadomasochism is an extension of that.'

'Then what about bisexuality?' Her eyelashes dipped demurely.

'Well, of course, he recognises that everyone's bisexual; so there's no simple division between aggressive males and submissive females; far from it. In fact—ah, yes! it's come to me!—the most interesting thing he has to say is that sadism and masochism are always present in the same person: a masochist is a frustrated sadist, and a sadist is a frustrated masochist.'

'I see . . . That could apply to Sophie. In her situation, as a menial, she wouldn't have much opportunity to give pain to others.'

I nodded. 'Opportunity—or perhaps willingness to do it. One could be frustrated by conscience too.'

She would like some coffee after all, she said. Decaffeinated. And maybe some toast, since she'd missed dinner. I rang room service. The waiter when he came archly avoided looking at Masha. Our amusement at his false assumption seemed to ease the tension between us. She questioned why, since our meeting this time, there had been a barrier of reserve.

'I think for my part it's because of Liubov,' I said. 'Ah, this coffee is good!'

'But why? What difference should it make? I was married to Shimon when we first met, and that didn't put a wall between us. Liuba doesn't try to own me.'

'I don't know why it is . . . I have the uncomfortable feeling that homosexual relationships exclude the opposite sex. As a woman, married to a man, you had a close relationship with other women—your own kind—and also with men. But living with another woman—it's like saying you can do without men altogether.'

'But that's stupid! I have loads of male friends.'

'Of course.'

'And I can still find some men sexually attractive.'

I took the plunge: 'Sergei, for instance?'

'Well, yes, he's quite attractive.' She became involved with scraping butter and marmalade on a piece of toast. 'Only since he came out of the *psikhushka*. And yet it's actually made him look much older and less attractive. But he has a new power, don't you agree?'

'Yes.'

'Sexual attraction is very strange. When you came to Moscow I found you intensely attractive; in Grindelwald too, with the mountains so atmospheric! But this time, all that is gone; and it's not because you have aged a lot, or changed. You still have the same elements of attractiveness, but I simply don't find you desirable anymore. I can sit here by your bed and simply feel affection. I hope you're not offended.'

'Of course not.'

'Well, I'm glad. So now we can be real friends.' She paused, hesitated. 'I wasn't telling the truth yesterday.'

'About what?'

'My fall. There was none. Well, I fell in bed rather than in my bath.' She gave a slight, sad smile, stood up and took a few paces round the bedroom. 'I must tell someone. I've been unfaithful to Liuba.'

I said, 'Well, that's not a surprise to me. It's pretty clear you and Sergei—'

'Sergei? Oh, no! I wouldn't consider that being unfaithful. With a man, I mean. No—another woman . . .'

She sat on my bed, her face strained, her hands clenched. 'With Maria.'

'Maria?'

'Maria Sanchez.'

I exclaimed, bewildered, 'But she must be seventy.'

'Sixty-eight. But she has such power, such spiritual power. And those eyes . . . You won't tell anyone, will you? Because of her marriage and her religion, she's terrified of a scandal. She comes to my room each afternoon. She won't see me at night, because sometimes her husband rings up then. She's so quiet—yet also terribly passionate.' She touched her bruised cheek. 'She did this to me. It didn't seem wrong or perverted. It was quite a heavy blow, quite out of the blue— yet I enjoyed it!' Her eyes flashed defiantly. 'I can't say whether I invited it or—or not; it just happened.'

'But why should she want to hit you?'

She shook her head. 'I don't know. She's angry. For not being Márquez. For having spent most of her life, most of her energy, looking after her husband and children and grand-children. For not having the obsessive singlemindedness—the bloody-minded selfishness—which permits a few male artists to be geniuses. To be brigands of the wood. But I'm guessing. Maybe she just sensed what I needed—as you did, I'm sure, when you introduced those letters.'

It had disturbed her, though, she said: being struck hard on the face and finding she enjoyed it. She'd felt emotionally shaky after; that was why she had given dinner and the theatre a miss.

She drained her coffee cup and put it down. 'I must go and try to get some sleep. You won't tell anyone, will you?'

'Of course not.'

She bent, in a waft of musky scent, to kiss me on the cheek; rose, drawing the hem of her dressing-gown about her, and left, shutting the door quietly.

On a grey-miniskirted lap rested copies of *Ararat, Swallow* and *Sphinx*. Fiona Hayes-Drummond of the *Times*, languidly beautiful, confessed to having only dipped into them.

'Isn't it unusual,' she asked the Russians, 'for a novelist to make open use of real, living people?'

Surkov: 'It is unusual, but perhaps it should happen more often. Perhaps every novelist should be compelled, by law, to write only about real, living people. It would remove a lot of tedious fiction.'

Rozanov: 'It is unusual, but I don't object to it.'

She turned her cool gaze on me. I felt a helpless desire stirring. I have always felt helpless and hopeless desire for beautiful, rich, elegantly dressed women. 'Why did you do it?' she demanded.

'When I first met Sergei and Victor, six or seven years ago, they made a big impression on me. As honest and honourable Russian writers, they seemed to me to be emblematic in some way. I couldn't have got the same effect if I'd fictionalised them.'

'You say'—she searched for the first page of *Ararat*—'*Sergei Rozanov had made an unnecessary journey from Moscow to Gorky, simply in order to sleep with a young blind woman.*' She turned to Rozanov. 'Did that happen?'

'Certainly not. It's clearly symbolic. Every time a writer opens his notebook, or puts a blank sheet in a typewriter, he is making a journey to a young blind woman.'

She scribbled shorthand and asked, 'So this isn't a sexist episode?'

'In terms of the fiction,' said Rozanov, 'she is a sex object to Rozanov, clearly. In the sense that he desires this unknown figure, he craves her warmth, her yielding flesh, her mystery. Juliet was a sex object to Romeo, and vice versa. It's simply a reductionist cliché used by feminists, it really has no meaning.'

'You're a sex object to me at this moment,' said Surkov. 'Probably to all three of us. What comes across to us most obviously is your electricity, your erotic charm. Frankly I would love to go to bed with you; but that doesn't mean I fail to recognise that you have a mind, a spirit. Indeed, I would not desire you if you did *not* have a mind and a spirit. Why should we separate sex from the soul? "Sex object" can be another word for "soul object". Sex is the soul's chief communication channel. I would love to have yours open for me.'

Disconcerted, the young reporter recrossed her shapely, miniskirted legs and sat up straighter.

'Did you have a—a threesome in bed with your mistress and a Canadian woman?' she asked Rozanov.

'Of course not.'

'And did you attend a sex club in Washington?' she asked Surkov.

'As a matter of fact, I did; but like the novel says, I didn't take part. It was research.'

She switched to me: 'Why did you invent the threesome involving Rozanov?'

'It was a symbolic act.'

Her biro hovered, waiting for more.

'I don't believe in explaining symbols.'

Her biro dipped; a torrent of chestnut hair hung between her lowered brow and her lamb's-wool-sweatered bosom. She raised her eyes to Surkov. 'Did you ever interview the American President?' she asked with a slight smile.

'No, no! But can I tell you something off the record?'

She hesitated. 'Okay.'

I have slept with Mrs Gorbachev.'

Her large brown eyes widened. 'How? When?'

'I'd have to know you a lot better before telling you such things.'

Ignoring the innuendo, she scribbled. I said, 'The novels are a mixture of fact and fiction. *Ararat* is mostly fact; *Swallow*, where Victor interviews the President, is mostly fiction. *Sphinx*, again, is largely true-to-life. Well, except for the Russian actress who has an affair with a cardinal.'

'In reality,' Surkov interposed, 'it was the Pope.'

She looked up sharply. 'You're pulling my leg.'

'No, there's this beautiful Leningrad actress who went to Rome for several months. There's reasonable evidence that she was trying to "turn" the Pope.'

'I didn't dare to be truthful,' I said, nodding agreement. 'It weakened it; everyone knows cardinals have mistresses. There's a fourth novel, called *Summit* . . .'

'I didn't know about that.'

'It's fiction. A kind of *divertimento*.'

'You've read all the novels, have you?' she asked the Russians. Yes, said Surkov, they took a great interest in my work; and Rozanov nodded.

She asked one or two cursory questions about their published work. I felt guilty and embarrassed. It was not enough that they had been questioned at length about a work in which they had secretly collaborated: they were now to be insulted by having their acknowledged work dismissed as of small account. Yet Rozanov, at least, was much better than I, though little known in the West.

I admired their good-humour, especially Surkov's. I had always thought him to be egotistical and attention-seeking; but apart from mentioning his invitation to the Dukakis Inaugural, he answered modestly, even humbly: praising his friends' work and disparaging his own.

Raising her eyes to Rozanov, she asked in lighter tones how he was enjoying his first visit to England. It was wonderful, he said. He particularly loved reading the *Sun*. He hoped she wasn't offended, as a *Times* reporter. Today, for example, was the seventy-fifth birthday of the brassiere; but for a *Sun* feature called 'All Our Breasterdays' he would not have known this. The poetry of England still flourished.

She smiled, scribbling then closing her notebook; said it was also coincidentally the seventy-fifth birthday of a family friend, Lord Monkton. She was having tea at the Dorchester with him; she had better go. 'Thank you for your time.'

Surkov: 'You're welcome.'

At the theatre that evening Masha, as a little-known

curtain-raiser to Márquez, read simple lyrics, accompanied by her own translations, about the flora and fauna of Siberia. She had used make-up skilfully to mask her bruise, and with the subdued stage-light it was scarcely visible. She concluded her performance—and rather stole Márquez' thunder—with a moving, powerful *Elegy for a Nuclear Physicist*.

I felt hostile towards her. I wished I had got in first by telling her I no longer found her sexually attractive. I was too courteous, I decided, too afraid of hurting people's feelings.

At the end of the evening Surkov was surrounded by a group of admirers soliciting autographs, and he shouted at us to go on back to the hotel, he would join us in a while. Sergei and Masha came to my room and I opened a bottle of mineral water: we all felt we needed to be abstemious. While waiting for Surkov to arrive, Sergei spoke of the need to move the story on realistically and swiftly. Masha had been fine last night, but we really couldn't afford any more dreams or letters.

The phone rang. I picked it up. It was Surkov. 'I'm going for a drink with Miss Hayes-Drummond. She wants the private details of my affair with Raisa.' His voice sounded triumphant. 'You'll have to count me out tonight, my friend. Apologise for me. I'll listen to the tape tomorrow. *Do svidaniya!*'

'He's seeing the girl from the *Times*,' I announced, stifling a black envy. 'He says he'll listen to the tape tomorrow.'

'*Bastard!*' said Rozanov. 'How does he do it? Well, it's between you and me, Don. We'll toss for it.' He plucked a coin from his pocket, spun it into the air, and called correctly. I felt a great relief at having lost the privilege of performing.

'Okay. How did it end?' he asked.

'Anna was running a bath, recalling her erotic dream about Switzerland. Dmitri was still in bed, drowsy—I guess he was going to have another dream!' I smiled rather malevolently at Masha, who lay on a bed, her chin cupped in her hand.

'Well, then—let's see . . .'

Silence fell and endured. He began to rub his jaw as if he was in pain; his normally pale face had turned white. I asked him if he was okay. He nodded, still clutching his jaw.

'It's cold,' said Masha; 'is the heating off?'

I felt the radiator, said, 'No.' Yet I shivered.

The lamplight suddenly went out. We were in darkness, relieved only by a chink of light under the door. From the direction of Rozanov came a voice, but it was unlike his. It was the voice of someone old, with a speech impairment, and it was in German.

· II ·

Existence almost unbearable. Fortunately Schur promises to keep his promise.

'Is this the war to end all wars?' he asks. 'For me at any rate,' I reply.

There will be a measure of relief even in Anna's sorrow.

I dream that we live in a mare's field. It must relate to my first sight of my mother's genitals—but not the last, for we lived in just one room.

I could never see her thick black tuft of pubic hair without longing to go with my father into that dark Moravian pine forest, stretching all the way from the Carpathians, which surrounded our home. The constant view of so much hair excited in me a love of nature, wild nature, that has never waned. The hairs prickle on my nape whenever I see a picture representing a deep, dark forest. I must go there.

If my past work has any value at all, it lies in my having exhorted my readers to love the forest depths; to feel the enchantment of their vast silences, their cunning hidden flowers; their murky scents; the sighing of their leaves; the teasing hints of sunlight or moonlight through the tree tops.

Happy is the infant whose father fills him with a passion for forests by coupling with his bride in full view.

My mother was a woman of great piety and orthodoxy; and when she allowed me to look into her forest depths I found them good. Our room was an ark; and I had no wish for the dove to bring home a green leaf. I hated the dove; I preferred the raven, that black leaf torn from the dark forest.

The other children, my playmates, meant little to me; so little that one day they all rose from the field and vanished, like angels.

Like my patient the Wolf-Man, I was fortunate or unfortunate enough to be lying awake in the night when the five candles of my destiny glimmered on the tree outside. The candles glimmered on the moon-blanched tree like Christmas candles. I have heard it denied that the candles— different candles—glimmer for every child when he or she reaches the age of three or four; but of course that denial is nonsense; simply, most children are asleep in the depths of the night when the candles shine out.

They represent the hand we have been dealt in life, for life. In my case, the first and most important candle stood for the dark forest. Ever and ever, as I have said, I return to it. Another candle stood for the trivium, the place where three roads meet. I know beyond question that I am Oedipus and he is I. I should make it clear that I hold no truck with the theory of reincarnation; it is just as clear to me that I am Marie Romanov, whose life overlapped with mine. But that past tense, 'overlapped', is simply a necessary fiction. All life is contemporaneous, is now. At this very moment, Oedipus stands at the crossroads, killing the testy man, his father. I am at that crossroads.

As with Oedipus, often we are compelled to relight the candle against our will. It was the case with my first sexual experience. The young woman in question, a casual acquaintance of my family in Vienna, had inflamed me with cunning caresses. She was the type of young woman who loves danger; and she insisted that we lie down in the entranceway to a park. At night, carriages containing prostitutes and their clients would come hurtling out of the park towards the entrance, and they could come from two directions. Because the drives curved, it was impossible to see the carriages before they were almost on top of you. We lay down and made love, in extreme danger.

Since I was unprepared, lacking a condom, she and I were endangered from two directions in another sense also: from disease (for we were strangers to each other), and from a pregnancy desired by neither of us.

It would have been so easy and commonplace to move into some bushes; but my partner insisted that I light my second candle.

A third candle was ambivalence, and usually takes the form of two women who are close allies and rivals. The woman Rebecca, my father's childless and rejected wife, haunts my early years. I would often see her watching me as I played in the fields. She was close at hand at my birth as well as at my conception; and she and my mother were often together. What my father felt about this conjunction I can only guess. When we moved from Freiberg, Rebecca followed us at a distance. I don't know where she lived, but years later, as I walked to the *gymnasium*, I would often turn a corner and see Rebecca's burning eyes.

I hated Vienna, because we now had several rooms and so I was further from the forest.

Days and nights merge in a common pain, relieved scarcely at all by Schur's drugs.

I dream that I am visited by a poet called T. S. Eliot. This is surely a babyhood memory, slightly corrupted, of seeing the word 'toilets' reflected fleetingly in my nurse's spectacles, when we travelled from London to Dover to sail for the Continent. A great fuss was made of us on that trip, according to my mother. As well as our maid, Martha, we had her sister

Minna with us. I was very upset, I have been told, because we had to leave our chow, Lün, behind, owing to quarantine restrictions.

En route for Austria, we stayed overnight in Paris. For many years I was convinced we stayed with a lady by the name of Marie Bonaparte. I think it likely that some enthusiastic exponent of Paris's history must have spoken the names Marie Antoinette and Napoleon Bonaparte in my hearing.

It would be extremely tedious to go through my life chronologically; therefore I shall break off, from time to time. 'From time to time' is a meaningless phrase, all time is instant. The fly, which has settled on my forehead and reads to me from the Sixth Book of the *Aeneid*, is the same fly which buzzes round the head of Vergil in Mantua. Man is more individuated than a fly—but not by a great margin. I know, for instance, that I am Marie Romanov, struggling through snowdrifts in the Winter Palace in Petersburg, and finding the gold clock still ticking at her bedside. I have even dreamed as Marie Romanov: a nightmare in which I and all my family were taken down into a cellar and shot.

They say the child is father to the man; yet looking back, across those immensities, those eons, separating myself now from myself then, I can see almost nothing that I owe to him, almost nothing we have in common. Yet also, at the same time, I smile with his smile, weep with his tears.

And my beloved mother—can it be that she ever existed? The years without her stretch away; years in which I have done without her well enough, have been sometimes happy, sometimes sad for other reasons than her eternal absence.

And yet the years have lessened the gap in age between us: she is more like a sister to me now. Sometimes I find myself calling her, in my thoughts, 'Anna', as a brother would, or even a father. When I am being helped into a bath of hot water, however, I draw in my breath and cry out for her: 'Mama! Mama!'

To tell you something very strange, there are times when she returns, and fusses over me as before.

I said to Schur, after reminding him of his promise, 'Tell Anna.' Isn't that odd?

I understand life, and the family ties that make up almost all of it, much less than I ever did. Families are like constellations of stars: we see each one as an entity, because they make some recognisable design, yet the individual stars are scattered all over the universe, apart.

And marriage? It is like an endless, exhausting game of tennis, deuce after deuce. No wonder its most common term is love.

Anna, my mother, is standing beside me now, I sense it. She has returned again, and feels lost, unable to do anything for me.

A dream I had not so long ago took me back to my first year in Vienna. I am waiting for my mama, and neither Martha nor Minna can comfort me. She is away for hours; perhaps a whole day. I think she has left me forever. She went away with some men in brown uniforms, and will not come back to her little boy.

I do not understand the memory. I scarcely know which is memory and which the recent dream. The men in brown uniforms must belong to the dream: an image of defecation. My mother would never have left me without telling me when she would be back. She was not the kind of mother who by carelessness would make her child feel insecure.

I was quite sick at the time. I was a very sickly child, and so my memories of those first years are dark. I was in bed almost continuously.

There was something wrong with my mouth, which stopped me from talking properly.

I remember I had a dream, when I was five or six, of all the books in my mother's library being thrown onto a bonfire with piles of other books and burnt. I must have been jealous of her life away from me, and wished to have her entirely to myself.

Ah! a very early memory . . . Just a flash. An autumnal garden bordered by shrubs . . . A maid, Paula, trimming them. I am in a swing-couch. The garden resembles what I have been told of Primrose Hill.

Nothing connects. Nothing—

The clumsily articulated, yet effortlessly accurate, German came to a sudden halt. I was aware of Sergei and Masha only as invisible presences in the blackness. I was bathed in a cold sweat. Startlingly, then, a voice rasped in an American accent:

War is a sonofabitch. I was a crew member of the *Enola Gay*, the B-29 that dropped the bomb on Hiroshima. That's a big enough weight to carry. But there's something else. I was in Sydney for a few weeks, and had an affair with this broad. She was nice—well-stacked. Her old man was away fighting. They had a little baby, a girl. I was fond of her, she reminded me of my own kid back home. This is going to sound pretty stupid, but before I left I put one of the kid's diapers in my kitbag. I knew there'd be some big raids. I had an idea that if I dropped this diaper when we unloaded our bombs, it might help some mother. You know, kids get shit-scared when the bombs are falling.

It sounds crazy. Well, I was more than a little crazy in those days. I'd flown too many missions, seen too many of my friends blown to pieces. It sounds crazy to think some Jap mother might see a diaper floating down out of the sky, lit up by flares and fires, and grab it to put on her crying baby. You could say I meant it as a gesture. Of human feeling. So I took it with me on the Hiroshima mission.

But this is what really gets at me: when we started our run in, and I picked up the diaper, I found it was already stained. It was yellow and shitty. I thought I'd picked it up off a clean pile, but I was mistaken.

I still dropped it, just as the first shock-wave struck us. We turned round for a look. It was a beautiful, clear day. The cloud was already at our height, 33,000 feet. And below us, it was like boiling tar in a barrel. I thought, Somewhere down there is a shitty diaper. I couldn't even get that right. Fuck it! Anyway, why should I care about those yellow motherfuckers?

· 12 ·

My eyes shut, I could see that napkin fluttering down through the mushroom cloud. There was a thud—opening my eyes I saw that Rozanov had pitched to the floor. The lamplight flickered on. He lay still, pole-axed. Masha and I rushed to him. We tried to rouse him but to no effect. We became alarmed; I felt for his pulse, but could feel none. Masha unbuttoned his shirt and slid her hand in. After a few moments she said, 'My God, I think he's dead.'

Jumping up, I lurched to the phone. I have never been competent in an emergency, and time was lost as I tried to figure out whether to dial 999, or 9 for an outside line, then 999. Masha, kneeling, was pressing her mouth to Rozanov's, attempting to force life into his body. At last I got through, demanded an ambulance, and had to ask Masha for the number of the room.

She pulled back from him, sitting on her haunches. 'It's no good. I'm not even sure if I'm doing it right, or if it's the right thing to do.'

I helped her to her feet and hugged her. She started to cry. She snuffled into silence and we stood there, facing each other, feeling helpless. I sensed, from her wide, fearful eyes, that she was dreading the prospect of having to ring Moscow and wake Sonia up in the middle of the night, telling her Sergei was dead.

'We must try to contact Victor,' she whispered. 'Did he tell you where he'd be?'

'He was going back to her flat. I'll see if she's in the book.' I reached for the thick directory.

'He'll have to call Sonia,' she said.

'She must be *ex* directory.' I put down the book and accepted a drink.

'What's going on?' asked Rozanov, opening his eyes, staring up at us.

'Sergei! Oh, thank God!' We fell joyfully upon him, Masha devouring him with kisses. 'We thought you were dead! Are you all right?'

'Perfectly. I could do with a drink.'

We helped him get to his feet and into a chair.

'I saw Freud,' he said, gulping a brandy.

'We know.'

I went to the phone, dialled the front desk, and awkwardly explained that an ambulance would be coming. But the patient was okay, it was a false alarm, please thank them and send them on their way. The uninterested male voice promised to do so.

'You spoke in German,' I pointed out to Sergei. 'Can you speak German?'

'Not a word.'

'That's extraordinary! There was even a Viennese tinge to your pronunciation.'

He had met Freud in a dark forest. The spirit, wearing wolfskins and an eagle's mask, had read to him a kind of autobiographical fragment. 'He told me he wrote it to distract him from pain in his last days. His daughter destroyed it. I'd like to hear what came out. Will you translate it for us?'

I stopped the still-running tape, then ran it back. We heard the wail of a siren approaching the hotel, below us. It stopped. A couple of minutes later the night-silence outside was broken by the sound of a vehicle, presumably an ambulance, starting up and moving off. It might have been carrying Sergei's lifeless body: so thin a line divides the dead and the living.

Playing the tape, I paused it every few seconds to translate. They listened in fascination, but it was the American airman's account that spoke most deeply to us. Rozanov had not seen the man, in any form, nor had he been aware of speaking those words. He was very affected; he blinked rapidly as if warding off tears.

Perhaps, Masha said, he had been influenced by Surkov's story of London's near extinction. But I pointed out that Sergei's Southern States accent had been perfect.

We were silent. Exhausted. Agreed to call it a night. We rose, from chair or bed, slowly and stiffly. Masha hugged Sergei, thanking God again that all was well. We said our good-nights.

I had a dream in which my ex-wife, Ingrid Bergman, suggested we sit in class with our son, to make sure he was getting along happily at school. It felt quite pleasant sitting at a desk, being taught Geography and Physics again, and keeping an eye on our son. The only problem was that my present wife, Isabella Rossellini, also insisted I come to lessons with our daughter, to make sure she was happy. I felt embarrassed, being in different classes with two different women. And before I could resolve the problem I was struggling up in bed, in the pitch-blackness, reaching for the shrilling telephone. It was Surkov. His agitation seemed an aspect of my fading dream, and it was several moments before I could take in what he was saying. He was at a police station, being questioned. He had been accused by Fiona Hayes-Drummond of raping her. He was innocent. The woman had allowed him to make love, but afterwards had started crying and screaming. She had to be crazy. He had left and walked back to the hotel, and by the time he reached it the police were waiting for him in the lobby. This was the one call he was allowed. He had tried his/Sergei's room first but could get no answer; presumably Sergei was with Masha. Could we for God's sake do something? I caught a man's voice behind him, low, authoritative, then the link was cut.

I paced around smoking while I decided what to do. I thought I'd try their bedroom again, and the call was answered by Rozanov. I gave him the bad news without preamble. He uttered a Russian oath. I said Victor had tried to call him first but could get no answer. There was a momentary hesitation before he explained that he'd only just got to the room, he'd felt too disturbed by the shamanistic experience to sleep and had sat in the Hospitality Suite reading. It sounded lame, but his nocturnal practices were his own affair; we had something serious on our hands.

We agreed that the accusation was obviously nonsense; but I warned him that rape, like child abuse, was a powerfully charged topic at present in England. We had to hope the police would release him after the questioning. There was nothing we could do for poor Victor at five in the morning; we should meet for an early breakfast and decide then what we could do to help. Sergei said he would ring Masha and tell her.

We gathered, the sole figures in the restaurant, gaunt-eyed and pale. At this murky hour the luxurious hotel had a seedy, spiritless air, matching our mood. None of us had slept in the intervening hours; Sergei had not been idle; he had gone to the lobby for a chat with the night-porter. Yes, a couple of policemen had turned up, at around two, and waited for Mr Surkov. On the latter's arrival, they had talked to him for a while and then he had gone off with them.

'I slipped him a tenner to keep quiet. We don't want this to get around if we can possibly avoid it.'

Rozanov, it was decided, would head for the Soviet Embassy; Masha and I would visit a friend of mine in Holborn who knew one or two influential people. I went back to my room and took a long bath. Just after nine we set off in a taxi and dropped Rozanov off outside his Embassy in Kensington Gardens.

My friend in Holborn rang a friend who rang the Chelsea police and found they were taking the accusation very seriously. Mr Surkov would get the chance of seeing the duty-solicitor. My friend's friend advised us on the best solicitors for a rape case, but warned that the final bill might be enough to buy a flat in Mayfair. In any case there was no point approaching anyone today, a Friday: they'd all be intent on an early departure for their weekend retreats. Best to let Mr Surkov see the duty-solicitor on legal aid.

Depressed, Masha and I found further cause for depression as, walking in search of a tube station, we came to a major intersection, a roundabout of relentless, screeching vehicles, three and four abreast: for in the centre, on the small concrete island, we saw a man lying on his side. A tramp, a derelict. Presumably he was drunk, but he might have been ill, or even dead. There was no break in the mad traffic pouring from half-a-dozen streets; no way to reach him. And no one else seemed to notice him.

So much, said Masha, for 'No man is an island . . .'

We ourselves did nothing. We felt helpless.

Rozanov was back before us. He'd had little luck with the Embassy. They couldn't interfere. He'd managed to persuade them to get a message through to British Intelligence: the words 'Prime Minister' and 'Cadogan Square'. Victor had bragged, absurdly, that he'd had a 5 A.M. rendezvous with her at a private house in Cadogan Square, just before her flight to Poland, and that 'the earth had moved'. 'He was almost certainly lying,' Sergei said, 'but it seemed worth a try.'

We all confessed ourselves exhausted, and headed for our rooms: though I guessed Masha would not be resting. It was time for her afternoon appointment. I didn't imagine Surkov's misfortune would entirely spoil her amorous pleasure. For myself, I lay down with nothing more erotic than the *Guard-*

ian. I turned to the Arts page which, every day this week, contained interview-portraits of two Festival writers. Today they were Jack Lamont, a novelist from Canada, and Geraldine Porter. Lamont turned out to be an egotistical womaniser who had selfishly kept his marriage of twenty years intact; Porter, a woman of integrity, now on her fourth marriage and deeply fond of both her disturbed children.

I dropped the paper to the floor; I closed my eyes. The pressure, not of this day alone but of all our nights of little sleep, overcame me.

Darkness had fallen—in fact it was approaching midnight—when I joined the others in Sergei's room. They too had slept; had missed both dinner and the theatre performance. I brought grim news, and I delivered it with a certain mournful pleasure. There is always a mournful pleasure in being the messenger of bad news, unless it affects you or the recipients intimately. The duty-solicitor had contacted me at Surkov's request. He had been charged with the rape. He would be appearing at Marylebone Magistrates' Court on Monday.

'The police are opposing bail,' I said, tossing back a whisky. 'They're afraid he'll skip the country, or try to intimidate the victim. In any case, you're almost never bailed for a rape charge.'

'Did this man tell you what's supposed to have happened?' asked Masha.

'According to Hayes-Drummond, Victor drank too much and started pawing her around. She tried to fob him off tactfully at first, but then he became brutal. She has bruising on her wrists from where she says he held her down.'

'Jesus!' growled Rozanov. Masha touched her cheek involuntarily.

'Victor's story is that she was willing, she undressed and led him to the bedroom. When they started making love she protested a little, but he thought this was just talk, since she was kissing him and caressing him. It was only later on that she started protesting strongly, and by then it was too late, he was close to coming. He's quite badly marked too.'

Masha: 'So it's bad.'

I nodded. 'Victor's a disreputable alien; Hayes-Drummond a respectable columnist, ex-Cambridge, aristocratic connections, her father an Old Bailey judge. Who will the jury believe?'

'Shit!' murmured Rozanov. 'It's crazy. Victor's no rapist; he can get any girl he likes.'

'They believe he took his revenge on Imogen,' I continued. 'This woman's a similar type to his English wife, and they've read that they've split up acrimoniously. The lawyer thinks it'll be a sensational case, and I'm sure he's right. All the feminists will be gunning for Victor.'

Secretly, though I had every sympathy for Surkov, I thought him much more likely to have raped a woman when drunk than Miss Hayes-Drummond was to have made a false accusation. I had observed with what relish he had improvised a rape—of a Soviet actress—for a scene in one of our novels. I had heard how lightly he dismissed the horrific offence of incestuous abuse. And I had read many of Miss Hayes-Drummond's pieces in the *Times*—admirably rational, objective and sincere.

I thought it probable the police were right, he had sought revenge against Imogen Surkov for separating him from his nice third wife, Vera, and their son. Which would make it a *crime passionnel*, and therefore deserving of compassion; but he would get none. I expressed these feelings, in a censored form still more sympathetic to Surkov.

'It may be so,' said Rozanov. 'Love is the most irrational of instincts, and Eros infinitely subtle.'

Masha: 'It's perfectly possible for a woman to be responsive to a sexual advance and yet feel she has been compelled. I've experienced it myself.'

'So have I,' said Rozanov thoughtfully. 'But the law is pre-Freudian, crude—even in this country: right?'

I nodded.

'So—what sentence can he expect?' asked Masha.

'Five years. No judge would dare to give less. It's a bad time to commit rape.'

Rozanov groaned.

He was in a Black Hole, reflected Masha. If it was some horrible misunderstanding, he couldn't talk to the girl to try to clear it up; instead, he had to be kept in prison to prevent any possibility of contact.

We thought of him lying in a cell. That first night of captivity, said Rozanov, was unforgettable. I tried to imagine it. The nearest I could get was my first night in a barracks in Shropshire, at the start of National Service.

Should Victor's daughter be told? Katya Surkov was living in Rostov; Sergei could probably find her number in Victor's address book. Yes, he should probably call her—later, around breakfast-time in Rostov. Though she wouldn't be able to do anything. And what about telling the Festival people? Jock would go crazy; Surkov was due to perform tomorrow night, to a sell-out audience.

'We must change our plane tickets, Sergei,' said Masha. 'We have to be in court on Monday; he must see that we're right behind him.'

He nodded. 'Of course.' I saw the outlandish figure shuffling into the dock. The word 'rape', enough to freeze the bones of everyone there.

'Will we get a chance to speak to him?' she asked me.

'I don't know. I doubt it.'

'Can we at least get some fresh clothes to him? Some books?'

'I don't know. I'll ask the solicitor—he's given me his home number.'

We lapsed into depressed silence. Then Masha said we should improvise, for Victor's sake. It meant a lot to him that we try to create a novel. Rozanov said, Yes, we must go on.

I agreed. In any case, none of us felt like sleep. Was it to be Masha or I? She and I would toss for it?

The task fell to me. I dragged my mind back into the world of Anna and Dmitri Charsky. They had got lost along the way. We still knew very little about them. Our 'novel' was almost certainly a write-off; but that in a sense gave a kind of freedom. It didn't much matter what I came out with. My stomach rumbled; I was hungry; but room service was extortionately expensive, and it would do me no harm to fast for one night. The lamplight was dimmed; I withdrew into my reluctant imagination.

· 13 ·

Anna lay back in the bath, staring at the wall tiles.

Threads of blood mingled with the foam and hot water. She agitated the water and dispersed the traces. The sign of her barrenness filled her with depression, and as usual she couldn't prevent an irrational moment of anger with Dmitri for being sterile.

Dunya, the cat, was perched precariously on the rim of the bath, gazing at her with ancient green eyes, her paws extended sphinxlike. She always liked to watch them bathing, for some reason.

Lying back, sponging soapy breasts, Anna wondered if she really loved her husband, and if he really loved her. He'd as good as admitted he'd gone off her sexually by saying he preferred just resting in her, motionless. Emotionless? Oh, he was very good with compliments, but what did they mean? No longer did he ask her for cuttings of her pubic hair!— Now that, she could see, it was thinning out.

No, it's not his fault, she said silently to Dunya; he's a good husband and I do love him, I suppose. But there's no language for love after twenty years of living together, mostly in the same rooms. If we'd had a child there would have been movement; we'd have watched him growing up, seen him change, worried about his schooling, and so on. There would be family snaps. You can't have family snaps when there's just the two of you and a cat.

There has to be some dynamism in love. She thought of the Richard–Sophie letters. That relationship did not stay still; the man and the woman tugged at one another, and fought one another, like earth and moon. She and Dmitri could still be here when they were seventy. He might still be saying— lying through his teeth—that her breasts were as firm as ever.

She kneaded her sagging breasts, searching anxiously for a lump; all was well.

And I still don't feel I know him, Dunya! He's too familiar. I must seem just the same to him. A long marriage is like the bath-foam covering the water—until, in the end, it's all foam and no water.

These women he slept with casually when he was touring— they knew him better than she, because they got an instant, naked impact. He *must* sleep with other women; he was charming, and found women desirable, so inevitably he weakened from time to time. Why, Anna herself had weakened once, and she had far fewer opportunities. She'd received only two or three serious propositions throughout her marriage—serious in the sense of coming from a man of intelligence and sensitivity—and to one of them she had yielded, in a matter of weeks. And Dmitri must sometimes get propositioned two or three times a week!

This film director, Bella Kropotkin, was undoubtedly after him, and undoubtedly he would take advantage of it— tonight! The casting couch, they called it.

Bathing always made her think of childhood. She could vaguely remember her mother bathing her, but mostly she recalled her grandmother's strong arms. She felt, at this moment, like crying out, 'Mama! Papa!' They were lost almost beyond memory. She shivered with cold, even though the bathwater was still warm; and she pulled herself up, causing a big splash and sending Dunya leaping for safety.

Death . . . She had a sudden fearful vision of everyone in the world, the untold billions, including Gorbachev and Reagan, engaged in desperate meaningless activity to stave off the horror of death in life, the accident of life. Life was a cinema screen, in an infinite darkness. There was no projectionist nor projector, nor audience, nor theatre, nor a surrounding city. Just a cinema screen. Where characters appeared and disappeared at random, and the plot was therefore ever-changing and never got anywhere. Many with whom she had shared the screen for a brief while, people whom she had revered, who had even seemed to define life—such as Akhmatova and Pasternak and Vysotsky—had already slipped out of the plot, and the film churned on as if they had never been.

There were others, friends, who had not died, but had departed from Russia, never to return. Glasnost had come only just in time to prevent all the interesting, intelligent spirits from vanishing. Unless, indeed, it actually increased the incidence of emigration! She thought of three couples, friends, who had managed to get to Israel, after a bitter struggle. They had left a gap in the life of the city. She contrasted their fortitude and determination with her own weaknesses.

Filled with world-weariness and self-disgust, she towelled herself zealously, as if wishing to flay herself.

Squatting, she performed the familiar ritual of menstruation.

She returned to the bedroom, slipped on pants and bra, then the overalls she wore for the factory. Dmitri was breathing nasally. It was almost like an old man's breathing—almost as old Yury had breathed during sleep. Perhaps her husband was faithful to her, as he swore; in her present mood, that seemed just as deplorable as his imagined infidelities.

She sat on the bed beside him, putting on her socks. His chin and cheeks were stubbled, his mouth was open. Who are you? she asked silently. What's in your soul? Supposing there were a heaven, I couldn't stand an eternity with you. I'd want to see you often, but not in a special way.

Rather viciously, she jerked a comb through her short hair.

In the living-room she picked up a couple of wine-glasses from the floor and set them down on a coffee table. After this slight rearrangement of the chaos she paced restlessly up and down. Pausing by the window, gazing at the apartment building opposite, she had an urge to punch her fist through the glass.

'I'm having two poems published in *Novy Mir*,' she said aloud; 'Dmitri's had some good luck too. The Summit looks like being a success. It's a lovely day out. I ought to be pleased. Well, it's only the time of the month.'

Or the menopause! That thought horrified her.

Mixed up with magazines and newspapers were the proofs of a book she had translated—*Eiger, Wall of Death*. Dmitri had been checking it for misprints and left it to get messed up like this. She tried to gather the pages into order. The work had been incredibly boring; even with her husband's help it had taken an age to find out the Russian terms for the jargon of mountaineering; and the subject simply left her cold. Heroism should have a moral or social purpose. Dmitri agreed with her, and they had had a passionate argument last night with Marchak, who drove racing-cars, and Frolovna, who had loved a matador for two weeks in Spain.

Yet now, today, she could feel the attraction of hacking one's way almost perpendicularly up an icefield, in imminent danger of being swept away. Anything for some excitement!

She had always assumed that something would happen, sometime, to sweep away her marital comfort. Perhaps Dmitri would find someone younger and more beautiful while on tour abroad, and would defect. Perhaps—it had seemed for a short while—she herself might leave him. Or else she and her husband would find some way of getting out of Russia and would share the entrancing hardship of starting afresh in the West. And these possibilities had made her cling to her actual existence with pleasure.

Whereas now . . .

Now they would go on lying together, here. And the years would pass . . .

She crouched before a coffee table on which rested, between a wine bottle and a dirty plate, a copy of *Hedda Gabler*; imagining she was feeding a manuscript into a stove, she murmured fiercely: 'I am burning our child, I am burning our child!' She felt destructive, like Hedda.

She felt tired of her life, tired of her self-consciousness. How lucky Dmitri was to be able to stride onstage and become someone entirely different. She supposed it gave him his equanimity. He seemed to engage in a continuous *carezza* with himself.

A glance at her watch told her she would have to leave to catch a tram in half an hour. She wandered into the study, thinking she would work on a poem, whose first line would be, *Yes, I remember the Stockhausen*. But seeing the confusion on her desk, all the things that had to be done, she lost heart. There was so little time to write. Mind you, it was partly her fault; they could afford to live without her factory work, but it gave her some company and a feeling of contributing to society.

Sitting on the studio bed to the right of her desk and chair, she recalled old Yury lying there, for most of the hours of the day and night, and felt relieved, for his sake, that he was gone. Death had been a merciful release for him. Even Dmitri's sorrow had been mostly used up by the fading of his father's life, remorselessly, year by year.

His psyche had chosen to fly during what was to have been a two-week visit at their flat—rather than fifteen storeys up in his own dismal, run-down tower-block, alone with his nagging wife. Just the day before the fatal collapse Konstantin,

Dmitri's brother, had come for a meal. His family all together. It was good. Still, she might have been nicer to the kindly old man. There was always a certain resentment, whenever they came to visit, at having to give up her study.

She thought of Yevdoxia, his wife, dragging his decayed body and bruised mind around. She was a hard-nosed bitch, but she'd had to be, to survive.

Gradually these musings dissolved into the main current of her thoughts, that vague depression and dissatisfaction. An absurd idea took hold of her. The more absurd it appeared, the more appealing it became. Smiling to herself, she walked into the kitchen, switched on the kettle to make a drink, picked up the phone and dialled.

Charsky woke up to find his father, vividly present a moment before, vanished from the room. Yet he felt convinced it had been more than a dream. I must ring my mother, he thought, and tell her about it. He stretched and picked up the phone, but before he could dial he realised he had cut in on a conversation. Anna was talking with an old friend of theirs, Irena Ignatiev. Irena was saying, in her quavery ancient voice, 'Of course, I'll be in all evening, my dear; these days I'm always in.' The grand old lady of the Arts Theatre was finding retirement almost unbearably tedious. He thought of saying, 'Hello, Irena!' but it would have been a rude interruption and he replaced the phone. He lay back, closing his eyes, and tried to reconstitute the extraordinary image and speech of his father.

He opened his eyes and sat up in bed as Anna came in holding a mug of coffee. 'Thanks, darling. I cut in on you. I'm sorry.'

'I thought I'd drop round to see Irena after work,' she said. 'You'll be very late, I guess?'

'I guess so.'

'Irena gets lonely.'

'I know. Invite her for a meal sometime.'

'I'll do that.' She circled the bedroom, tidying, picking up

dirty clothes, ashtray, dirty plates, the glossy Italian magazine. She stood with arms full. 'Well, I'm leaving now. The
lounge is your job. I hope it goes well with Kropotkin.'

'Thanks.' She leant over and he kissed her on the cheek.
When she had left the bedroom he heard her feet scurrying
for a few minutes, then the door slammed.

At one of the tram stops on the way to the industrial estate
where Anna worked, she saw an old lady in a shabby grey
coat pull herself on, and recognised with surprise and a sinking
of her heart her mother-in-law. Yevdoxia revealed the same
blend of feelings: the two women had a healthy disregard for
each other. Hatchet-faced, tough as the city's granite,
Yevdoxia plumped herself down at Anna's side. She'd just
been visiting the widow of an old army friend of Yury's,
who had a bad attack of flu. Lots of people had flu. Yevdoxia
put it down to Chernobyl. Now she was on her way to see
a second cousin, who had the double misfortune of being a
cripple and being married to a horrible man. 'Butcher by
trade and butcher by nature,' said Yevdoxia tartly. She stared
at Anna's face: '*You* don't look too well. You've got terrible
shadows under your eyes and you're very pale, my dear.'

'Oh, it's just the time of the month.'

'You still have *them*, do you?' Her eyes expressed incre-
dulity that Anna hadn't reached the menopause.

'I'm not *that* old!' Anna snapped.

At once regretting that she had let herself become riled,
she delved into her bag and came out with a bar of soap.
'Here,' she said, 'I managed to get some soap at—'

The bedroom door opened and Surkov burst in. We exclaimed our astonishment and relief, and rushed to embrace
him. Rozanov himself, in last night's shamanistic trance, had
not risen more miraculously from the dead. As befitted a

resurrection, Surkov looked shattered. 'Yes, I'm free,' he confirmed. Pulling off his black leather jacket and kicking off his shoes, he threw himself onto a bed. Sergei thrust a drink into his hand.

'I have to leave the country by Monday, but that's no problem,' he growled. 'What a fucking day!'

Hours of questioning, blood tests, sperm tests, photographs, examination of every inch of his body. He'd been charged eventually and thrust into a cell for the night; then, half an hour later, without explanation, given his belt back and told he could go.

But what, we asked, had really happened? Had she really changed her mind in the midst of having sex?

'It seemed that way. One minute she was enjoying it—oh, with a few protests thrown in, like she didn't know me well enough, she shouldn't be doing it, and so on—nothing serious. And then, suddenly, she was struggling and screaming and I had to hold her wrists to stop her from scratching me.' He pulled back his open shirt-collar, showing us scars on his neck. 'I just didn't see why I should stop, it was too late. Maybe I did, technically, rape her.'

Surely not, we said, since she had plunged into it willingly.

'—Perfectly willingly. We started necking on the sofa, and she undressed, and suggested the bedroom. The bitch denied that, of course. But why? Why did she suddenly start screaming and scratching, and swearing that she'd get me?'

'You touched some nerve, I guess,' Masha offered, shrugging.

'I tried to reason with her after, but she locked herself in the bathroom, crying. So I dressed and left. I wandered around for a while, in a bit of a daze, and then strolled back here. They were here waiting for me. She didn't waste any time . . . Does anyone else know about this?'

We reassured him; no one knew, the night-porter had been bribed to keep quiet.

'Thank Christ. Maybe we can keep it out of the papers.'

He accepted a refill. 'She could be an old friend of Imogen's. I wouldn't put it past that bitch to have set her up to frame me.'

We drank quietly; faintly Big Ben struck one.

'It looked curtains for me,' he sighed. 'They told me her bra was torn. But she turned to let me undo it and I got impatient with the damn thing. That could happen to anybody.'

'Still,' said Masha, 'you're free. Thank God!'

'I'm starving. I've had nothing to eat since four o'clock. A fucking cheese sandwich and tea with milk.'

'Have something sent up,' I suggested. 'This is on me.' I was feeling guilty, still, about the poor royalties they had had, as well as genuinely relieved at his freedom. 'I could eat something too; I'll have a hamburger.'

Surkov glanced through the room-service menu. 'I'd like a filet with french fries. And maybe a Waldorf salad to start.'

'Fine. I'll ring down.'

Masha and Sergei said they could eat a sandwich. 'And why don't we have a bottle of champagne sent up?' Surkov suggested. He looked again at the menu and chose a Dom Perignon.

My blood froze as I looked at the prices. This would cost me a fortune. Then I accused myself of ungenerosity. I could be a mean bastard at times. I had had endless hospitality in Moscow, and it was only natural Surkov would want to celebrate. I rang room service and placed the order.

'So why do you think they let you go?' Masha asked.

'God only knows.'

'I guess they realised she was telling lies,' said Rozanov.

Unseen by Victor, he mouthed to me, 'Maggie?', lifting an eyebrow in query.

That possibility had already occurred to me. And I became conscious that, alongside a genuine pleasure that he had been released, there was also a resentment that he had got away with it. Whatever 'it' was. Even by his own account, he had continued to make love to her when he knew she didn't want him to. That behaviour demanded more suffering than just a few uncomfortable hours.

His cockiness would be unbearable from now on.

After a couple of glasses of champagne and a hamburger, and under the influence of my friends' euphoria, I cheered up. Aware that he had broken in, Surkov urged me to go on improvising. He was exhausted but not sleepy. Masha sketched for him what had happened so far.

'We'll dedicate this section to fucking Fiona Hayes-Drummond,' he said in English, raising his glass. The ambiguous obscenity seemed crude and callous. His eyes gleamed malevolently. At that moment, in my mind, the scales lurched against Surkov's version of events. The others looked uncomfortable too, and none of us joined him in his toast.

When her mother-in-law got off the tram, Anna, waving to her, felt glad she had given her a bar of Zoya's soap. And remorseful that she didn't like her more. She wasn't a bad woman. She was feeling her loss much more than she revealed; she was schooled in hiding her emotions. There was no malice in her; on the contrary, she was kind. These sick-visits were genuinely meant to be helpful. It wasn't her fault if she had a gift for putting her foot in it. Her negative attitudes were the result of a harsh life: a sickly, poverty-stricken childhood, the horrors of the war, the struggle to bring up two children and look after an invalid husband. I must be kinder to her, Anna thought. She remembered an American Indian saying, that you shouldn't condemn a man until you had walked a mile in his shoes.

Dmitri, trying and failing to reach his mother through the bedside phone, was also thinking about her a little more charitably. She had had no life of her own for several years; if she went out for half an hour, she had to leave messages all round the flat, telling Yury she'd be back soon, otherwise he would panic. And she could never be sure he wouldn't turn the gas on and forget to light it. So now she was having a splendid time visiting friends, and who could blame her?

He rang his brother, who was in. 'I've had a strange experience, Konstantin! I'm sure Father was here! . . . Well, yes, I was just waking up, but . . . I'm sure it wasn't a dream! Much too vivid; my dreams are always so nondescript I always forget them, you know that . . .'

I can't really blame her either, thought Charsky as he reclined in a hot bath, for feeling a sense of relief. And yet—it's rather cold-blooded. She could at least pretend some sorrow. She had superhuman control of her feelings. If either or both of her sons had decamped to the West, she'd have shrugged her shoulders and got on with existence.

'Well, anyway, there's no question of trying to get out now,' he said aloud, addressing the cat who had come and perched beside him. 'We shan't have to look for another home for you, my friend. Gorbachev is a good guy. He'll drag this country into the West, as Peter the Great tried to do.'

The cat gazed sphinxlike into his eyes with every appearance of understanding.

It was a great relief that they would no longer have to scheme some way of getting Anna out, at the right moment, while he himself was touring somewhere. They could go on living in this flat they both loved.

He would probably die here. The thought was pleasing and oppressive at the same time. They could become like the old couple in *Fathers and Sons*—so entwined they would even look alike. This thought, too, caused him a few moments of depression before it was drowned by feelings of tranquil pleasure.

Sliding deeper, he let the warm water lap around him. Was this, he wondered—thinking of Freud—the amniotic fluid? In the Leningrad of 1942, besieged by the Nazis, explosions everywhere, he could imagine himself shrinking from birth. He hated seeing wartime documentaries; they didn't seem to affect Anna in the same way—she seemed to thrill with excitement as the guns flashed and the tanks churned through ruined streets.

Only now, he reflected, was he beginning to feel really secure.

He pulled himself up, the scattered water making the cat leap for safety. He towelled himself dry, then slipped into his dressing-gown. A peaceful lunch, some bread and cheese— or should he perhaps tidy the lounge first? Neither: he would get dressed. Slowly: he felt pleasantly languid, a shade hung over still. From long experience he knew the hangover would pass before it was time for him to stalk on stage and rebuke Hamlet for grieving overmuch for his father. Halfway through dressing, wearing his shirt and underpants, he looked for *Moda* in the workroom, where he assumed she would have thrown it on their pile of magazines; he wanted to gaze at Bella Kropotkin again, but he couldn't find the magazine. Well, it didn't matter.

Komarovsky! That would be a splendid role! To sit in a plush cinema with Anna, Mama and Konstantin on the first night, watching the titles unroll! Dmitri Charsky! Then observing himself as he fluttered and flustered the teen-aged Lara in a restaurant! Life was really opening up, thanks to Gorbachev.

He wondered if she would indeed try to seduce him? It was conceivable; she had a reputation. Well, she would not succeed; greater beauties than Bella Kropotkin had tried and failed.

The workroom was in a mess. She hadn't really had time to set it straight since his father's death. How strange, thought Charsky, that he had watched him fall asleep here on his last night on earth.

He'd been put to bed early, exhausted after a visit from

Konstantin and his girlfriend. Dmitri, typing letters of thanks for the Freud books sent by American friends, was a little irritated to be interrupted. His mother, undressing the panting old man, had told her son not to disturb himself—Yury was almost asleep already. Indeed, standing in his vest, his eyes closed, he was swaying like a punch-drunk boxer. Yevdoxia had rolled him into bed then, kissing him, whispered not 'Good-night' but 'Good-bye'.

His father rolls onto his side, facing him. One hand rests between his cheek and the pillow, cupping his head almost maternally; the other, hairy but oddly sensitive for so big and coarse a man, lies outside the sheet. He continues to pant for breath. His eyes open once, and he murmurs 'Dmitri' in recognition and greeting. Charsky gazes at him for a long time, sadly.

Recalling those moments now, he opened Anna's file of typed poems, seeking the one she'd written, only a couple of weeks ago, about the funeral flowers. There were several alterations in ink; she'd changed it again since he'd last looked. And now it had a title: *Varvara*.

> Varvara wants to put 'Rest in Peace' on Ivan's wreath.
> Her son begs her to write 'With Fondest Memories',
> But she refuses. 'I don't like lies,
> Not fondest memories. No, not the last few years.'
> She settles reluctantly for 'God bless you, Vanya,
> And keep you safe'. That's fairly meaningless
> In Varvara's eyes, not being religious.
> Then there are problems of translation;
> A distant relative's long-distant and fairly
> Meaningless tribute, 'We shan't forget old Vanya',
> Gets translated into funeralese as
> 'We shall never forget you', which in turn
> Gets translated by a deaf florist into
> 'We shall love you forever'. So the world
> Maintains its confusion round the silent corpse
> Of the old warrior; and the flowers,

Beset by astonishing messages,
Wear his familiar, wry and bemused smile.

Charsky sighed. The poem hurt him. There was something cold-blooded about using his father's death to make a poem; she had changed the names so that she could attempt to get it published—and it was going to be. Her response, when he'd said he hadn't read *Varvara*, had shown guilt.

Do I really know her? he thought. There was something a little cold at her heart—as when she had picked up that book to read while he was fucking her. Having been blessed with a cold mother, did I seek a cold wife?

He heard the phone ring. He padded to the kitchen to answer it. He recognised the drawling, somewhat condescending voice of Bella Kropotkin. For a moment his heart sank, as he thought she might be cancelling their meeting. But she was merely changing the venue: 'I'm moving from the hotel. It's perfectly dreadful! Luckily some friends of mine, who are in Georgia at the moment, have said I can stay in their flat for a couple of nights. It's very sweet of them. Can you meet me there? It's Flat 5, 238 Kirov Street. Good! It will be much quieter and more pleasant and there's always plenty to drink. I'm looking forward to *Hamlet*, but I won't bother you at the theatre; I'll see you at the flat. I look forward to meeting you *immensely*. Good-bye.'

Charsky poured himself a glass of apple juice, then wandered back to the bedroom to finish dressing. The change might be entirely innocent, the hotel might be dreadful—though it was the smartest in Leningrad; on the other hand it might confirm Anna's suspicions about the casting couch.

He would have to be careful. He drew on socks, a pair of tight Italian jeans, and plimsolls, combed his receding hair before a mirror.

He mustn't foul up tonight. He addressed to the mirror a few noble lines of the ignoble king.

· 14 ·

The workers on the shop floor at the radio factory, who were all female, had become used to treating Anna as a bit of an oddity. They knew she wrote poems, and that this often made her absent-minded, prone to mistakes which others corrected, and silent while they were discussing such subjects as the best way of getting stains out of carpets, where to get hold of a plumber, how to deal with a dictatorial schoolteacher, how to get rid of their children's head nits and so on. They would say, 'Comrade Charsky is composing something!'

Today, however, as cheerful music blared over the loud-speakers, brightening the afternoon shift, a subject came up that aroused Anna's interest and distracted her from thoughts of *Yes, I remember the Stockhausen.* As a reward for quality work and exceptional nonabsenteeism, two of the workers had been given tickets for a play currently showing at the Maly Theatre. The women would have much preferred tick-ets for the Circus, but of course one couldn't look a gift horse in the mouth. They had gone on the previous evening, and for the first half-hour of the shift they entertained their com-rades with their and their husbands' opinion of what they had seen.

Actually the work at the factory wasn't too demanding.

Since no one expected radios to work perfectly, it was quite possible to plug in a few parts while Tanya or Lisa gave you a perm or a manicure. Their lives at home were so deadly, one nonstop round of cooking, cleaning and queueing, that they really came to the factory for a rest and a gossip. This afternoon, Tanya was dexterously removing a corn from Anna's right foot.

The play seen by Vera, Masha and their husbands was *Stars under a Morning Sky* by Alexander Galin. It was causing a sensation among Party members and the intelligentsia. Having been performed briefly at the Moscow theatre festival, it was now attracting droves of the fashionable from both major cities; Muscovites were coming up by plane or overnight train just to see the play or just to say they had seen it. Anna had managed to see it, thanks to Dmitri's influence, and had loved it. Not for nothing, in her view, was it being described as the first theatrical child of glasnost.

Set in the 'Brezhnevka' in the year of the Moscow Olympics, it described some of the people at a special deportation centre, where the social dregs were congregated before being sent out of the city. The main characters and victims were women: a former ardent Communist turned alcoholic whose children had been taken from her; and a prostitute who still had faith in love, somewhere in the depths of her sad being. She fell for one of the militiamen entrusted with purging the streets of undesirables, and they started an affair.

The young policeman's mother, a 'strong' Stalinist type who had already had her unconventional Tartar husband consigned to a lunatic asylum, intervened once more to save her son's career. Nemesis for the fragile and immoral love affair enters in the form of an official car, riding through all the roadblocks, and playing on its expensive tape deck—very ironically—music of Vysotsky, that modern Villon of the underground whose sudden death and emotional funeral in that summer of '80 had almost stolen the Olympics' thunder.

The two ladies from the factory had found the play deeply

shocking. 'It's disgusting,' said Vera, her double chin wobbling and her spectacles flashing indignantly. 'The whore was stark naked. Yes, and face-on to the audience—isn't that right, Masha?'

Masha, beside her, nodded, her fingers flying over wires and transistors. 'You could see everything, everything. It should be closed down. There were boys and girls of sixteen, seventeen, in the audience.'

'Yes, it's no wonder you hear of so many rapes, when they see that kind of thing.'

The workers who listened avidly expressed themselves appalled by such obscenity.

Anna, rolling on her sock, felt bound to intervene. 'But what's indecent about seeing a woman's body onstage? Isn't it the temple of the holy spirit? Why should it make a man want to commit rape?'

But only one or two timid voices agreed with her. God! she thought: if only Alexandra Kollontai could walk through that door and tell them what rubbish they're talking! What's happened to the early ideals of the Revolutionary women? The faith in emotional generosity, free love, passion, destruction of old dead taboos?

Vera and Masha hated the whole play. You could tell, they said, you were supposed to feel sympathy for the alcoholic and the whore; which was disgraceful. There were enough girls taking to the bottle or going on the streets without encouraging them to do so. They thoroughly approved the actions of the young policeman's mother. She was only doing what any decent mother would do, yet she was shown in a bad light. 'You would think the whore was a nicer character than the mother!' said Masha, to a general tut-tutting.

'Well, she was!' Anna exclaimed. 'For God's sake, look at Tolstoy's *Resurrection*! Look at Dostoievsky!'

But none of them had read *Resurrection*; and though some of them had read Dostoievsky, they claimed, not unreasonably, that you couldn't compare a girl in Tsarist times, forced into prostitution through dire poverty, with girls of today who had shelter and plenty to eat, and who were just lazy or simply corrupt.

'And what about the poor man who was shoved into a lunatic asylum?'

'I don't think that could happen,' said Vera. 'If he wasn't mental he'd have been sent home again. They don't keep you there unless you need treatment.'

On this point, however, Anna—blazing with secret anger because of her friend from Moscow, Sergei Rozanov—got some support. By no means was everyone sure there weren't any quite sane people in mental hospitals. There was no support for her argument that it had been wrong to expel social misfits from Moscow during the Games. It was natural you should want to show your best side to foreigners—who must have been happy not to have to suffer drunks and pickpockets.

Choking, as if all the air vents had been stopped, Anna fled. She needed to ring Dmitri. After that, she went to the toilet. Taking a book from her overalled bosom, she spent a few precious minutes reading.

Berlin

My dear Professor,

Oh, I am so bored, so unutterably bored! I am sorry you have not been well. If only your invitation had come earlier. I would have accepted without a moment's hesitation! But now it is too late. I know I should be grateful to my husband, who is kindness itself, but I am so bored with the routine of the day, in which I scarcely see anyone other than Heinz, perhaps a neighbour, and a few shopkeepers. And the bed side of things is dull! He is so gentle with me!

I know my way of life before was dangerous but it was thrilling. I would gladly give up my present safety for just a touch of excitement. I can't help feeling that you should be my Master. Since that cannot be, I am sorely tempted to go into the city one day and stand in one of the streets near the Opera, where I am told the bad women carry on their trade. Just to stand there and be brushed against, not to actually go with anyone. May I do it? If I don't do *something* I shall die of boredom. Truly! Give me your permission, will you? Better still, your command. If I have that little outlet for my yearnings, I am sure I shall be a better wife to Heinz.

> Yours affectionately,
> Sophie

> Vienna

Dear Sophie,

I cannot think of you as Frau Stolz, married to a railwayman. Yet you must be good and kind to him, and I do see your point that if you had some outlet you might find it easier to be an affectionate wife. I can't see much harm in what you propose, just so long as you promise me not to let it go further. You must never go home with one of those men, do you hear me? I feel extraordinarily responsible for you, in some way; and very anxious and concerned. So, yes, I give you permission to stand near the Opera, now and then. No—all right—I command you to! But I also command you to take great care of yourself.

I once, in my youth, walked along those streets you mention: merely out of curiosity, with a Berlin friend. I recall Leopoldstrasse was a favourite haunt; but of course it may have changed. My youth is far distant.

Be very, very careful.

> Sincerely yours,
> Richard von Krafft-Ebing

> Berlin

My dear Professor,

I have stood in Leopoldstrasse! Men have come by and spoken brutally to me, they have pawed my breasts and thighs! It was wonderful! I came home full of life, and cooked my husband a lovely meal, and was nice to him!

Thank you! Thank you!

Your obedient servant,
Sophie

Vienna

My dear Sophie,

I am glad your experiment was successful—and above all that you are safe. You may repeat it, but not too frequently, and always with my (*sic*) safety uppermost in your thoughts.

I still wish I could cure the original perversion. As a matter of fact, a young colleague of mine has developed a theory that such perverse desires are connected with the womb. It may be that you have some minor disease of the womb. Would you please send me, in a plain package marked Personal, one of your used napkins at your next menstrual period. I shall subject the blood-stains to analysis.

Sincerely yours,
R. von Krafft-Ebing

Berlin

Dear Professor,

I am sorry to go against any request of yours, and I know you mean to help, but really I could not send what you ask for through the mails. It would seem rather dirty. Apart from which, as I've told you many times, I have no wish to be cured.

Yesterday, one of my fantasies came true! I was standing along with the other—I was about to write 'prostitutes', but I am not one—in one of the alleys, when a man brushed past behind me. I felt a fierce pain in my bottom, and when I put my hand there it came away covered in blood. I had been stabbed to the depth of about an inch. I almost fainted, not with the pain or loss of blood but from sheer delight! I was just an object for him to hurt.

At first, when I stood there, some of the girls were unfriendly, but now they know I'm not in the business of stealing customers from them they're okay.

Affectionately,
Sophie

Vienna

Dear Sophie,

Of course I can understand your reluctance about sending such an item through the mails; however, it seems a little ironic that you wish me to be your Master yet the first real request I make to you is rejected!

Anyway, we won't dwell on it. It does not matter. I have little faith in my colleague's theory. What is much more important is that I am going to be in Berlin for three days next week, attending a conference. We can meet at last. Most of my time will be taken up by the conference, but I have a couple of hours free on Thursday afternoon. I will meet you in Leopoldstrasse at three o'clock. We can go and have coffee and cake somewhere. There is the problem of recognition; I do not want to confuse you with the other *filles de joie* who will be standing there. Therefore you should carry your copy of my book.

I don't mind confessing that I am stimulated by the prospect of our meeting at long last; I hope you will feel the same.

Cordially,
Richard von Krafft-Ebing

Berlin

My dear Professor,

I do not know if I shall be able to meet you next Thursday. Perhaps I will, perhaps I won't. My mother-in-law often comes to visit me on a Thursday afternoon, and it could be difficult to get out.

Affectionately,
Sophie

Vienna

Dear Sophie,

You can surely make an excuse to your mother-in-law. You can see your mother-in-law any time. I shall expect to meet you in Leopoldstrasse at three on Thursday.

Richard von K.E.

'We are ghosts,' thought Charsky as the two watchmen greeted each other on the battlements of Elsinore. Gazing from the wings, he could see how insubstantial those battlements were. By the logic of mathematics, in which two negatives make a positive, the Ghost was the most real character in the play. Perhaps the author had thought so too, and for that reason had, so tradition said, performed as the Ghost.

Then, with his Queen, Hamlet and others, it was time to make an entrance. He plunged into his first speech. Charsky believed in letting the language dictate the meaning of a character and of the play in general; he didn't believe in a lot of fussy 'business'. In the case of Claudius, the words he spoke were orotund, seeming thoughtful and impressive, but gave no sign of soul. He thought Claudius the emptiest man he had ever personated. He had filched the crown so that power could provide him with a spurious density. Love or sex, in Charsky's view, meant little to him, and the Charsky interpretation emphasised his erotic torpor: he made him appear slightly ill at ease with the Queen.

The most powerful moment of his Claudius characterisation came at the end of the play-scene: his cry, *Give me some light:—away!* evoked desperation, as though he were an earth-worm begging for light.

When he huddled in prayer at the side of the apron-stage, he stared through his hands at a family trio in the front row: father, mother, and a boy of about eleven. The order in which they sat, and the way mother and son leaned slightly towards each other, clearly revealed to the actor that the father was of small account. He looked like a prosperous businessman. Perhaps he spent most of his time in the fleshpots of Helsinki. As for the boy, he looked revoltingly fat and spoiled. *The Queen, his mother / Lives almost by his looks*, the actor recalled. Even though only a few people could see his face—which in any case was almost masked by his hands—he tried to act as if the whole theatre could see him. He sweated in the agony of his vain remorse. He could see that the man and woman were entranced, but the boy started to make faces at him: poking out his tongue, then swallowing his lips and rolling his eyes. Charsky closed his eyes in order to concentrate.

'*Pretty Ophelia . . .*' He gave a tinge of desire to the words. Whatever affection had attached him to Gertrude was waning already. He couldn't understand how Hamlet could turn away from such a charming young creature.

Dmitriev was on top form. Sweat rolled off the Prince of Denmark. It must be like climbing a sheer mountain-face, every performance. Charsky had no interest in mountain climbing. But there was that book he had helped Anna with: it had touched a faint chord.

As Hamlet and Laertes prepared to duel, Charsky had a moment's panic, feeling he was going to faint. His robes were heavy and hot; but it wasn't only that. Something about Elsinore tonight made him see it as the vast, stinking cor-ruption that was Russia; that was even the world, as man had made it. The poison ran too deep for any Gorbachev-Fortinbras to cure it. Lydia, his queen, noticing his momen-tary frailty, dipped her handkerchief in a ewer of water and bathed his brow, making it appear an act they had rehearsed and performed a hundred times. He came back to himself.

Not until the poisoned chalice had killed him did he remember that a famous blind film director was somewhere in the audience, staring at the blackness, perhaps holding an unreadable programme in her lap. What had she thought of him? Well, he had been no better nor worse than usual.

A small group of autograph-seekers waited outside the stage door. The prosperous businessman was among them. He offered Charsky a programme. 'Could you please sign it for Nikolai? He's our son. He was here tonight and really loved it, even though he's only ten.'

'Why didn't he come to me himself?' Charsky asked, scribbling his name 'for Nikolai'.

'We wanted him to, but he was too shy. Thank you, Comrade.'

The boy could hardly have been more shy than the red-headed girl-student waiting in line behind the businessman. She blushed as she handed Charsky her programme. He chatted with her for a few moments. Before turning away she pressed a piece of paper into his hand. Glancing at it by the still-clear light of the low sun, he saw she had written her name and a phone number. He kept the paper in his hand as he strode along the street thronged with deferential theatre-goers, nudging one another as he passed, but then crunched it up and tossed it into a litter-bin.

'Comrade Charsky! Dmitri!' An obvious drunk stepped into his path and placed both hands on his shoulders. 'That was wonderful! Honour me by having a glass with me!'

Charsky recognised fresh-faced Punin, an unpleasant companion of his schooldays. Punin had tried to initiate him into masturbation; Charsky could still visualise Punin's red knob poking through the opening of his rather grimy underpants.

Flinching from the man's sour alcoholic breath, disengaging his hands politely, Charsky said, 'I'd love to, old friend, but I have another engagement. Sorry! Some other time.'

. . .

He rose in the juddery lift of a gloomy apartment building. In a windowless passageway he confronted a door which had lost its number, but he assumed it was five because the door adjacent to it was marked four. He knocked. After a lengthy interval he heard footsteps and the door was opened. Bella Kropotkin stood in the light, her eyes, hidden behind dark glasses, seeming to look over his shoulder. 'Comrade Charsky?' she asked uncertainly.

'Yes.'

'Come in, please.'

Feeling her way adroitly with a long white stick, she led him into a living-room. 'Please sit down.'

'Thank you.'

He eased himself into a faded and lumpy armchair, and the blind beauty sat on a sofa opposite. Folding and laying aside her stick, she gestured towards a bottle and two glasses on a small table between them. 'Help yourself to a drink. Is vodka okay?'

'Of course: what else?'

'That's good, because I find it's all my friends have got. It's unlike them.'

While he poured the drinks, Charsky continued his observation of her. She appeared slenderer in face than in her photograph, and her long curly golden hair was even more resplendent. The scarlet of her lipstick was matched by a red velvet dress, the neckline scooped to show off an exquisite throat, and the knee-length skirt generously cut. A hint of white lace petticoat gave way to black stockings, probably silk, and her high-heeled red shoes had also not been bought at GUM. His eyes swept up to her face again, staring past him blindly. He gazed as at a beautiful picture in the Hermitage. She really was as wondrous as everyone said.

'They actually don't spend all that much time here,' she said. 'They're in Georgia all summer, and at other times too. They have a lovely dacha there.'

'Yes, it feels unlived in,' Charsky observed, gazing round. The curtains and carpet were shabby, the walls could have done with a coat of paint, the furniture was strictly functional. The window, giving on to the side of another apartment building, let in little of the murky midnight light, and added to the depressing effect of the room. At least his parents' flat—he corrected himself, his mother's flat—was crowded with pictures and ornaments. Here, a saturnine picture of a Cossack campfire was the only decoration.

'It feels that way to me too. Uncared for.'

'Do they have a child?' He couldn't imagine children living here.

'No, there's just the two of them. So they simply don't care. They exist here when they have to, and take off as often as possible for their real life in the sun. Still, it's very nice of them to let me stay. Do you have a nice flat, Comrade Charsky?—look, may I call you Dmitri?'

'Please do.'

'And please call me Bella.'

'Bella. Yes, a very nice flat.'

'You have a child?'

'No. No. It's just the two of us.'

'And what's your wife like? I've heard she's a poet: is that true?'

'Yes, she is. She's not very well known. She's published mostly in samizdat. But today she had some good news—*Novy Mir* are going to publish a couple of her poems.'

'Oh, that's wonderful! I bet she's thrilled.'

'She is, yes.'

Bella nodded, smiling, and reached into a leopardskin handbag, taking out a silver cigarette case and lighter. Charsky sprang to light a cigarette for her. She nodded in thanks as she breathed out smoke. 'But what is she like? I imagine she must be beautiful.'

'Not exactly beautiful,' Charsky replied cautiously; 'but very attractive.'

'Young?'

'Not young. Slightly older than me, in fact. She's rather quiet and self-contained; deeply committed to her work.'

'Is she good?'

He hesitated. Honesty impelled him to say, 'She's pretty good. She certainly deserves to be better known.'

'Well, that's enough about wives,' said Bella, removing her cigarette from the centre of her mouth and loosing a languid coil of smoke. 'I'm more interested in you, Dmitri. You gave a wonderful performance tonight.'

'Oh—thank you!' Charsky breathed a silent sigh of relief.

'Do you know why your interpretation is so good?' Not waiting for a reply she went on: 'Because it has tremendous sex appeal. It's obvious Claudius and Gertrude go at it like muskrats. Do muskrats go at it? Well, never mind—you know what I mean.'

'Yes.'

'Claudius has to be very sexy; and so does Gertrude, but Dorinskaya let you down. Much too tame. *That* Gertrude wouldn't have let her sleepy old husband be killed, so she could have a real man to fuck every night.'

'What did you think of Hamlet?'

'Oh, Dmitriev was quite good. But Hamlet is such a dull character, don't you agree? He takes after his father. No sexuality. Ophelia was well off losing him, if only she'd realised. I thought the whole production was quite good, though of course there were many things I'd have done differently.'

She stretched forward, offering her empty glass. He filled it and added a little to his own, leaving it still half-empty, resolved to stay reasonably sober.

'Oh, do fill up your glass,' she urged.

'That's extraordinary! How did you know it wasn't full?'

She smiled sadly. 'One is given certain compensations for blindness. My other senses are acute. I knew you had drunk quite a lot, and then you poured in just a very little. It is not so extraordinary! But let's think about *Doctor Zhivago*.'

Charsky strained forward in his chair.

'As I told you, I'm considering you very seriously for the role of Komarovsky.'

Charsky's heart sank. So it wasn't certain. He knew from bitter experience what 'considering very seriously' meant: it meant there were about ten others equally in the running. He drained his glass with one gulp and slurped in more vodka.

'*Very* seriously. Would you like to do it?'

'I'd love to,' he replied fervently.

'Good. It will be a huge production; no expense spared. Have you seen the western version?'

'No, I'm afraid not. Anna's seen it, I think. At a private screening.'

'You've missed nothing. It's rubbish. Completely Hollywoodised. An actor called Omar Sharif plays Zhivago as if he were a gigolo. A very beautiful man; but a poet? Not in a million years. Lara, played by a young woman called Christie, is not the least bit Russian. You couldn't imagine drawing a line around the immensity of Russia, as Pasternak says, and calling it "Lara". And there's the most ludicrous little jaunty theme tune, called "Lara's Song"! In my production you will see all of Russia in Lara, and Zhivago will be a true poet. I'm thinking of asking Surkov. What do you think?'

Charsky's heart fell again, though not quite so low. 'An interesting choice,' he offered.

'*I* think so. But the real problem, of course, is how to weave the actual poetry, Zhivago's verses, into the narrative. One can't just have them quoted. Somehow the sense of them has to be poured into the images. It will require a different kind of film altogether, something quite new.'

She reached her glass out again and Charsky recharged it. 'It would be very exciting to be part of such a venture,' he said. 'And you're having no problem with the censorship and the bureaucracy?'

She shook her head. 'Everyone's being very cooperative. The order has come from on high.'

'That's wonderful.'

'To Comrade Gorbachev!' she intoned, holding her glass up. He echoed her words, and they clinked glasses.

'For me, the role of Komarovsky is central,' she proceeded. 'He is the untransformed Zhivago, the Tsarist Zhivago. There is a lot that is good in him, otherwise Lara would not fall in love with him as a girl, and especially she would not go off with him at the end. He's more than just a rake. So if there is a possibility of our working together in this film, first of all I must know everything about you. Everything!' she emphasised. 'So you must portray yourself to me. Paint a picture of yourself, your life, your background.'

'Difficult. There's nothing very remarkable about me.'

'Try. Take it from your childhood. Tell me about your parents, and so on.'

After another gulp of vodka, Charsky launched into an account of his life. 'I was born during the Siege of Leningrad,' he said. 'My father was in the Red Army and received a head wound from which he never really recovered; my mother wielded a rifle too and cooked rats so we could stay alive. My father died just a few weeks ago but had been seriously ill for years; my mother is a very difficult woman, but who can expect otherwise? I never knew my grandparents; on my father's side they were Caucasian gypsies; my mother's parents both perished in Siberia before I was born. Anna has a similar background. Her mother died of wounds during the war, her father died a few years later from the effects of disease and starvation.

'Like most Russians, we are children of violence . . .'

· 15 ·

Rozanov emerged from his newspaper to say, 'Good morning! How do you feel?'

'Fine.'

'That's good,' said Surkov, seated opposite, wiping egg from his chin. 'Last night you looked pretty sick.'

At the end of my improvisation I had developed nausea and migraine, and had to stagger away to bed.

Surkov looked remarkably fresh after his day of ordeal, and confirmed that he felt fine. Our English autumns were marvellous, observed Rozanov, turning his gaze to a high, broad, light-filled window. 'Have you seen this?' he asked, flexing his newspaper. 'Victor's mistress is wowing Lech Walesa!'

I saw Thatcher's and Walesa's faces, leaning close, smiling. 'You can see she's very happy,' Surkov said with a sigh. 'Look at the sparkle in her eyes! It's because her cunt is still tingling from our session together. But what can I do? There's no future for us.'

'Thousands of shipyard workers in Gdansk were cheering her,' Rozanov reported.

I commented that she was a remarkable lady, popular almost everywhere except here in Britain.

'The scourge of your unions! It's rather ironic.'

'Well, there's a big difference. We have a democratic government, and the union bosses had become barons. But yes, it's a little ironic.'

Surkov: 'Did I tell you she has wonderful taut nipples? She loves having them sucked, it sends her wild.'

I still felt too fragile to discuss Thatcher's nipples. Instead I praised her sincerity and plain speaking. She was hardly Plato, but she said what she thought. From there we drifted into a discussion of the language of politicians. I remarked that in some of Gorbachev's speeches, as reported in Britain, he seemed to strike a humanistic, philosophical tone quite different from the traditional dreary, shrill propaganda jargon; a tone, moreover, to which our politicians were incapable of responding. That was because truth, in the West, had become slowly corrupted, Surkov said; whereas in the Soviet Union it had had to go underground for seventy years. Therefore when it was tapped it was still pure, like a spring.

'But let's wait and see,' he concluded. 'We've had false dawns before.'

Maria Sanchez stopped by at our table, on her way out. Dressed in black, she was setting off for Mass. Confession too, perhaps. It was hard to imagine the demure, wrinkled Bolivian poetess lying in passion with Masha, striking her and raising bruises. I should have made an effort with her. I felt a brief pang of regret that I'd stuck so closely to my Russian friends, neglecting almost everyone else.

She carried a copy of the *Times*. There was a good piece about us, she said. She spread the newspaper on the table, open at Miss Hayes-Drummond's interview. Having expected it to be cancelled, we scanned it nervously. Surkov, 'an ageing vodka-battered roué trying to look like the Botticelli Venus . . . A faded charm . . . Cross between Jimmy Saville and Chaucer's Pardoner . . . Mountebank, hooligan . . . Texas University T-shirt . . .' Rozanov in a 'crumpled navy suit. Cadaverous face, bald, eyes sunken, badly fitting dentures . . . Impression of sincerity . . .' Thomas, 'defensively aggressive and arrogant . . . Squashed, rounded features, like a Dylan Thomas who had survived—just—the New York alcoholic poisoning . . .'

'Why, that's really not bad at all,' said Surkov, relieved.

'It's quite good,' I agreed.

'Who are Jimmy Saville and Chaucer's Pardoner?'

I explained.

'Well, I'm a pretty charitable guy, and all poets are pardoners.'

Later, he and I set off for the Tate. In the Underground we talked about Sergei. Victor warned me he was in a pretty crazy state. It was the effect of the mind-changing drugs in the *psikhushka*. I was right about him and Masha, there was nothing going on between them. Sergei was obsessed with his 'spirit-wife'. He obviously believed in her, and all this shaman nonsense.

'But the Freud!' Surkov had listened to the extraordinary tape recording.

'Do you really think Freud would be wearing wolfskins and an eagle mask?'

'Maybe not, but how do you explain the fluent German?'

'I'm sure he knows some. No, Don, I'm afraid the poor guy is crazy. I don't know how Sonia stands it. She's been terrifically loyal.'

We fell silent. Blank faces all around, crowded. Black, white, yellow. All the women were wearing trousers. It was hard to tell the sexes apart, these days. There was one sex and a dozen races in the tube train. I didn't like it, felt stifled and depressed; wished back the England in which everyone was patently English and women enjoyed looking different from men.

We didn't stay long at the Tate; Surkov charged around with all the discrimination of a restless bull and then said he must get back to the hotel, as he had to prepare his stuff for tonight. 'They tell me it's standing-room only. It ought to be the last night tonight; tomorrow night will be an anticlimax.'

'With Sergei performing? And Bellow?'

'Bellow just reads from a book; I've heard him; there's no excitement.'

'I read from a book too.'

'Yes, you should memorise your stuff, my friend.'

We decided to grab a taxi, and drove through darkening streets crowded with Saturday afternoon shoppers. And not shoppers alone: turning a corner, we were confronted by a mob of young men in Union Jack shirts, their heads shaven. Spread across the street, they came at the taxi like the peasants marching towards the Winter Palace in 1905. The driver, cursing, had to stop. Fists hammered on our roof; blank, chalk-white faces stared in, grimacing. They withdrew on hearing our cabby's cockney obscenities. 'Football hooligans,' I explained. Surkov wound down the window, adding sound to vision.

'England's a shit-hole!' floated in.

'It's a piss-hole!'

A cropped youth wearing an earring and Mohican face-paint confronted an Asian lady carrying shopping bags. He stepped to the right and left, blocking her as she tried to pass. She looked frightened.

'Hitler should've won the war,' we heard him say; 'he'd have got rid of the bird-slime from the streets.' He stepped back into the street and the lady scuttled past. The last remnants of the crowd leered past us and we began to move.

'We ought to have Joe Stalin here,' growled the elderly driver. 'He'd have given them what-for.' He glanced at Surkov in his mirror. 'Ain't you got someone like him you can send over, mate?'

Later, late down for dinner, I found that my friends hadn't saved me a seat and I was forced to join some of the others.

It was awkward having to converse with authors I had been studiously avoiding. But in fact there was no problem, they had just come from a fringe event in one of the hotel reception rooms and were ecstatic about it.

The event, I gathered, had been a talk by an English writer, Reg Wilson, on *The Re-assembly of Crash Victims*. Legrand, the French poet, asked me about him; why wasn't he reading at the Festival? why was he restricted to the fringe, and not mentioned in the programme? I had to confess my ignorance.

Well, he had been *formidable, merveilleux*. Helmutt Hauptmann, bulky in brown leather, agreed. It was the best talk to date. 'But if I had not seen it announced on the lobby notice-board, we would all have missed it! It's outrageous!'

Marie-Pierre Duval, fixing me with her thick-lensed glasses, said, 'You missed something very special. *C'est difficile de . . .* it's hard to describe its effect. It was literary criticism entirely through metaphoric language.'

'What was he saying?' I asked, picking at a lettuce leaf.

'What was he saying?' she repeated, turning to Hauptmann for support.

'He was arguing for synthesis.'

'*Oui, exactement*—synthesis.'

'It was a work of art in itself,' murmured Legrand. 'Overtones of Robbe-Grillet, but with a much greater dynamism. I want to ask him if I can translate it into French, but he's not around.' He swivelled in his chair to survey the tables again.

'And you say you've not heard of him?' demanded Hauptmann.

'No,' I said.

'You will, you will. The man is a genius.'

Duval, nodding, said, 'He really showed up the session at the theatre. Antinuclear protest would be much more effective if it were couched in metaphors.'

'In the Wilsonian metastyle,' I offered.

'*Exactement.*'

Hauptmann repeated the phrase 'Wilsonian metastyle' at the theatre, in a stumbling introduction to an extract from his novel *Luther*. As most of the foreign writers were doing, he read a page in his own tongue, then an English actress continued the extract in English translation. Maria Sanchez employed the same technique with her highly coloured religious lyrics. Neither of these mostly mute performers brought the house down. As the Bolivian left the stage, signalling the interval, a man in a pin-striped suit, with a nod at her in passing, headed for the microphone. The confused audience, checking their programmes, settled. 'Timothy Bartlett,' the man announced in a thick Brummie accent. 'Droitwich. Oi should apologise, moi train was two hours late, oi've rushed straight from the hotel. Also, oi didn't expect such a big gathering.' He dropped one of a sheaf of papers he was holding. 'You must excuse me, oi'm a little flustered.' Crouching to pick up the paper, he lost his balance, had to save himself from falling off the stage. A ripple of amusement was followed immediately by shushes of sympathy.

Rising to his feet, smoothing his jacket, he announced, '*The Preservation of a Cadaver.*' He read, then, quite fluently if without much expression. Relieved to be hearing authentic English tones, and stirred by a forceful, rather deliciously macabre narrative, the audience gave him a warm hand as he stumbled off. I heard Legrand, sitting in front of me, refer to Borges.

In the concourse, where books were on sale, people looked for Bartlett's name, in order to start a queue. It wasn't to be found. The man in charge of the book sales flapped around, saying, 'Nobody told me.' Reluctantly people drifted to the tables where Hauptmann and Sanchez were sitting.

Fiona Hayes-Drummond made a surprise appearance, thrusting herself in front of Surkov, staring coldly into his eyes. Interrupted in a pleasant chat with some students who wanted their books signed, he reeled back. Regaining his composure, he asked her with a smile, 'What are you doing afterwards?' She turned and walked away, heading for the exit.

The second half of the programme was to belong to Surkov. He was given an enthusiastic reception as he strode onstage, his jeans skintight, his T-shirt embossed with a dove of peace, his yellow hair flapping. There were a few empty seats, which would have been unheard of in the great days of the Sixties, when Yevtushenko and Surkov had circumnavigated the globe, poets of longed-for reconciliation. Yet the ageing hooligan-poet still managed to evoke an air of excitement. It was increased by a series of muted explosions during his performance, for it was Guy Fawkes Night.

'It's good to be back in Great Britain,' he intoned, standing very close to the mike. 'This is a wonderful Festival. Great writers. Well, you've just heard three of them. And there simply haven't been any cliques among us, as there often are. It's wonderful to have so many writers, from so many countries, eating together, talking together, lying together. From East and West, North and South—friends. It was good to hear an English writer, Bartlett, tonight; I'm just sorry some of the English failed to turn up. Mr Aimes and Mr Parkin. They would have seen the Cold War is dead. *Long live peace and friendship!*' He raised his arms aloft; then waited for the applause, punctuated by the echoing boom of a loud firework, to die down before resuming:

'I wrote a poem after watching the Seoul Olympics on TV. I was thrilled by that great run by Ben Johnson. Yah. And then I saw his gold medal taken away because of drugs. I'll recite the poem, it's a rather long poem, it's about three, four hundred lines. I've translated it myself, but you'll have to forgive my poor English.'

His poem, recited from memory, full of sympathy for an exploited black athlete, received tumultuous applause. When it had died away, Surkov said, 'Now I'd like to give you some prose, from a novel in progress.' He set the scene: a hopeful actor meeting a blind film director. 'You know, *Zhivago* has been published in the Soviet Union at last. Well, it's not before time. I have to tell you I don't at this moment know how my narrative is going to continue; I'll be making it up as I go.' A ripple of interest ran round the audience. 'Some of you may know I improvise a little. Well, it's very risky, but I'll try . . .'

He began . . .

· 16 ·

'. . . So you actually tried to commit suicide?'

Charsky nodded; remembered she couldn't see him, and said, 'Yes.' Gazing at Bella's square-shaped dark glasses, he felt his foot pressing on the accelerator and the narrow stone bridge leaping to meet him. He added, thinking of his Freudian readings, 'Of course I may have subconsciously noted the railings as I drove to and from Stratford. Maybe I knew I would hit them before the stonework of the bridge. But I don't think so. I think I really intended to die.'

'Thank God you failed.'

Her voice, strident and condescending earlier, had become full of sympathy.

'My hosts' car was a write-off; they weren't very pleased about it. I told them I'd been drunk. You're the first person I've ever shared this with. Yet I hardly know you. Isn't it strange?'

'Dostoievsky says somewhere that there are things we won't reveal to everybody, but only to friends. There are things we won't reveal to friends but only to ourselves. And finally there are things we are afraid to reveal even to ourselves. All that is true. But there are also secrets I might tell a complete stranger that I wouldn't tell my friends.'

'Such as?' Charsky asked boldly.

She looked startled. 'Well, such as . . . I thought seriously of leaving my husband a few years ago, when I got involved with another man. I can tell *you* that, but I couldn't tell anyone who was close to me—least of all my husband, who knew nothing about the affair.'

'A woman was involved when I tried to kill myself,' admitted Charsky, becoming expansive through the warming effects of vodka. 'I became very fond of one of the English backstage girls, and she of me. Nothing happened; but I think if I'd defected we might well have ended up living together.'

'What was she like?'

He strained to remember, but could not recall her features. 'She was very sensitive, very intuitive and kind. Rather plump, with big breasts.'

'You like women with big breasts?'

'I enjoy looking at them; but I don't know that I'd want them to engulf me, in reality.'

'I wish mine were bigger.'

'You have a perfect figure.'

'Oh, you flatter me! Excuse me a moment, I must go to the bathroom.' She stood up and, not bothering with her stick, took cautious steps towards the door. Charsky half-rose.

'Can you manage?'

'Of course I can bloody well manage!' she said with a good-humoured asperity. 'I've had quite enough practice at finding my way to bathrooms!' She felt for the door, found the handle, and went through. Charsky stretched his legs under the coffee table and relaxed. His thoughts reverted to that memorable, disturbing visit to Stratford with the company in '78. How spellbound the audience had been, even though they hadn't understood a word of their *Macbeth* and *Lear*. The sheer power of the productions and of the sonorous Russian language had overwhelmed them. But then, as that girl had explained—he wished he could recall her name—Shakespeare was all Russian to most people in the audience anyway.

He heard the toilet's flush. Bella returned, groping her way towards the sofa. 'There was no toilet paper,' she said with a smile, sitting and arranging her skirt. 'Luckily I found a magazine. From the feel of it I would guess it was *Krokodil*. I hope so. It deserves to be used for wiping arses! You can top me up again, Dmitri.'

'We're almost out.'

'You'll find another bottle in that cupboard.' She pointed, and he went to the cupboard and found the vodka.

'So you didn't think of leaving your wife and setting up with this English girl?'

'Oh, I thought of it!' he said ruefully. 'I thought of little else for a week. But it simply wasn't on. Anna would have been absolutely devastated. She has no family, you see. If I'd defected, she'd have had nobody.'

'But if you'd committed suicide, she'd have been in the same boat.'

'I know!' He chuckled. 'One doesn't think logically in that situation.'

'In the event, you sacrificed your happiness to her.'

'No, no. I knew I loved her very much. There was no comparison between my feelings for her and my feelings for— Shirley: yes, that was her name. She wasn't the main reason for my wanting to stay in England; she was just a bonus. No, I was sick of the deadness of our life here. Our static theatre. The sickening privileges which I, as a Party member, enjoyed. And of course the greatest privilege of all was my ability to travel. Closely chaperoned, of course. I've been to the West six times. I was sick of it all. If only my wife had been with me. Still'—he spread his hands, then again realised the expressive gesture was pointless—'it's just as well. Here we are, planning to film *Doctor Zhivago*!'

Bella failed to take the bait, but sipped her drink quietly.

To break the silence he said, 'Anyway, I learned my lesson that night. Our lives aren't our own to take away. My brother's closest friend committed suicide, and I've seen how it's damaged him. He's never been the same.'

'We think of our lives,' she said reflectively, 'as bounded by the space we occupy. But it's not so, is it? We are like force-fields, with very indeterminate boundaries.'

'That's true, Bella.'

'Come here.' She signalled peremptorily. Sensing his startled look, she explained: 'I want to touch you. I want to trace your observable field. Do you object?'

'No, not at all.'

He stood and came round the table to her. 'Kneel down,' she ordered. Clumsily, feeling slightly the worse for drink, he knelt. With her right hand she started to stroke his face: first the cheeks, then the forehead; his eyes closed as she touched the eyebrows, the lids. Charsky had never experienced such infinitely gentle and sensuous touches. His lips tingled as her fingers drew across them, then moved to his plump chin, his throat. She repeated the caresses, in a different order. The tingle in his lips spread throughout his body. His eyes felt heavy, drugged. He was almost drowsing, and it took him completely by surprise when he felt her moist, plump, tacky, scented mouth pressed to his. It was a moment before he pulled his face away.

'The reports were right. You are a handsome man,' she whispered. She kissed him more lightly; again he pulled back.

'I'm sorry, Bella,' he said. 'It's not possible.'

'What isn't possible? You don't mean your wife would object to a kiss?'

'Of course not. But you're too attractive. We know where it could lead.'

'So? Would that be so terrible?'

'It would probably be wonderful,' replied Charsky, still tremulous from her touches and kisses. 'But I love my wife. I couldn't be unfaithful to her.'

'But you must have affairs? *Every*one does.'

'I don't.'

'That's incredible!' she exclaimed, with a jerk of her hand which knocked her glass over.

As he curved a stream of urine into a cracked toilet bowl, Charsky observed that the bathroom, too, looked abandoned, almost derelict. There was a razor and a stub of a shaving-stick; two toothbrushes in a drinking-glass and a well-squeezed tube of toothpaste; a sliver of soap.

If Anna and he had been lucky enough to own a Georgian dacha and could spend most of their time there, doubtless their flat would soon look almost as comfortless.

The ripped-up magazine was indeed *Krokodil*, and was at least five years old. Charsky gazed at crude caricatures of Reagan and the Iron Lady.

It took three tugs of the handle for the flush to work.

He glanced in at a gloomy, narrow kitchen, its brown paint badly needing to be refreshed. A tin of coffee, a saucepan, two mugs by the draining-board. And the bedroom, when he peered in, was equally stark. The bed was made up, but there was nothing to suggest home comfort: no bedside radio or books; a solitary comb and brush on the dresser; a familiar photograph of Lenin glared down.

As he turned towards the living-room door he reflected that he must be nice to her; what would a few kisses matter? After their last topic of conversation, it was important she didn't get the idea he was some sort of puritan—or it would be good-bye Komarovsky.

He prepared himself to cuddle against her, which would be no hardship, and to put his arm around her again. But she had reclined against a corner of the sofa; it was impossible to get close. He perched on the sofa's edge, half-turned to her.

'It's not,' he said in a lively voice, 'that I don't feel tempted. I do, constantly. And I get lots of opportunities. If one is in the public eye, one does—I'm sure you know that. But some of these women can be very dangerous; they can lure you into bed and then cry Rape! Just for the chance of some publicity. So I feel I have to be careful.'

'I can understand that.'

They sipped their drinks as one of those unpredictable silences fell on them. Charsky became aware of it, felt that the friendly atmosphere was in danger of cooling, and plunged in heartily with: 'So tomorrow you're being presented to Raisa and Nancy!'

'Yes; yes,' she said in dismissive tones. 'I've been thinking about the problem of depicting Yury Zhivago. He is not simply one person in the novel, is he?'

'No, of course not.'

'You take the poem *Hamlet*. How does the second verse go? *The darkness of the night is aimed towards me / Through the sights of a thousand opera glasses. / Abba, Father, if it be possible, / Let this cup pass from me.* Have I quoted it correctly?'

'I think so. I'm not sure. Anna should be here, she knows almost all the poems by heart. She knew all of Pasternak, Mandelstam and Akhmatova by heart when she was seventeen. From samizdat. It was the only way.'

'It's the pivot of the whole work, of course,' she continued, ignoring his praise of his wife. 'And the speaker of the poem is multiple. He is Hamlet, sick of what destiny has prepared for him. He is also the actor playing Hamlet, terrified of the responsibility of carrying through such a difficult role. He's Christ at Gethsemane, praying that the cup pass from him; he is of course Doctor Zhivago; and he is also Boris Pasternak, living in Stalinist times, faced with painful choices of courage or compromise. Five people! How do we handle it, my friend?'

'More than one actor?' he suggested.

'Well, that's an obvious solution, though it presents its own difficulties. We could have a stage, bare, with just one spotlight. Yury moves from the wings, his face caught for a moment before he moves again into shadows; when he is next seen, he has the refined bearded face of Christ. Maybe he's carrying the Cross. Shadows again. When we next see him he is Pasternak. God knows how we would do it. And then finally he is in doublet and hose: Prince Hamlet. No, I don't like that. Shit, it's so difficult!'

She swung her knees onto the sofa. Her skirt had got caught in her folded white stick, propped at her side. She had no way of knowing, he realised, that her thighs were exposed to him above the black silk of her stockings; he could see the strained arc where an inch or two of red garter strap was revealed. Such images of free-market sensuality were rare even in Gorbachev's Russia. They reminded him of magazine stalls in Naples; but this was rich, creamy, three-dimensional flesh, exciting and disturbing. 'Of course the poems are deeply religious as well as deeply erotic,' she continued. 'The two forces fuse into one.'

Charsky was faced with a dilemma. Should he tell her, lightly, that her skirt had got caught up—which might embarrass her, although, heaven knew, she was no prude; or should he refrain from telling her, and therefore go on gazing at her thighs like a voyeur? Or he could fix his gaze on her beautiful face. Before he could resolve the moral problem, she ran her hand over her skirt, found the impediment and corrected it: all the time smoothly carrying on her musings: 'The one about the candle burning is a prime example. I shall do this simply with a candle flame and shadows reflected on the ceiling. *Crossed hands, crossed feet, crossed fate* . . . Are you religious, Dmitri?'

He pondered for a moment. 'I have a vague sense of something beyond us,' he replied finally. 'I'm not religious in a conventional sense, I've never been in a church; but when my father died I kind of wanted to. I hated to see him just go up in smoke, like trash. I wanted some sort of ritual, you know?'

'I know.'

'How about you?'

Like him, she said, she believed in something beyond this world, though she didn't know what it could be. Her blindness had perhaps allowed her to penetrate more deeply than sighted people into the mysterious dimension which seemed to cross our world at a tangent. And she was very aware of the approaching millennium: 'I believe we're entering a period which will be reminiscent of Petersburg before the Revolution. You know, all sorts of mystical experiences will occur. There will be seers and soothsayers and mediums, and even a Rasputin. There will be false Messiahs. The life of dreams and of reality will become confused.'

'I'm sure you're right!' Charsky exclaimed. 'It's already happening to Anna and me. At times—well, it's actually when she has her period—we become extraordinarily telepathic.'

'I can quite believe it. The blood of a woman's womb *is* magical. My intuitive powers are most intense when I'm menstruating—as I am now, as a matter of fact.' She swung her feet onto the floor and sat up straight, groping for her cigarette case on the coffee table. 'And because the earth is feminine, don't you think she could be having her period? Look at all the bloodshed there's been!'

Charsky threw back his head in pleasure at the whimsical yet strangely compelling idea. 'You should make a film about it, Bella!'

'I intend to. *Millennium*. Or perhaps *The Second Coming*. But imagine, if Christ comes, how devastated the churches will be!' She gave a husky chuckle.

'Yes!' he agreed delightedly. 'We'll have chat shows in which the Metropolitan, the Roman Pope and Christ are interviewed together!'

Bella laughed. 'And they'll row like mad! It reminds me, I heard yesterday a good joke about the Pope . . .' He was desperately ill; only if he slept with a woman, it seemed, could his life be saved. Feebly the Pope agreed to this sacrifice, for the sake of his flock. Twice he summoned the cardinal back to his bedside, to ask that the girl chosen should be blind, and also dumb: she should see nothing, nor be able to report what had happened. Then a third time he feebly called the bowing, retiring cardinal back—Bella imitated the feeble summons: 'One thing more—big tits and stiletto heels.'

Charsky roared with laughter, and Bella laughed at the success of her joke. 'Wonderful! Wonderful!' exclaimed Charsky, picturing vividly the scene in the Pope's bedroom.

His laughter died away, and there was silence as they sipped from their glasses; but then Charsky barked another laugh, and Bella sniggered. He relaxed, stretching out his legs, savouring the potent vodka and the remarkable woman's company. He felt his anxieties, and some of his repressions, fall away. He permitted himself to stroke her back as he let out another, weaker laugh. 'Big tits and stiletto heels! Wonderful!'

In the brief murk of the white night, Charsky and Bella, sprawled on the sofa, were kissing. They were not locked together like Rodin's lovers, but kept breaking off to take a drink, or for Bella to have a few puffs at her cigarette. During one such pause she murmured, 'Well, my dear, you won't go to hell for this, will you?', and smiled. Her teeth were beautifully even and snowy white, like Anna's.

He smiled back, having almost forgotten her blindness. 'I wouldn't think so.'

She had unbuttoned his shirt and was stroking his hairy chest. 'Are you very suntanned,' she asked, 'from your Italian tour?'

'It's faded a lot.'

'Did you kiss any Neapolitan beauties? I bet you did.'

'No.'

'Liar.' Her lips clove to his again, her tongue penetrative. He eventually drew away, and she stretched to pick up her glass.

'I was pleased to go to Naples,' he said, attempting to steady the mood. 'In Pushkin's *Egyptian Nights*, if you remember, a Neopolitan *improvisatore* visits a gentleman-poet called Charsky in Petersburg. So here I was, one of Charsky's descendents, so to speak, returning the compliment! I kept looking for an *improvisatore*!'

She did not appear to be listening. Her blind eyes seemed to be staring towards the window. 'You've just given me a wonderful idea for another film, Dmitri,' she exclaimed. 'A life of Pushkin, but inhabiting our modern world. Sorry—I interrupted you.'

'No, go on.'

'The dialogue will be all Pushkin. For his birth we'll show a real baby, gazing up at a portrait of Lenin—like the one in the bedroom here . . . And you will hear, voice-over, his lines to Anna Kern: *I remember the moment of wonder: / You appeared before me, / Like a momentary vision, / A spirit of pure beauty.*' She gave a joyous laugh.

'You can actually tell there's a portrait of Lenin in the bedroom?'

'Of course. Please don't interrupt me. You will see him as a student, surrounded by Komsomol banners, doing physical jerks. You'll see him bravely fighting in the Great Patriotic War, then being arrested and put in a cattle truck; and you will hear his lines from *19 October* which go: *But I deceived myself; for though I gave / My heart with all the ardency of youth, / Bitterly I found that trust, and truth, / Were far away in Petersburg or the grave.* Next, documentary shots of Stalin, that smirk under the turned-up moustache, while you hear: *Do not sing to me again / Your songs of sad Georgia!*'

She uncoiled from his embrace, stood up and took a few steps round the room; at one point bumping into the coffee table and knocking over an empty bottle. Consumed with excitement, she took no notice, but continued: 'You'll see him in a Siberian camp and hear: *And then, here in this haunt of freezing winds / And blizzards, hope renewed itself, I found / Green shoots emerging from the stony ground; / A brief, sweet solace.*

Three of you, dear friends, / I embraced here! I could not speak for joy! . . . And you'll see four skeletal, toothless old men shaking hands and embracing . . . Light me a cigarette.'

Charsky obliged, and passed it into her hand. He noticed it was trembling.

'We'll have him laying a flower on the grave of Khrushchev, and hear: *I loved you once; perhaps I love you still* . . . I don't know what poetry would suit the Brezhnev reign. Can you think of anything? It's hard; Brezhnev is Pushkin's antithesis.'

She paced, smoking. 'We need Anna here,' he said; 'she's the Pushkin expert.'

'Well, we'll put him in a *psikhushka*, being injected with torturing, mind-destroying drugs, and hear: *Dear God, don't let me go mad!*' She bent, searching blindly for an ashtray, and Charsky held it up for her; angrily she stubbed the half-finished cigarette. Straightening, she stretched her arms behind her back. He saw her dress fall away from her shoulders and bosom, then her bra came away. Almost hurling herself onto Charsky, she exclaimed: 'Can you only think of Anna? Suck my breasts!' He was so shocked, and so dazzled by her flights of imagination, he felt it impossible to disobey her; but buried his head on her bosom, kissing a cold erect nipple surrounded by its brown aureole. Stroking his hair she murmured huskily: 'Suck! Chew!'

He found himself drowning in her perfume, in her sweet round flesh, yet at the same time was filled with horror. This was far beyond the line he had always drawn. But there could be no stopping. His brain was spinning from the mingled effects of Bella and vodka.

'At some point we'll bundle him on a plane to the West,' she murmured while stroking Charsky's hair. 'And there we'll show him walking through Harlem, or down Sixth Avenue, surrounded by crude adverts, porno signs, and drug pushers. He'll lecture in a dark suit to gum-chewing or pot-smoking students, then drive back to a neat suburban home, and watch more inane adverts and quiz shows on TV. In fact we'll have him appear on TV, promoting his latest book. *How heavy is the pressure of his stone hand!* we'll hear as the chat-show host crushes his fingers at the end. And finally— that's beautiful, you suck so beautifully!—we'll show a hand-ful of bored people at a crematorium; and as he goes up in smoke we'll hear: *I shall not wholly die . . .*'

Charsky took his lips from her nipple and with a sigh buried his face between her breasts. 'Do you think that's how we'll turn out?' she asked. 'If perestroika succeeds? Can we change our own fate, yet avoid the spiritual emptiness of the West?'

He didn't reply. She asked him what was wrong. He told her he was thinking of his father.

'Ah, the crematorium! That was stupid of me.'

'No, no! It's just that I thought I saw him this morning. I was waking up. He sat by my bed, looking incredibly well, and told me he'd found a new body. I thought, God, Mother will be furious when she hears he's still around. It didn't seem like a dream at the time, though I suppose it must have been.'

'Not necessarily,' she said, kissing his hair, his ear. 'If only you hadn't been against us making love, I could have brought him to you. I told you I have magic powers when I'm menstruating.'

In Charsky's fuddled, drunken state her claim seemed en-tirely reasonable. Slurring the words, he said, 'I'd do anything to see him again. Why didn't you tell me that before?'

'Because I would rather have persuaded you by my own charms. But it doesn't matter. You're willing to be unfaithful to your wife?'

'Yes.'

'Then come. Let's go to the bedroom.'

She helped him lurch to his feet, and they took a few steps. Then she stopped. 'No, not the bedroom. It doesn't seem fair to my friends. The sofa's all right, isn't it?'

· 17 ·

To loud applause, mingled with a few chuckles and gasps of frustration at being cheated of a sizzling sex scene, Surkov strode from the stage. I led the rush from the writers' boxes to reach the bar before the crowds piled in for the book signing.

A few minutes later, as I queued for drinks, Victor rushed up, flushed with triumph. 'How was it?'

'Terrific! Quite a surprise!'

'Well, I heard there was to be a party, so I thought I would—how do you say?—kill two dogs with one stone, huh?'

Fans were already starting to paw at him: 'When will the novel be out?' 'What will it be called?' To which he replied genially, 'Wait and see!'

He skipped off towards the rapidly lengthening queue of people eager to seize one of his two books available in English, *Leningrad Awakes!* and *Black Days, White Nights*, copies of which were piled on a table.

I carried drinks from the bar for Masha and Rozanov, but the latter had disappeared. Yet more Amnesty people, who had helped get his release, had turned up, she said, and he'd felt obliged to go off with them for a quiet drink. He would see us at the party.

'You know why Victor did that?' she asked, dabbing wine from a taut-bloused breast.

'So we don't miss the party.'

'No—he couldn't give a shit about that. He wants to put his mark on our text. If and when our novel appears, there'll be some readers who'll remember tonight's performance.'

'Ah! Of course! They will think I plagiarised him. Well, I guess the collaboration will have to come out.' I didn't feel too perturbed, since I thought there was very little likelihood that our chaotic improvisations could make a successful novel. 'Maybe he would like to organise it himself this time,' I said rather starchily.

She lowered her eyelids, and blushed. Mumbling her words, she said, 'Well, you've done a lot; we can't ask you to do any more. Perhaps *we* could look at it. But in any case, I'm sure it should go out under your name as usual.'

I felt, vaguely, dismissed.

Maria Sanchez came into view for a moment; she was talking to a Spanish novelist and two or three people clutching copies of Surkov. I saw her eyes and Masha's connect; there was an almost imperceptible softening in the Bolivian poetess's gaze. Masha turned away and clutched my arm. 'It's over,' she said with a deep sigh.

We went out to a night of brilliant stars and an explosive cascade of fireworks from across the Thames. We climbed aboard the coach. An hour later we were crammed into the Hospitality Suite. I found myself pressed up against the Festival organiser, still dressed in his Superman outfit. His eyes were glazed. 'Thanks,' he said to me, clutching my arm. 'I enjoyed your reading—when was it? Wednesday? Thursday? The nights rush by.'

'It's all gone well, Jock, thanks to you.'

'I just hope Bellow and Finn arrive. Tomorrow night I shall collapse. But yes, it's gone pretty well. That was a nice interview in the *Times*. When we heard the Russians had agreed to come, we just had to invite you.'

'Well, I'm glad you did.'

'We never know who's going to accept. So we invite about three times too many. That's why there was the cock-up tonight. I didn't know Timothy Bartlett was coming; I don't know who invited him; to be perfectly honest I'd never heard of him. But anyway he was bloody good.'

'Tremendous.'

He sighed; puffy eyelids fluttered. 'D'ye ken how much we've spent on booze this week? The *Guardian*, that is. Eight thousand quid. We could've kept a thousand Ethiopian babies alive for that money. Ah, well . . .'

He must say good-bye, he said, to Maria and Helmutt, who were catching early flights in the morning. He slapped a friendly hand on my shoulder as he turned with some difficulty. Seeing no one near me whom I wanted to talk to, I decided to go to bed.

Rozanov, breathing a sigh of relief as the admirable Amnesty guys dropped him off at the hotel, made his way to the Queen Mary Suite. To his amusement he found himself in the same throng of dark-suited funeral directors as on his first evening. The writers' party must be in the other suite this time. Before he could withdraw he was collared by familiar figures: Bromley and Davenport.

'How have you enjoyed the conference?' the latter asked.

'Very much.'

Rozanov lifted a glass of red wine from an offered tray as Bromley said, 'I think it's been useful, don't you?'

'Extremely.'

'Did you get that word processor?'

'No, I decided against it.'

'Probably just as well. Our customers like the personal touch when we send our bills, don't you think?'

'I'm sure you're right.'

Bromley, a look of alarm crossing his face, said, 'Excuse me, a sudden call,' and rushed off towards the toilets.

His colleague touched the Russian amiably on the chest. 'You know, you've made a big contribution. I've heard you spoke to good effect at the seminar on Sikh funeral services. I couldn't make it myself but I heard about it.'

'Thank you. I did my best.'

'But apart from that, it's just been good to have you amongst us. One gets pretty fed up, frankly speaking, seeing the same old faces.'

'Well, it's been an eye-opener to me.'

'Good. I'd like to talk to you about Russia. I think it's a fascinating country. Shall we try and find some seats?'

'I'm sorry but I just dropped in for a few minutes. I must ring Moscow—a funeral.'

'Ah, well! Business is business!'

On his way to the door Rozanov was confronted by two stately figures barring his way. His eyes were staring straight into theirs, and it was impossible to avoid a greeting, though it was clear they wished it no more than did he. 'I'm Sergei Rozanov,' he said.

'Kington Aimes,' said one of the figures.

'Douglas Parkin,' said the other.

After an uncomfortable silence, Rozanov asked if they had enjoyed the Festival. Very much, they said; it had been mercifully and surprisingly free of cant, free of sex, free of European pseudo-intellectualism. And almost free of women, thank God. They had at first been concerned about the absence of major writers, but they had enjoyed the down-to-earth discussions.

'Are you a writer or one of the organisers?' Aimes asked Rozanov uninterestedly.

'I try to write.'

'Ah! It's been organised extremely well, don't you think?'

Another couple, bearded, scowling, dressed in tweed jackets and roll-neck sweaters, drifted up. Rozanov found himself introduced to Fullerton and Birtwhistle. It was clear that no love was lost between the two pairs, yet to the Russian they seemed to have much in common. The bearded pair lectured the Russian for a while on Marxism and Structuralism; Aimes and Parkin took the opportunity to sidle into a neighbouring group. Rozanov overheard them discussing someone called Rumpole.

Suddenly a murmur of concern ran from group to group: old Bromley from Luton had been found stretched out in the loo, clearly having a heart-attack. As soon as the rumour reached Rozanov and the two English literati, Rozanov pushed his way towards the exit and came across an excitable scrum outside the toilets. 'Let me through, I'm a shaman,' he cried, and their ranks parted for him. Bromley was on his back near the urinals, his face blue; he appeared not to be breathing. Rozanov broke into song: a Tungus Healing Song. Everyone was startled by the wild mysterious sound. Almost at once Bromley breathed again, his colour became normal; he sat up, bewildered. He stretched up his arms to be helped to his feet; he was led away. Davenport said to Rozanov: 'You shouldn't be in our profession! We wouldn't have any customers.'

'I could see that his spirit hadn't yet left his body,' Sergei explained next morning, relating the incident to me. 'It was fortunate I was there.'

'Well, you had a livelier time than us. I didn't stay long. Did you make the right party eventually?'

'No, I went to bed.'

We were taking an early stroll near the hotel. The sun shone low but brilliant from another clear sky, dispersing the overnight frost. The Sunday streets were uncrowded. Rozanov lapsed into silence after his account of the healing. He looked distant, absorbed, sad. 'Did you ring Sonia?' I asked.

'What?'

I repeated it.

'Oh—yes. She's okay.'

But everyone has ambivalent feelings about going home. We drifted, each in his own thoughts.

Our reflective mood was shattered when, on entering a newsagent's so I could buy cigarettes, we saw Surkov leering from the front page of the *News of the World*. The headline: SEXY SOVIET SENT PACKING. We grabbed a copy and bought it. Leaning against some railings we scanned the 'Exclusive' by Stacy Diamond . . .

Celebrity Russian writer Victor Surkov, close friend of Raisa, wife of Premier Gorbachev, has been given 24 hours to quit Britain.

Surkov, 57, who lives near Moscow, was involved in a middle-of-the-night visit to the Chelsea police station following a date with an attractive brunette at a flat in Cheynes Walk.

Neighbours of the girl reported her screams and found her naked and in a distressed condition.

The Russian, a matinée idol to millions both East and West, is one of the star-turns at a Festival of Writers taking place at the Riverside Theatre.

But it appears he has not confined his activity to the front of the stage.

Fellow writers at the Festival describe him as remote and standoffish.

Since his early tours of the West with his friend Yev-tushenko, he has had the reputation of being a lady-killer.

His fourth wife, Imogen Walters, 23, daughter of Lady Anabelle Walters, Labour Education spokesperson in the Lords, recently filed for divorce in Moscow following reports that Surkov was escorting a Georgian film star.

Earlier this week Surkov was among a panel of Iron Curtain experts advising Mrs Thatcher on how to handle the Poles.

He once described the British Prime Minister as 'very sexy, not nearly so stiff as she's painted'.

Of attractive Raisa Gorbachev he said, 'We were very,

very close a few years ago and she still calls me now and again.'

He has very cleverly gained a reputation in the West for being a political moderate, yet remained on cosy terms with his own government—for instance, he won a Lenin Prize in 1979 for his war novel *Leningrad Awakes!*

Getting into trouble with the law is not new to him. In 1973 he was arrested in New York for being drunk and disorderly, and two years later, in Paris, gendarmes had to break up a bar brawl in which he was involved.

But this is the first time action has been taken. Released by the police after being held for sixteen hours, Surkov was ordered to leave the country by tomorrow.

The woman involved, a well-known journalist and almost-nightly denizen of London's chic-est media-haunt, the Groucho Club, a friend of Princess Margaret, was too distressed to comment on the affair. She is being looked after by friends in the country.

We found Surkov still in bed, smoking. He looked pale and disturbed. 'Have you seen it?' he groaned.

'Yes.'

He reached down beside the bed and brought up a section of the *Sunday Times*. 'Isn't it foul? She's really fucked me up.' Rozanov grabbed the paper from him. Victor said, 'I thought you'd already read it. What's that one you've got there?' Sergei tossed the tabloid to him. 'Holy shit!' Surkov groaned.

Sitting down on his own bed, Rozanov spread the pages of the quality newspaper for me to read too. GLASNOST: A SOVIET POET'S VIEW, ran the headline. The author was Fiona Hayes-Drummond. Our reading was punctuated by Surkov's groans and imprecations.

Victor Surkov is no longer the impressive, handsome poet who took the West by storm twenty years ago, rivalling even his friend and Moscow neighbour, Yev-geni Yevtushenko, even though he would probably still like to be. Now in his late-fifties, battered and bleak—despite the vivid daffodil-yellow of his uncertainly tinted shoulder-length hair—he has the flamboyant mannerisms of the 'star' without the substance. He has been visiting London this week as a guest of the Writers Internationale.

Sometimes slightingly characterised as 'Russia's tame liberal', Surkov gives a candid and disturbing picture of the reality of glasnost. He hopes it will succeed, but he is fearful. As he talked to me, he drank as if prohibition was just around the corner, and chain-smoked.

He traces the beginning of glasnost to former KGB chief Andropov. 'Andropov was a wily Greek; his name was actually Andropoulos. I knew his daughter. He forced his way to the top, doing awful things to get there, so that he could bring about changes. I am not certain his death was from natural causes. But before his death he chose his successor—Gorbachev. Gorbachev owes everything to Andropov.'

Yet in Surkov's view the dice are loaded against the Gorbachev reforms succeeding. In the first place there was the atmosphere of revolt in the suppressed, colonised 'republics', Latvia, Estonia, Lithuania, Armenia; even perhaps Georgia and the Ukraine. There was a powder keg, or indeed several, just waiting to explode.

Secondly, the people were too used to inertia. You could get by in the Soviet Union if you didn't take responsibility, initiate action. Yet here was Comrade Gorbachev suddenly begging them to do just that. But they wouldn't, partly from habit and partly from fear: for the organs of state repression, notably the KGB, were still in place. 'What guy is going to run the risk of taking unpopular decisions when the KGB might decide to pounce at any moment?' Surkov asks.

Thirdly, there is the military, he says: commanders of nuclear installations who are intensely conservative and inured to Cold War thinking. It would only take one officer to decide to launch a strike. 'I'm afraid there's going to be great bloodshed. It might even be best if

Gorbachev initiates it; it may be the only way of ensuring the success of glasnost and perestroika.'

The fatal flaw in Russia's de-Stalinisation was that there had been no Nuremberg Trial of left-wing Fascists. They were still around. 'The cruellest guy of all, a man who told Stalin he was too soft, is still living comfortably in Moscow. Kaganovich. He plays draughts, draws a nice pension.'

Life for the ordinary people in his homeland had not improved. People tried to stifle depression by manufacturing psychedelic chemicals. And what about the artist, the poet? 'Well, there is little actual censorship now, but there's something even more dangerous, in a way—self-censorship. Gorbachev is saying, Look, you guys, I'm trusting you; don't let me down! So we try not to let him down by censoring our works in our minds, or even our subconscious. It's very dangerous.'

Surkov, winner of a Lenin Prize for his novel *Leningrad Awakes!* (published here by Penguin) lit yet another cigarette, took yet another gulp of whisky, and stared towards the east. Perhaps he was wondering how his frank speaking will be regarded in Moscow, to which he is due to return tomorrow.

'She's fucked me up! That bitch has really fucked me up!' Surkov kept groaning, his eyes fixed on the tabloid's leering portrait of him.

I tried to calm him. No one would take a rag like the *News of the World* seriously.

'But look, it sells over five million copies!' Surkov moaned. 'That means about ten million people will have read this.'

'Thirteen million, actually,' I corrected.

Another groan. 'Thirteen million. And what about the *Times* piece? Bloodshed! Suppressed colonies! Kaganovich! Trigger-happy officers! . . . Christ, I'll be slaughtered!'

'Did you say these things?'

'Oh, some of them, yes; but she's distorted a lot. For instance, I said there was also self-censorship in the West.'

'Did you say it was off the record?'

'I just fucking assumed it would be! It was private, we were having a drink. My arm was around her! I wasn't gazing east but down into her cleavage! Of course it was off the fucking record!'

Rozanov paced obsessively. He paced with shoulders hunched forward, as he might have paced in the *psikhushka*. Something was troubling him, and I didn't think it could be Surkov's problems. It occurred to me he'd become increasingly preoccupied as the week had progressed. I was fairly sure Sonia was the problem. Marriage had not softened their stormy relationship. Anyway, he paced, like a caged tiger. At length he muttered, 'We need some diversion; I'll ring Masha.' He dialled her room number. 'Hi! Did I wake you up? I'm sorry. Do you feel like improvising? Time's running short; we won't want a late night. Victor's been dragged through the newspapers, he needs to be entertained . . . Okay, we'll see you . . .'

Replacing the phone, he said, 'She'll be down in half an hour. She doesn't sound very cheerful. I'm going to finish packing.' He showed me the purple basque and black fishnet stockings he had bought for Sonia.

Surkov had a caseful of Earl Grey tea. He wondered if he would be allowed to take it to Siberia.

· 18 ·

'Won't you take off your glasses?'

'No, I couldn't, darling; you wouldn't like my eyes. I never take my glasses off.'

Naked, she stretched back along the couch, her right foot in contact with the floor. Charsky approached her awkwardly. From a mixture of causes—fear of failure, a sense of the enormous betrayal of Anna, chilliness upon undressing, and perhaps above all, vodka—he found he couldn't get an erection. She kissed him passionately, probed an ear with her tongue, and caressed him intimately, all with no effect.

'Don't worry about it; it will come.'

Smiling, she began to tickle and tease his nipples. Charsky's nipples were very sensitive; he hated to have them touched and squeezed, it made him angry. But anger could turn into lust, and as he squirmed he also felt himself hardening. He had forgotten that having his nipples stimulated and tormented could have this effect on him. Only Anna had ever done it, and only in their earliest days together.

'Oh, yes!' the blind woman cried. 'Now you're Komarovsky!'

Maddened by having his nipples tweaked and vibrated, he tore into her. The vaginal tightness so familiar from Anna during menstruation soon yielded, becoming moist and deliciously receptive.

'Is it good?' she gasped.

'It's good, it's good!'

'I'm beginning to know you!'

He slowed after a while, his head resting against hers as he drew breath. A sharp-nailed finger touched him near the base of his spine and made him shiver as it ascended to his nape.

'Do you and Anna make love like this?' she whispered.

'No.'

'Is it as good as this?'

'No.'

She reacted by quickening her movements, caressing him more tenderly and lasciviously. 'Was it *ever* as good as this?'

'No! No!' He groaned.

She panted in delight, 'Ah, wonderful!', bucking under him like a wild mare; she gripped his hair, and screamed. Thrusting rapidly again he felt her palpitate against him, tightening on him, and he came.

His portly frame sagged and he gulped for breath. He was still quite hard. 'Stay inside me,' she commanded. She moved both of them further from the edge of the sofa and wound her legs around him to help keep him in. His eyes were closed; he felt wonderfully peaceful.

His erection weakened but then grew strong again. There was no movement nor sound in the room, except for their quiet breathing. After a while he felt the dissolving of boundaries between them which he had experienced with his wife a few hours earlier. He saw in a blurred close-up her lips, curved in a half-smile of fulfillment. The image endured; he wanted to go on and on gazing at those sweetly curving lips. A minute or an hour passed: he had lost all sense of time.

And then something still more extraordinary happened: not only was he at one with Bella, but he could no longer find a precise boundary between himself and everything which existed outside them, such as the walls of the room, the window—he sensed it without needing to open his sleepy eyes—and the murk of the white night outside. Nothing in the visible universe or beyond it seemed completely separate from him.

The voice which whispered to her seemed to come from one of those distant suburbs: 'I'm falling in love with you!'

He heard her give a sigh of pleasure; her arm tightened around him.

'So do you want to be Komarovsky, darling?' she murmured. 'Or one of the Zhivagos?'

'I don't give a shit about Komarovsky or Zhivago, so long as I can be with you.'

Instantly he was aghast at what he had said. This was madness!

'Has your father come to you?'

'In a way.'

'In a way?'

'Everyone's come to me.'

Everyone except Anna, he thought. My God, what have I done? Just when everything seemed calm at last, when our lives were opening out, and we no longer had to think of exile . . . And Gorbachev and Reagan are getting it together . . . I have to go and create a new balance of terror! . . .

And the terror weakened him; he slid from her.

He felt a desperate need for sleep, even though Anna would be expecting him home and he ought to dress. He heard a rustle which was Bella groping on the floor for her cigarettes.

Now that this terrible and beautiful event had come to pass, he realised that for some time there had been a lurking hunger in his mind. He had known and yet not known it at the airport in March, waiting to fly to Italy: staring at a queue of slim, shapely ballet-dancers from the Kirov; and, only yesterday, at a bookshop, gazing at a bad reproduction of an Impressionist painting which showed a young woman reclining in a boat by a riverbank. A hunger for a new source of vitality.

He had never imagined she would come to him in the form

of a blind film director: in whose naked embrace he was now drifting closer and closer to the rapids of sleep.

He had been encased in ice for he didn't know how long. A living death. Deep-frozen. When he had given up all hope of ever being released, he heard the sound of a pick-axe. The pressure of the ice began to ease; then it was breaking up around his face like the ice of Russia, stirring after winter.

He could see his rescuer: a massive, mighty-shouldered man.

'Thank you,' Charsky gasped.

'You're welcome. I'm John Harlin.'

'Charsky. Dmitri.'

'Russian? I didn't know there were Russians on the wall. I knew there are some Germans. Are there others, or were you doing a solo?'

'A solo.'

'Ah, that's brave. I'm with Haston. We're going for a direct. How long have you been up here?'

'To tell you the truth, I don't know. Forever, it feels like.'

The American offered to stay with him awhile. His ropemate was in no hurry. He would melt some snow and they would brew up. 'Then I suggest you bivouac here, my friend. You look done in. You won't get much further today.' He gazed into that vast space where early-evening cloud and mist were beginning to obscure the Grindelwald valley and Kleine Scheidegg.

'That's a good idea. Thanks.'

Harlin unhooked his rucksack, took out the small stove, broke off a piece of ice and dropped it into a saucepan. Once or twice he looked up and shouted, hoping to catch Haston's attention; but the British climber had disappeared from view, and the wailing wind snatched the shouts away.

'When will you reach the summit, do you think?' asked the Russian.

'Oh, tomorrow.'

'You shouldn't have any problems. I don't imagine there's a finer team in the world.' He paid the compliment gracefully, and it was as gracefully accepted, with a shrug of All-American, football-playing shoulders.

'Dougal's a great climber,' Harlin said.

'And you're no slouch!' said Charsky with a feeble smile of his frost-hardened lips.

'I just wish,' said Harlin, 'I'd been around thirty years ago, when the North Face was a real test. Now it's a cinch, so long as you take reasonable precautions, like not attempting the Spider in the afternoon when the sun's melting the ice. The *direttissima* is its last challenge.'

'It's always tough,' said Charsky with deep feeling. 'Like marriage. My wife doesn't like me climbing. Are you married, John?'

'Uh-huh. And I have two kids.' He handed the Russian a mug of coffee. 'It's hard on them, I know.'

'I, thank God, have no children.'

They drank then in silence, gazing at the snow-filled valley where the lights of Grindelwald were beginning to twinkle hazily. Below them stretched a mile of empty space, but it held no terrors for Harlin. It wasn't the first time he'd been on the North Face; he would have liked to be able to set up home on it.

'Well, I'd better get going,' he said at last; he emptied some coffee dregs, which turned instantly to ice. Standing up, he swung the rucksack onto his back and clipped himself into the rope. He gave it a tug to test it. 'See you at the top.'

'Maybe.'

His feet swinging against the rock, Harlin began to climb. Charsky stared up after him. Then something drew his gaze higher still, to where the rope curved over a rounded projection. Something nagged him about the rope.

Frayed!

He shouted a warning. Harlin didn't hear. He shouted

again, and this time the American heard but it was too late. The rope snapped, and Harlin's blond head was rushing past Charsky's, turning upside-down. There was a crunch as the body struck a rock and bounced off, and then it was plunging downwards, a fragment of red anorak, blue rucksack, and puffs of snow.

It dwindled until it was too small for the naked eye to follow, but Charsky travelled still with the lifeless body scattering equipment over the valley floor.

His legs like jelly, the Russian managed to stand up. It was no use staying here. There was no way down except Harlin's way. The only faint hope was to go on climbing.

Then—such is the nature of dreams—Charsky was dining with his mother. She complained about the filthy state of the kitchen. People had no right to be taking up valuable housing space if they were always haring off to Georgia and leaving their flat in a mess.

She had cooked him a steak, and surprisingly, for she was a poor cook, it tasted good. They talked about Bella Kropotkin, with whom he had started an affair. His mother was pleased he was betraying his wife, such a dead-weight with no ambition; but she didn't know why he wanted sex with this other woman. That was one thing his father had not troubled her with, since their early years: she would say that for him. She had never seen any of Bella's films—how could she have, when she'd slaved for his father for forty years?

He had paid her a visit too, this morning. She complained that his hair had been filthy, he obviously hadn't had it washed since his death. Well, he wouldn't find anyone else who would wash his hair and tend to his every want, as she had done, all these years.

'So what did you talk about?' he asked, forcing down a piece of fat. Fat was good for the heart, his mother insisted.

'Oh, nothing much. Did he ever talk much? I could go a

whole day and never get a word out of him; even when he *could* talk. Where are you going? What's wrong with it?'

'Nothing,' he said. 'It's wonderful. I just want some water.'

'Water is bad for you when you're eating.'

He sat back down. 'So you just told him he was a filthy old gypsy—that's all you said?'

The old woman nodded. 'I soon got rid of him.'

'Oh?' He rolled a mélange of potato, mushroom and beef round his mouth.

With a sly smile, she brandished her knife.

'You chased him out with a knife?'

'Not exactly. I pretended I was going to shave him, and I slit his throat.'

'You *what?*' He stopped chewing.

'I slit his throat. He had no right to come back. Once you're dead you're dead.'

This was your husband . . . So excellent a king!

He dropped his knife and fork. 'So where is he? What have you done with him?'

That was none of his business, she said.

'Excuse me, but I think it *is* my business, Mother.'

'Just eat your dinner before it gets cold. Cold beef is very bad for the digestion, dear.'

He picked up his knife and fork and began eating again, slowly. He insisted she tell him where his father was. Was he still at the flat?

'Most of him,' she said.

'*Most* of him! What the hell do you mean?'

'Don't swear. You never used to swear as a boy. You never heard your father or me swear. You only started swearing when you married that awful woman.'

'Sorry. But what did you mean, *most* of him is there?'

She gave another sly smile, revealing her metallic teeth. 'Because a bit of him is here.' She cut off and stabbed a piece of steak and waved it over her plate.

'You don't mean—?'

His mother nodded triumphantly. 'You didn't think I'd pay those fancy black-market prices, did you? We've got enough meat to last us a year or more. You and your brother and me too. It's good quality, I gave him nothing but the best.'

Charsky cried out, and gagged chewed-up beef back onto his plate.

'What was wrong with that piece?' she demanded. 'It wasn't too rare, was it? I tried to fry it as you like it. You weren't so fussy when you were little, my lad; you ate human meat often enough then, and it wasn't always fresh!'

· 19 ·

Victor approached the last formal meal of the Festival with fear. The intense feminists, having read the *News of the World* story, would eat him up. But we received the usual polite greetings, on sitting down, and thereafter were ignored. Evidently none of them had read the tabloid.

As he pincered the legs of a lobster, Sergei said to me across the table: 'I believe Masha has had a word with you about the novel?' Masha looked away. 'It's time we took the weight off your shoulders.' He'd taken the liberty of asking one of the theatre technicians to duplicate the tapes, so I could have a set as a memento; all except today's, Masha's finale. They wanted to get to work as soon as they reached home. They might possibly set it in the framework of the Writers Internationale. They'd get Imogen to translate it.

Surkov took over: 'She'll do anything for a few roubles. We plan to make you the narrator, my friend. We can be a little more objective if we see this crappy Festival through your eyes. Don't worry, we shan't embarrass you, you'll be the neutral, admirably well-behaved observer!'

Masha smiled reassuringly: 'We won't mention—you know!'

'We'll send it to you. You can correct my ex-wife's shitty

English, and of course feel free to make any suggestions. We don't want you to feel left out.'

A tall, cadaverous man, as old as the century, was being led around the tables by the *Guardian* editor, and was shaking hands with each writer in turn. It was Finn, former Secretary General of UNO and a winner of the Nobel Peace Prize. As I gave him my lobster-reeking fingers he stared down at me with a sinister expression. Doubtless he knew he had figured in our fiction from time to time. I caught a sick-sweet odour from his breath.

At the coffee stage, Finn was formally introduced to the whole assembly and invited to say a few words. The old man swayed as he stood before us, fingers pressed to the table. Since there were so many present from African countries, he said, he would speak about the success of decolonisation within black Africa. He recalled with pride the standing ova- tion given at UNO, during his period of office, to Idi Amin. Amin had perhaps been the most outstanding creator of a new mood in Africa, a new justice, a new political maturity, a new innocence. The threat, which had seemed very real forty years ago, that several African states would join the lotus-land of capitalistic softness and so-called democracy, no longer existed. They belonged, and would continue to be- long, to the uncorrupted Third World.

If he himself had played any part in this process—most notably through his friendships with Amin, Gadafy, Bokassa, and other wonderful leaders, it would be one of his proudest achievements—ranking with the pacification of the Arme- nians, of the Russians under Stalin, of the Jews during the Second World War, of the Tibetans by the Chinese, of the Cambodians by Pol Pot, to name just a few of the great enterprises in which he had played a modest part.

Enthusiastic applause rang out, and the old man smiled his thanks. When the clapping at last died down he said he had had little time for writing during his active life, but he loved literature. Works such as *Mein Kampf* and the writings of

Lenin had had a seminal influence on him. Now he had written his autobiography—he lifted a glossy book from the table and displayed it to us. The cover showed an execution, from a sketch by Goya, under the title, *Tomorrow Is Coming*. There was more applause as he was assisted to sit down.

We finished our coffee quickly, for it was time to board the coach. Surkov had almost to be dragged on, he was so terrified of confronting the tabloid-reading public. I tried to reassure him that few patrons of a Finn-Rozanov-Bellow recital would have read the tabloids. He was not convinced, but joined us out of loyalty to Sergei.

The foyer was packed, and there were queues outside. The crowds had come, of course, mainly to hear Bellow, who had flown in overnight.

Yet the reception for Surkov, as we shouldered our way through, was immensely enthusiastic, almost as if he were the star turn. He was surrounded by admirers seeking his autograph. I overheard him say to one good-looking girl: 'Of course, you know, I write my best signature in white ink . . .' She blushed and looked coy, not knowing he had lifted the phrase from Pushkin.

Several said, 'I loved your article in the *Sunday Times*. It was very brave of you.'

'A writer has to speak the truth,' Surkov would reply.

Wishing Sergei luck, we followed the crowds into the auditorium.

Finn, assisted onto the stage, read in a tremulous voice from his autobiography, a vivid account of his first experience of a massacre. Then, after the lively applause had died down, Rozanov recited poems from memory but without zest. He looked exhausted. Yet a considerable queue—not much shorter than the one for Finn's *Tomorrow Is Coming*—formed during the interval for copies of a dissident anthology, in which a few of Rozanov's poems appeared. The bar and concourse heaved with people, and the noise was staggering. I saw Victor and Masha engaging attractive women in talk; for myself, I felt that 'remoteness' and 'stand-offishness' which is often a prelude to some creative idea. And it was not slow in coming, imprecisely at first, then more concretely: a way of developing and concluding the story of the Charskys which struck me (at the moment) as brilliant.

So often such ideas crumble at the first exposure to light; it was vital to test it out in my mind while it was fresh. It could be jotted down later and used when they sent me their draft to check and add to. I successfully fobbed off several attempts by lovers of literature to distract me; but then a couple, gliding up arm in arm, proved impossible to shake off. The man, auburn-bearded, barrel-chested, looked like a middle-aged Moses; his younger, fur-coated wife had the build of an East German field athlete, and was heavily pregnant with it. Listening yet not listening, I gathered that they were the old friends of Rozanov for whom he had reserved seats. Russian-Israelis. How greatly Sergei had aged, they lamented. Those swine who had done this to him. What kind of books did I write? Had I ever visited/would I like to visit Israel? Their broken English droned; I nodded and smiled and chatted, while my mind was in Leningrad.

The annoying couple were themselves from Leningrad. They had emigrated to Israel ten years ago, together with his parents. This year was both happy and sad; his father had died, but their second child (he had two older children still in Leningrad) would soon be born. This was a temporary transfer to London; he was a computer programmer at the Embassy; soon they would go home and settle on the West Bank. Thank God Likud looked like being victorious: the Arabs would be kept in their place.

I looked despairingly towards Rozanov, but he was still signing books. In fact he was in sombre conversation with the handsome, terminally ill young man. My brilliant idea was dying too. The tongues of the Israeli-Russian couple clacked on. London was too rainy, though they had a nice flat in Richmond, by the Thames. They enjoyed watching athletics at the White City. She was a fine shot-putter; would have been in the Israeli Olympic team but for her pregnancy.

'We can't be sure of that, Misha.'

'You'd have made it, my love.'

He kissed her solid neck, and a simper registered on her stolid face. I disliked them intensely. Relief, as Victor and Masha approached, became dismay as I realised I would have to introduce them. It is a constant problem: I talk to people without noting their names, and then have to introduce them to someone or else sign a book, For . . .

'These are old friends of Sergei's,' I said. 'Misha and . . .' I paused helplessly. To my relief Rozanov came shouldering through the crowds at that moment, beaming. 'Anna! How nice!' He clasped the pregnant fur-coated field athlete. 'Dmitri!' His sallow face brushed the thick auburn beard. 'You've met my good friends,' he said, turning to us: 'Dmitri and Anna Charsky!'

I caught the momentary confusion and horror on my friends' faces before I too composed my face: though with a roaring in my ears and a sense of total unreality, as if the room or indeed all London were dissolving. I had too intensely imagined the Charskys to be able to endure these imposters—these simpering, fascistic, philistine impostors. I could have killed them.

Gradually I was able to take in flashes of the conversation. How memorable that first meeting, when Konstantin had dragged them along to the open-air performance, the Neva's bank, Sergei's poems accompanied by Nina Rozanov on the harp—wonderful! Summer of '74, during the Brezhnev-Nixon Summit in Moscow.

Yes, they knew Pushkin had used the name Charsky. It was actually Polish, Chorazycki, his ancestors were from Danzig. But always that pull towards the ancestral land—next year in Jerusalem.

They wouldn't stay for Bellow. The smoke was troubling Anna; she needed her sleep, and he had a busy day tomorrow.

. . .

'You bastard, Sergei!'

His dentures flashed; he'd had the idea when they told him over the phone that their flat overlooked the Thames; he'd recalled Leningrad and their first encounter. Another summit. Which he guessed was why he'd set this story back in May, when Reagan was in Moscow.

They were hardly friends. He had only met them two or three times.

'I thought it would interest you, knowing you'd meet them, if you'd spent the week imagining their existence. He was a real lively dissident in Leningrad, whereas his brother is much more conformist. But I prefer the brother. I'm surprised you've not heard of him; he's quite a good poet.'

Surkov: 'That guy'—he nodded towards the exit— 'couldn't have improvised poetry.'

'Anything is possible in dreams.'

Masha: 'You didn't give us many clues.'

'That's true.'

The interval bell sounded.

Bellow read from *Humboldt's Gift*.

As we joined the surge-out, my arm was grabbed fiercely. Pain shot through it. I turned to see Finn staring down with a cadaverous smile. Smelt the sweet-sour breath. 'I wanted to tell you, I read your *Ararat*. My son said I should read it. Well, of course, I was most flattered to find myself in it!'

'You didn't mind?'

'Of course not. But I can't honestly say I enjoyed it. I wonder was it necessary to include so much sex and violence?'

'Possibly not.'

'The Armenian episode, for instance. Well, it was perfectly accurate, but did you have to be so graphic, so brutal? It struck me as *verging* on pornography.'

Smiling still, he allowed himself to be led away through the crowds. Leaving the theatre for the last time, we saw the two Nobel Prize winners—so utterly different—side by side, frozen-faced, in the back of a black limousine, edging out into the traffic.

We were silent in the returning coach. There were empty seats; I saw Masha brush her eyes. Surkov stared out at the darkness and neon; the reception he had had was fine, but the real test would be Moscow, tomorrow.

In his and Sergei's bedroom we poured vodka and were still silent; I could sense our imaginations turning back to the Charskys. Masha voiced it: 'That couple—they're irrelevant. They don't exist.'

'What couple?' asked Surkov.

When she realised Charsky had fallen asleep, Bella eased herself from under him and sat up. She picked up her petticoat from the floor and slipped it on over her head. She fumbled in her handbag, took out an object shaped like a candle and left the room.

While she was away, Charsky turned onto his side, facing the room, and drew his legs up into a crouched position.

Returning, she sat at the further end of the sofa, lit a cigarette, and leaned back.

She finished the cigarette and was thinking of lighting another when she heard the sound of a key turning in a lock. She froze, sank deeper into the sofa.

Two men stood in the doorway, stopped dead in their tracks by seeing a naked man and a woman in a petticoat. The visitor who had nonchalantly thrown the door open was about fifty, tall and slim, dressed smartly in a grey suit with white shirt and blue-striped tie. He was clean-shaven; his black hair was greying. His thin, sensitive, rather striking face bore a network of fine wrinkles. Behind him stood a skinny youth of about twenty, bizarrely attired in baggy yellow trousers and a pink-and-blue-striped T-shirt. His face was chalky, evidently from make-up; a bronze earring hung from his left ear. His skull was closely shaven. Though as surprised as his older companion at finding people in the room, he went on chewing gum as if nothing were amiss.

'Who the devil are you?' asked the grey-suited man.

Bella, striving to curb her panic, said in a trembling voice, 'I'm sorry, you have the advantage of me. I'm blind.' She gestured vaguely towards her white stick.

'I see.'

He stepped into the centre of the room, and the chalk-faced youth came up to his shoulder, staring intently at the woman.

'My name is Sakulin,' said the gentleman. 'Captain Sakulin. And this is my flat. I don't know what you're doing here.' He stared at the peacefully sleeping Charsky. 'Ah! I know this fellow—he's an actor.' He glanced at the youth. 'You must know him too. Charsky, a member of the Arts Theatre.'

'Never heard of him.'

Bella cut in: 'I'm sorry; I feel extremely confused and embarrassed. You say this is your flat?'

'Yes. But I'm sure this isn't your fault. I think I know what must have happened.'

Seeming to gain in confidence, Bella sat forward on the sofa and groped for her cigarettes. Sakulin leapt forward to pick up her lighter and clicked it for her. She thanked him. 'Are there two of you?' she asked.

'Yes. This is—' He stared closely into her face. 'Forgive me; it's just occurred to me who you are. You must be Bella Kropotkin?'

'That's right. But please, I'd be grateful if you could forget about this. Both of you.'

Sakulin, smiling, said, 'Of course! We haven't seen you. Have we?' He glanced at the gum-chewing chalk-faced youth.

'We ain't seen a thing.' The youth spat his chewing gum into an ashtray, opened Bella's cigarette case and helped himself. He said to Sakulin: 'Would you tell me what the fuck is going on? What are they doing here?'

'I used to be friendly with the Charskys,' he replied very

quietly, turning away from Bella as if, by so doing, he was ensuring she wouldn't hear. 'Well, particularly with his wife. She had a key; still has it. He must have got to know about this place and filched the key.'

'You screw women too? Shit! you get around!' exclaimed the youth, and Sakulin blushed. The youth, removing his cigarette, pulled him into an embrace and kissed him. 'I don't object,' he said. 'I'm all for a bit of variety myself.'

'Please!' Sakulin begged. At that moment Charsky jerked his legs and made a gagging noise in his throat. 'Comrade Kropotkin,' said the Captain rather formally, 'it looks as if your friend is out cold. I don't mind him sleeping it off here tonight. We only called in for—for a fleeting visit. I'm not actually living here. Your friend can find his way home in the morning. But can we drop you somewhere? My car is outside.'

Bella replied that it was kind of him, but if he didn't mind she would stay awhile, take a shower if that was all right, regain her composure, before going back to her hotel. It was not far; the walk would do her good.

'Of course, stay as long as you like. We'll leave you, then.'

'I must have a piss first,' the youth said. 'Where's the toilet?'

'It's through there.' Sakulin pointed. The youth signalled with a jerk of his head that he should follow. In the bathroom the youth threw his arms round the older man and kissed him with open lips. Sakulin eventually drew away, gasping, his eyes closed. Feeling for the zip of Sakulin's trousers, the youth said, 'Come on, a quick one.'

The nuclear submariner drew back. 'We can't. Not now; not tonight, my dear. Believe me, I'm disappointed too.'

'Then I'm going to have a bit of fun. You can join in if you want, it's up to you; only don't try to spoil it, or else . . .' He left the threat unspoken. Lifting the toilet seat, he unzipped himself and urinated. Sakulin sombrely watched.

'What are you going to do?'

'You'll find out. Just sit down in the room and keep dead quiet, Ivan. I'll do the rest.'

He unscrewed a wrinkled tube of toothpaste, squeezed, and swallowed. 'This is good, man, you should try it.'

When they returned to Bella and her sleeping lover, the youth said loudly: 'We're off then, Comrade. Good-bye.'

'Good-bye. And thank you, Captain Sakulin.'

'Don't mention it,' he said, sinking quietly into an armchair at a silent signal from his companion.

'I think your friend may be beginning to come round,' announced the youth. 'Cheers!'

He walked through into the passage, opened the outside door and shut it again with a bang. Slipping off his shoes, he crept silently back into the room. Bella, as if in relief, sank back against the cushions. The youth warned Sakulin with a finger to his lips, then started stealthily, in silence, to undress. A thin red penis, like a dog's, jutted. He crept up to the reclining woman and stroked her arm. She smiled. 'Ah, so you've woken up! You were asleep for a long time, darling!'

The youth touched her chin, tilting her face, and kissed her. He slid his hand under her petticoat to fondle her breast. Then, placing both hands on her shoulders, he turned her roughly onto her side; from there onto her stomach, her knees sliding down on to the carpet. Bella buried her face in a cushion. The youth bared, then parted, her buttocks. Seeing a wisp of white, he pulled. Turning with a leer towards Sakulin, he waved the tampon, then tossed it onto the floor. He prodded and entered.

'That's wonderful, Dmitri! God, you're a horny bastard! How did you guess I love it this way?'

The youth grunted and threw his head back, grinning, exposing wolfish pointed teeth. He set up a lazy rhythm of thrust and withdrawal. Sakulin, his face almost as white as the youth's, stared mesmerized. Then his young friend turned his head towards him and gave a jerk of invitation. The Captain, his white face flushing, shook his head. The youth jerked his head again, exposing his savage teeth in another grin; putting his hands behind him he slapped his buttocks and drew them apart.

Sakulin pulled himself to his feet, slipped off his shoes, took off his jacket, loosened his shirt collar, stripped off his trousers. Stepping up to the duo, he knelt. . . . The youth's head jerked back; he gasped.

'Wonderful! Oh, I love you, I love you, Dmitri!' Bella crooned. Her head, the long silky-gold locks, twisted from side to side. 'I'd like you to'—she panted—'oh yes! *there!*'

She screamed; gave a shuddering sigh. Later, the two men rose and started to dress, silently. The director slid to the floor, burying her face in her arms, her shoulders heaving.

Picking up their shoes, the visitors tiptoed from the room. Just as stealthily they left the flat.

Bella, slowly pulling herself to her feet, smoothed down her petticoat, then went to the bedroom where she picked up a blanket; returning to the living-room she laid the blanket over Charsky, tucking it in around him. She kissed his cheek.

She searched the floor for her tampon, found it, squatted down and inserted it. Then she gathered up her clothes and started to dress. She picked up a phone and dialled. Almost at once it was answered. 'Good heavens, you're still up, Irena, my dear!' she said. 'I was going to let it ring just three or four times in case you were asleep . . . You're sure it's not too late? I could bring them back in the morning . . . Fine, I'll be with you in about half an hour . . . Oh, amazingly well!'

Irena, the old, retired make-up artist, took a Polaroid snap of one of her more remarkable creations, before helping Anna to peel it all off. The blond wig, the white stick, the elegant clothes, the silver cigarette case—even a set of red underwear, relic of a French farce—returned to the old woman's fabulous collection of theatrical mementoes. Anna changed back into her overalls, picked up her shabby shoulderbag, slipped *Moda* into it, and set off to walk home along the embankment. She was still too tense and excited to feel tired.

On her right, she passed the University building where, a few weeks earlier, she had heard Fyodor Burlatsky, one of Gorbachev's aides, talk about the future of socialism. She had grown faint with disbelief and pleasure as the extraordinary lecture unrolled. Two Stalinist myths had been *on the whole* overcome: trust in the power of violence, and belief in 'the giant leap forward'. But one remained: the paramount role of the state in building socialism. The Soviet state, Burlatsky had said, must give way to a civil society, with the development of co-operative ownership and individual enterprise. There must be elections, a public opinion, mandatory rotation of senior officials.

And a passage which had brought the packed hall to its feet: 'What our people need is not Stalin's "new dawns" or monuments to political bosses. They need simply a normal, civilised life.'

Anna had never thought she would hear such quiet truths quietly stated in her lifetime.

And the speech hadn't been confined to an élite invited audience. Anyone could read it, a couple of weeks later, in *Literaturnaya Gazeta*.

Of course it might all fizzle out, Gorbachev might be swept away or his ideas tempered by the conservatism of power— and of people like her workmates. Yet these ideas had been openly and authoritatively expressed, for the first time in Soviet history; they could never be unsaid; any attempt to renege on this dawn would be regarded by millions as intolerable.

Gazing at the Neva's surges, she recalled some lines of Akhmatova: *As though, in night's terrible mirror / Man, raving, denied his image / And tried to disappear— / While along the historic river, / Not the calendar—the living / Twentieth century drew near.*

Petersburg, 1913. Well, perhaps, Anna thought, I'm seeing the beginning of the *living* twenty-first century, twelve years early. When man will make his face reappear in the mirror.

It was good to be alive at such a time. Then why this deadness, this flatness? Why, after tender embraces with Dmitri that morning, had she felt so dead and flat that she had rung Irena and then her husband, disguising her voice, setting up the perverse stage-performance?

Why had her heart sunk when she'd learned she was going to have poems published openly, and that *Zhivago* was going to be filmed?

Do I need secrecy and censorship? she wondered. Do I need the struggle for freedom and decency but not their realisation? Maybe I shall always be stirred by gunfire, as I was in my cot.

'Stop crying, little one! Or the Germans will creep in and get you! . . .'

Anna had reached the Sphinxes. She decided to sit for a while on the steps leading down to the water. Turning sideways, she gazed up at those enigmatic images, dredged from the Nile in the time of Pushkin. He must, many times, have scampered by, hurrying from a card game to a liaison, while they were being erected here. They would have seemed immeasurably ancient and mysterious to him even then. They would always be ancient and mysterious—even if the people of Russia attained a 'normal, civilized life'—even if, God forbid, they attained Utopia.

The bland stone heads, neither male nor female, Buddhalike, staring blindly. The gold crown, their fringes stretching down to their breasts. The powerful animal shoulders and bodies.

Egyptian Nights! she thought. Cleopatra and her Lovers . . . Heavens! it was just like it! How extraordinary! Dmitri would go crazy about the coincidence, if only he knew!

Yet at least no great harm had come of it. No deaths at dawn.

Sakulin. She still wasn't over him. She ought to have known it. That was why it had seemed so important to bring her husband there. An attempted exorcism. Yet she hadn't realised how much Ivan still meant to her until the moment when she should have taken Dmitri to the bedroom. Somehow she couldn't lie with him on the bed she had shared with Ivan.

He had always seemed a somewhat mysterious person. There were those years when he'd simply disappeared, and his wife claimed he had drowned. Then he had simply reappeared! He had been picked up by Icelandic fishermen, he had claimed, and had lost his memory. Well, it might be true. . . .

And now—this! She knew a lot of homosexuals, the theatre world was full of them, but she'd never for a moment suspected Ivan. It explained why he'd never been particularly passionate, preferring to talk and listen to music. She'd ascribed it to a fine, sensitive, spiritual nature!

It wasn't ended. Her heart leapt sickeningly. She would be forced to get in touch with him. His bisexuality made him still more interesting. And the way he had thrown aside all reserve and all decency, all 'normal, civilized' values, in sodomising the young man who was screwing her.

I was a sphinx to that boy, she reflected. A blind woman, a blind director. He had to screw me because I was totally unknown to him. And, in a way, he did get to know me. . . .

My God, I must be a masochist! I liked being treated with such contempt. I enjoyed it too when I was hurt by Dmitri's saying that sex with his wife wasn't so good, had *never* been so good. And the way my heart beat faster, and I wanted to open my legs for him, when he said I was only 'pretty good' as a poet!

Which means, according to Freud, I'm also a sadist. I needed to hurt my husband. God, how appalling!

To think that he once tried to commit suicide! One of the most important events in his life, and I'm his wife and I didn't know it! But I didn't tell him about the overdose when Ivan wasn't answering my phone calls. . . .

She wished she wasn't on a period. Otherwise, there might have been a chance the young man had made her pregnant. But hardly—she sighed; not at forty-seven. That was closed. Soon her periods would become irregular.

She stood up, tossing a cigarette stub into the river, and walked on. As she left the mythic creatures behind her, she saw the events of the past hours in a more prosaic light. She threw her head back and laughed, crying out loud: 'But people don't *do* that sort of thing!'

A worker, cycling by on his way to early-morning shift, caught sight of a middle-aged woman in blue overalls talking to herself, her head thrown back, her mouth spread in a grin. He turned to stare after, muttering, 'Crazy!'

Ah, but the light! The light was marvellous! She kept her head back and closed her eyes briefly, feeling the sun growing ever warmer on her face. That sun had no reason to exist, spreading warmth and light. There ought to be an eternal blankness. There was no reason for her to exist, with eyes to see that light.

She was a child of light, a child of history, of Russian history; and she did not even wish Stalin away. It was terrible for his victims; yet he gave a density to her life. *The children of Russia's terrible years.* Blok's phrase still echoed resonantly, and Anna didn't wish the terrible years away.

She just wanted more life. She wanted Fedorov's vision to come true: that crazy old philosopher who thought all the dead could be resurrected through electricity. She wanted Tsiolkovsky's vision to come true; that space pioneer who had dreamed of seeding all the stars and constellations with human life. Well, that was possible. Sometimes, when she made a mistake in the radio factory, she imagined she had created by chance a special radio which could communicate with outer space; and sometimes, at home alone, she would dial thirty or forty numbers on the phone, imagining she would hit on a phone number on a planet of Vega, say.

And she wanted more passion, more passion. In which you wanted the impossible *because* it was impossible!

A black car turned a corner further along the embankment and zoomed towards her. She followed its approach incuriously, but as it passed she became almost sure Ivan had been driving it. And that obscene yet fascinating youth, beside him. For a moment the driver's face had turned, staring, recognising.

When she reached home she stacked in the bathroom cabinet the toilet rolls Zoya had got for her—having slotted one onto the holder. She was sore; penetrating her there was something Dmitri would never think of doing. Well, that was good, that was right. She washed her hands and face, stripped off her overalls and tumbled straight into bed. Soon she was asleep.

Old Yury, her father-in-law, had been to the toilet—there was a proper roll instead of the usual newspaper—and was now wandering around looking for his bed. He felt unhappy; when, sitting at the kitchen table, he asked for tea, nobody took any notice of him—even less than usual. He might almost not be there. And he couldn't for the life of him find Yevdoxia. Also he was almost sure he was in the wrong flat. He spent all his time worrying about when he had slept on guard duty and cowering from explosions.

At last he found his bed—and Yevdoxia was there, asleep in it! And naked! She hadn't slept naked for years and years, yet he could remember her when she had been warm and fleshly and generous. The old man pulled back the sheet hesitantly and climbed in beside her. He couched into her warm softness and she didn't reject him. She was again his beautiful and tender Yevdoxia!

Gliding into her smoothly, deliciously, he passed out of the miseries of death-in-life and found peace and wonder.

Dunya leapt up, and nestled into the curve between two bodies.

· 21 ·

When Sakulin and his young companion crept out of the flat, taking the ramshackle lift to street-level and jumping into the car, the naval commander drove off with a screech of tyres and straightaway went through a red light.

'Hey, take it easy, old ducks!' the youth exclaimed. Sakulin braked, then turned into a narrow street marked 'No Entry'. Fortunately there was no traffic about. His mind was filled with the horror of what he had taken part in.

'Where are we going, anyway?'

'Nowhere. I just feel like driving.'

'Suits me.'

Sakulin zoomed aimlessly around Leningrad's streets. Barricades were already being erected in preparation for Mrs Reagan's brief visit. The lone car attracted suspicion; three times the naval officer was stopped, but his special pass brought salutes and he was waved on.

Eventually he drew into the kerb of a silent side-street. He rested his arms on the wheel and laid his head on his arms. The youth, reaching aside, started to fondle his groin, but Sakulin jerked away. 'How could you do such a thing?' he said.

'Because you turn me on. I like older guys. Don't you like me feeling you up?'

'No, I meant just now. At the flat.'

'Screwing the blind bitch? Oh, it was just a bit of fun! Life is short, so what the hell? It doesn't mean anything to me. I wouldn't have done it if I'd thought you were going to be jealous.'

'I wasn't jealous,' Sakulin explained tiredly. 'It was so—filthy.'

'Well, darling, you weren't exactly well behaved yourself.'

'I know. I was as bad as you.'

'She loved it. It was just the same to her as if her bloke had done it. But picture his face'—he uttered a wild laugh—'when he wakes up and she starts saying, That was really great when you had me up the arse! I'm disappointed, though; I was looking forward to going to bed with you. *Sleeping* with you. That's a great hideout. How did you pull that?'

'It belonged to my parents,' Sakulin replied tiredly. 'After my mother died I was allowed to keep it. When I'm ashore I need a place where I can make phone calls and so on in complete privacy. That's what I told them and they swallowed it. Well, it's true, in a way.'

'So you've got it to take your boyfriends to. Or your girlfriends. It's lucky for some!'

'I don't make a habit of this.'

'No? You could have fooled me. You were cruising the streets like a real pro. All I can say is, you're fucking lucky. *I* live in a poky little hole with five others. Hey!'—he grabbed Sakulin's knee—'I've got a great idea! You let me live in it and I can make it nice! Do a spot of painting to brighten it up. I'll even cook you dinners sometimes—I'm a great cook. What do you say to that?'

'It wouldn't be allowed. I run risks as it is. It wouldn't be so bad if I kept a woman there; but a male—no. I'd be under arrest before you could say Raisa Gorbachev.'

The youth pouted. Sakulin restarted the car. 'I'll drive you home. You must give me directions.'

Recovered, cooler, he drove at a steady pace. His young companion started to ask him about life in a nuclear submarine. Sakulin confined himself to generalities: the pressure of being under water for weeks at a time, the problems of close living, and so on.

'What would happen if the balloon went up? What would you actually have to do?'

'You know I can't tell you that.'

'Fuck—you've guessed I'm working for the CIA. What do you think of the Summit?'

'It looks promising.'

'Depends how you look at it. If I was in your shoes, darling, I'd be mad as fuck.'

'Why's that?'

'Go down here and turn off along the embankment. —Because it doesn't look as if there's going to be a war. Not that I particularly want to get blown up by an American missile; but if I was you I think I'd feel the old adrenalin flowing so long as I thought I *might* have to press the button. You know, I guess you have dummy runs in which you don't know at first if it's practice or for real. It must be terrific when there's just a chance it's for real. But from now on you can be pretty sure it's not going to happen. Dullsville, man.'

Turning left, with the Neva coming into sight ahead of them, Sakulin said, 'That's extremely cynical,' though in fact he knew there was a measure of truth in what the youth had said. Anger welled in him; his hawkish comrades were right, too much was being given away by Russia's leaders. Instantly he quelled the unreasoning emotion; he knew it was the voice of his unhappy, chaotic life, which had always found a certain self-excuse in the extreme situation of the Cold War frontline.

'Our task is to avoid war,' he added sincerely.

Scratching his shaven skull, the youth said, 'Actually I

wouldn't mind a war. The world's a shit-hole, we might as well all go out with a bang.'

There was a lone walker on the embankment, a woman in blue overalls. The driver turned his head sharply. 'I think that was Anna,' he exclaimed. 'Anna Charsky.'

'The cunt you used to screw?'

'Oh, it wasn't about sex. In that way it was no better than with my wife, God help me. No, it was just—she was a really good friend.'

'She's up fucking early. Or out fucking late.'

'Yes.'

The young man stroked Sakulin's thigh. 'Take the next right.' The city became more and more depressing. At length, dismal factories and apartment blocks rose above them. '*We* could be good friends, Ivan darling; and have a good time in bed too. Pull up here; I just have to nip down the alley.'

Sakulin braked and drew in.

'A good-night kiss?' said the youth.

Sakulin gave him a brief hug but turned his lips away.

'You're a bit coy, all of a sudden, aren't you? Ah well, it's your loss. Shall I see you tomorrow—tonight?'

'I don't think so. I don't think we should meet again.'

The youth drew back as if he had been struck. 'Fucking be like that, then. In that case I want some money.'

Already fumbling in his pocket, Sakulin stuffed a wad of roubles in his hands. The young man flung open the door and climbed out. He stooped and stared in, his eyes like flames in his chalky face. 'Perhaps it's just as well,' he said. 'I've got AIDS.'

He bared his pointed teeth in a snarl, and withdrew into the shadows.

He pulled himself over the edge and collapsed, his breast heaving, gulping the thin air. He was in too bad a way, and his heart was too filled with pain, to feel any sense of triumph.

It was merely survival. He was off the accursed face at last.

A terrible storm raged; each pellet of snow had the sharpness of a dagger. Night had fallen. But he would be all right, he had his bivouac tent; he would bivouac here tonight and then descend the easy south-western slope in the morning.

He was just crawling into the tent when he thought he heard, through the gale, a feeble cry. He listened; became convinced he had imagined the cry, and was settling in again when the cry was repeated, weak but unmistakable. He pulled himself out and set off blindly down the south-western slope in the direction from which the cries had come. He floundered through the snow. He was about two hundred feet from the summit when another cry stopped him. It seemed to come from right beside him. He felt on his left-hand side a mound of ice. His hand found a hole in it. He shouted: 'Is there anyone there?'

'Yes!' came a weak cry. 'Thank God!'

'Who are you?'

'I'm Günter Nothdurft; I'm with Franz Mayer. He's unconscious, and I've passed out a couple of times. We're in a bad way. Are you with a rescue team?'

'No, I'm just a solo climber. Dmitri Charsky. What happened to you?'

There was no reply for a while, as if the man was struggling to gain strength to speak. At last Nothdurft said, 'We were roped up with two Italians, Longhi and Corti. Longhi fell; we left him on a ledge and struggled on to try to get help for him. Then Corti got injured and we had to leave him too, with our bivouac tent and the remains of our food. We managed to get to the top. God knows how.' He stopped to gather breath. 'We knew we had to go straight down, to raise the alarm. But we floundered into a drift. We were exhausted; all we could do was make ourselves a snow cave. As you can see, it's frozen solid. We're trapped. It's been hell trying to keep a small hole open. Can you widen it with your axe?'

'I lost my axe on the climb. You'll just have to hold on. I'll get help.'

Nothdurft sobbed. 'Can't hold out. Almost gone.'

Charsky realised that was true. There wasn't any hope the two brave Germans could hold out until he brought rescuers up this south-western slope.

'Did Corti still have his axe?' he shouted.

'I believe so.'

'Then I'll go back down and get his. Courage!'

'Hurry!' came the weak cry.

The Russian struggled back the way he had come, scrambling on hands and knees in case he should reach the edge without realising it. At last his hand felt empty space. His heart misgave him. He would never find the injured Italian. Without an ice-axe he would be lucky to climb down fifty feet without falling. It was madness. Yet he eased himself over the edge, and started to climb down completely without aid, in the old style of mountaineering, relying on feet and fingers.

Two or three hours passed. To his astonishment he was still clinging on, in one of the Exit Cracks. The storm had eased a little. He had reached a point, however, from which further movement downwards was impossible. His only hope was to try for the summit again. In any case, it was clear to him that the Germans must long since have died. He found a toe-hold, stretched up to a fissure just wide enough to take his fingers, and pulled himself up. He flattened himself to the face.

When Charsky awoke it was bright morning. He felt stiff, but remarkably clear in the head. He looked around for Bella, but she was nowhere to be seen. There were no clothes, no suitcase—nothing. Bewildered and stricken, he wondered if she had returned to the hotel. He dialled the Leningrad, asked for Comrade Kropotkin, and was put through to her.

'Bella!' he said. 'Thank God I've got hold of you! I'm sorry; I just fell asleep.'

A cold voice said: 'Who is this? Oh, it's you, Comrade Charsky. Well, I shouldn't worry about it. I've decided to give the part to Fedotov. I saw him at a matinée. I think he'll be very good.'

Fedotov was appearing in *Stars under a Morning Sky.* 'I'm sorry. Thank you for calling.' And she put the phone down.

Dazed and nauseated, Charsky dialled his home number. After several rings Anna answered it.

'Darling, it's me. I'm sorry I never got home.'

'Why, what time is it? Good grief, is it that time already? You woke me up. Did you sleep with Bella?'

In his shocked condition Charsky could find no answer but the truth.

'Well, that's okay,' she responded in quite a gay tone. 'I told you I didn't mind so long as you were honest with me. It was inevitable, wasn't it? Look, could you pick up some cigarettes on your way home? I've run out.'

'Of course. I'll see you.'

'See you—oh, your mother rang. She wants us to come to dinner on Sunday. It seems she's got hold of some sweet-breads. I've said yes.'

'Okay,' said Charsky, and put the phone down. Well, life would go on, with or without Bella. He liked sweetbreads. He would try to persuade his mother to let Anna cook them.

Replacing the bedside phone, Anna immediately picked it up again. She hesitated for a long time, her thoughts churning, then dialled. If Nadia Sakulin should answer it she had, as in the old days, a ready chatter. They were good friends. But it was Ivan's voice.

'Hello. It's Anna.'

'Anna! Why—this is a surprise.'

'I was just wondering how you were. It's been a long time. I thought I saw your car this morning, very early.'

'Yes, it was me. We—I saw you. Well, I wasn't sure.'

'So how are you, Ivan?'

'Oh, I'm okay . . . I suppose.'

'You don't sound okay. Is anything the matter?'

'No. Probably not.'

But to Anna he sounded as if he had been crying. Clearly what had happened, what he had done, had upset him greatly.

'Would you like to tell me about it? Could we meet?'

'I'd like that, Anna. It's been too long. But I sail to-morrow.'

'How about today? I thought of having a migraine and staying off work.'

'Not today. Too much to do.' She could hear him breathing agitatedly.

'Are you sure you're fit to sail? You sound really upset.'

'I'm fine, Anna. I'll call you when I get back, in a couple of months. I promise. Thank you for ringing.'

'Well . . . good-bye.'

'Good-bye.'

Anna put down the phone but remained with her hand resting on it. 'He's in no kind of state to captain a nuclear submarine,' she reflected. 'Well, I don't suppose he can do any harm; except possibly to himself. . . .'

On an impulse she went to the study and typed a note to the editor of *Novy Mir*, saying the poems they had accepted were not ready, and could she please have them back. Anna wasn't quite sure why she was doing this; true, she felt a little guilty at publishing *Varvara*, but it was more complicated than that.

Her capital letters were higher than the lower-case ones. She must buy a new typewriter. Dmitri had offered to bring her back a fairly inexpensive word processor, programmed for Russian, from Naples but she'd said no. The technology frightened her. She would go on writing, for herself and a few friends, on a manual typewriter.

She sat in the bath reading the end of the Krafft-Ebing/Sophie correspondence . . .

Vienna

Dear Frau Stolz,

I don't know why I bother to write. I wandered up and down Leopoldstrasse for two hours, and to my acute embarrassment was forced to speak to the other girls. They told me you are almost always there on a Thursday afternoon. So much for your excuse about your mother-in-law. I wash my hands of you.

R. von Krafft-Ebing

Berlin

Dear Professor,

I deserve your anger. To tell you the truth I was frightened. Frightened I would have yet another disappointment. You see, if I was absolutely sure you were my one true Master, I would not have hesitated. You could command me to anything, anything. However degrading. However humiliating. Only—you care about me, you've admitted it. You feel concern for my well-being and I am grateful for that, but at the same time it's not what I want. I was afraid, if we met, you would show your care and respect, and I would lose interest. So it was better we didn't meet.

Affectionately,
Sophie

Vienna

Dear Sophie,

What then can I do? I can't help caring for you. But also, yes, I do want to give you what you crave. But all without *truly* hurting you. My mind is in a dreadful state. I must see you.

As a matter of fact I am almost sure I *did* see you, during my wretched visit. You were in a tram-car with one of the prostitutes I recognised from the Leopold-strasse. The girl sitting by the prostitute had brown hair, a large mouth, and turned-up nose, which was how you described yourself to me, a year or two ago. Was it you?

Give me a precise date and time and I will come to Berlin again.

Richard

Berlin

Dear Richard,

Yes, I think you probably did see me. How strange. There is nothing we can do. You cannot help caring for me, I cannot help not wanting that. Perhaps I could not be content with anyone unless he didn't care whether I lived or died. I may never find my Master, but I must go on searching.

Heinz and I are moving. We have found a slightly bigger flat, though in a poor neighbourhood. I am pregnant, you see. I am sure I shall be an awful mother. I shan't send you my new address. It is better this way. I shall always treasure your letters. I hope you will remember with some affection

Your obedient servant,
Sophie

Rimini

Dearest Sophie,

I have no idea if this will ever reach you. I am at the coast, taking a 'rest', but I can find none. I spend all night and all day gazing at the angry sea, and finding in it your beautiful, enigmatic face. You are the deepest experience of my life; I would do anything you wanted. Send me

just some message to assuage my hunger. Take pity on
a poor old man.

> Yours ever,
> Richard

She heard footsteps and called, 'I'm in the bath.' Charsky
entered, looking fearful, clutching a big bag. He took from
it three packets of cigarettes and some flowers. He lit her a
cigarette straightaway and said, 'Anna, I'm so sorry!'

'It's all right. It makes us equal.'

Then he had the painful experience of learning that she had
slept, not long ago, with a young drop-out. A casual encounter. She didn't even know his name, and he was of no
importance.

· 22 ·

'. . . So I said to him, "Okay, Mr Ambassador, I'll have bright-yellow hair for a year if you'll donate ten thousand dollars for those children's camps I'm involved in!" He said, "You're on, Victor!" So here I am, with beautiful long blond hair, huh?'

Surkov, in profile, grinned and stroked his locks. I watched him from my bed, a tray on my lap. The invitation to appear on breakfast TV had come at midnight, interrupting Masha's improvisation. A cab had picked him up at six.

The camera panned to the smiling, casually dressed presenter, herself a blonde. 'Some writers at the Festival have called you remote and stand-offish: are they right? It doesn't fit in with the picture of you I'm getting.'

'I think I'm very approachable. But maybe I've been preoccupied this past week. You see, four of us, who are good friends, have got together for the first time in years. Three Russian writers and an English writer. And we find we kind of spark each other off creatively. We've been improvising, mostly late at night, but of course it spills over into the day as well. I've been living mostly in my imagination; all four of us have.'

'We're going to take a break. Don't go away!'

'I won't!'

There was an advert for dog food, and another for Christmas games. I finished my orange juice and poured coffee. The presenter and Surkov came back. 'I'm talking to Victor Surkov, the famous Russian poet and novelist, who's been appearing this week at the Writers Internationale Festival at the Riverside Theatre, London. . . . Victor, you were saying, you live in your imagination. Does that create problems?'

'I guess it does. Let me give you an example. Like I said, we've been creating a novel, four of us together. My great friend and neighbour, Sergei Rozanov, a brilliant writer, set us going with a couple of characters called Dmitri and Anna Charsky. Unknown to the rest of us, he had taken them from life, they were real people, acquaintances of his, and he knew we'd meet them at the end of the week. He did it as an interesting experiment in the relationship of fiction and reality. Well, our English friend—I won't embarrass him by mentioning his name—actually talked to them for several minutes without even finding out who they were! Because he was thinking of our fictional characters! Well, it's pretty hard for those who have to live with us—'

The presenter had started to fidget while he was speaking, and her eyes strayed. This was getting too heavy.

'But reality,' she said, 'broke in during the week for you when—'

'—Fiction is lies, you see, but also a deeper truth. We're thinking of calling this novel we're creating *Lying Together*. There's a sexual pun there, of course: in sex there's the same combination of lies and deeper truth. When this novel—'

'I'm glad you brought up sex. I was going to say, reality broke in on you during the week, didn't it? A woman accused you of assaulting her—'

His eyes, red-veined and baggy from sleeplessness, flashed angrily. 'I was accused of rape, let's make no bones about it! I was dragged out of bed in the middle of the night, as if this was Stalin's Russia, and bundled off to a police station. That's what happened to me. And that's why, even though the charge obviously didn't hold up, I'm to be driven out of your country today, like a leprosy.'

'We'll come back to this in a moment.' She swung round in her chair: 'Fred, it looks as if the good weather has ended, right?'

'I'm afraid so, Sue!'

Fred, amiable, cardiganed, flourished his stick at the weather chart. I gulped coffee and brushed breadcrumbs from the coverlet. Rain swished at the still-dark window.

'I'm talking to Victor Surkov, Russian poet and novelist, who was accused of rape last week but later released on condition that he leaves Britain by today. Victor, why do you think a woman would make a false charge?'

His eyes flashed again. The anger he had largely suppressed in our company was obviously surging out. 'Do you think women are incapable of telling lies? Are human beings capable of lying? Are women not human beings?'

Her legs swished as they crossed. 'But that's a particularly vicious—'

'You're telling me it's vicious! She might have locked me away for years, being attacked by other prisoners! You wouldn't be so disbelieving if I said a man had done something vicious. Well, the whole sexual issue is riddled with problems and paradoxes. You can say that men are ultimately responsible—or at least more than women.'

'How do you mean?'

'I mean, men have always been terrified of the flesh. All over England, watching us, are men who are terrified of the flesh, of sex. And therefore they're rather—ah—turned on by the fact that we're discussing rape; and they'll be trotting to the front door to pick up the *Sun*, to see the page-three nude and read the latest scandal. But in themselves they're miserably scared and uptight. There's a poem by one of your great writers, Jonathan Quick—I was shown it by our English friend. This guy in the poem is madly in love with a woman called Celia, but he sees her commode just after she's had a shit and he can't take it; he can't take it that his beloved Celia shits just like everybody else!'

The presenter shuffled, glanced aside. 'Could we come back to—'

'You can't imagine Celia going off her lover if the positions were reversed,' Surkov continued. 'Women know that their lovers shit, just as babies do. What I'm trying to say is, though it's difficult with that guy waving at me madly, I guess to say we've run out of time, that women are essentially more at home with the flesh, more free and easy about our bodies. But men, who are happiest when they're building prisons or nuclear rockets, have crushed the free spirit out of women, so now they're as bad as the men, or even worse.'

'Thank you. It's fascinating, but we really do have to move on to—'

'Is this your Western free speech? A couple of minutes to deal with one of the most complex subjects in human life? The guy with the cat who's suckling a guinea-pig can wait a few minutes. Women have fantasies about rape and seduction—'

'That's a male stereotype.'

'I think your comment is a feminist stereotype, it makes me tired.'

'Well, you're entitled to your opinion. But we really must move on. Thank you very much for joining us. And now for something entirely different. Cats. Well, not your average cat, but a very special cat. We're going to meet her. If you can just bring her—' A phone trilled. 'Excuse me!' She picked it up. She listened. Her expression changed; her eyes widened, she licked her lips. 'Victor, don't go just yet—the Prime Minister.' The camera swung to Surkov, in the act of rising from the sofa. He sat again, took the phone from her hand. I put aside the tray and sat up in bed as the velvet, laryngal tones of the Prime Minister addressed Surkov and the nation:

'Mr Surkov, good morning!'

'Good morning, Marg—Prime Minister!'

'I don't usually listen to this programme, but Dennis happened to turn it on and I'm *extremely* glad he did. You were quite *right* to protest at being cut off. If one is dealing with an extremely complex subject, as you were, one is entitled to have enough time to deal with it adequately. Sue is a *marvellous* presenter, and I know she is always up against the clock, but I do hope she will let you carry on.'

'Thank you.'

'I was also extremely surprised that you have been ordered to leave Britain. If you were not charged with an offence, I cannot see how anyone could have the right to set limits to your stay. Unless there is a visa problem . . .'

'There's none.'

'Then I can only say I shall look into this very carefully—*very carefully indeed.* It will be sorted out within a couple of hours, I promise you.'

'Well, that's very kind of you, Prime Minister, but in fact I intended leaving this morning. There is work to do at home.'

'I shall still look into it. It's the principle.'

'Did you enjoy your Polish trip?'

'It was *marvellous*. Now I'll leave you to finish what you were saying. Good-bye!'

'Good-bye!'

He passed the phone back to the still-shocked presenter, who replaced it. 'Please continue,' she said. 'You were saying, you think women have rape fantasies?'

'Many women, not, of course, all,' said Surkov. 'Women know they have such fantasies. And it's perfectly healthy, it's a desire to be swept away, to fly away, out of this prison men have built, back to an ease about sex, back to the world of the witches. In my novel *Leningrad Awakes!* I describe a woman who grows up with a natural tolerance and sensual tenderness—she feels good about being a woman, having

doors opened for her, being seduced occasionally, seduc-
ing occasionally, and so on; but it's squeezed out of her bit
by bit.'

He lit a cigarette. A phantom hand placed a glass ashtray
on the coffee table in front of him. 'The fact that women have
these fantasies doesn't of course make it okay for some guy
to leap on them in a dark street or terrorise them in their
beds. Such guys need to be locked up and to have treatment.
But it's an additional reason for not taking a woman's word
on trust. Or a man's word, there's no difference. All of us—
men and women—very easily can come to believe that a
fiction is reality, and reality fiction: as my friends and I did
with this couple I told you about.'

He paused, leaning back, drawing thoughtfully on his
Marlboro.

'As for what happened to me—I think probably the woman
I was with wanted to seduce or be seduced, wanted to be
swept away, but then the other side of her, the male side,
got the better of her and said, "This is wrong, I shouldn't be
free, I'm in prison, so let's put this guy in an even tighter
prison." She wouldn't even be aware of it, she might even
be convinced I had raped her. I don't think it was deliberate
malice; she struck me as basically a nice person.'

The presenter waited. Surkov was silent.

'Victor Surkov, thank—'

'—But of course, these men building their rockets and prisons, or playing the stock markets, were largely raised in their
crucial years by women. On the other hand, they are women
who have grown up among men building prisons and rockets
and stock markets.'

He paused again, leaning forward to tip ash.

'Thank—'

'—It's like saying, who is to blame for your situation in
Ireland? The Catholic mama or the Protestant papa? All our
insolvable problems—the Jews and the Arabs, even Capital-
ism and Communism—are really war games for the basic

tension, which is between man and woman. I'd like to go into that more deeply, but I guess I must make room for the cat who's suckled a guinea-pig, yah? But it's a theme I've explored in *Leningrad Awakes!* and also my collection of poems, *Chorn'ie dni, biel'ie nochi—Black Days, White Nights*.'

'Victor Surkov, thank you.'

'It's been a pleasure.'

· 23 ·

It was the love-train, the home-along train; and therefore there was always a touch of melancholy mixed with pleasure. It was so on this cold, dark, drizzly November morning. Sergei and Masha—Victor was to be rushed from the TV studios to Heathrow—had felt it too, waiting for their taxi: *toska*, sad-sweet yearning; in old Cornish, a dead language, it was *hireth*. English has no single word for it.

The three-quarters-empty Inter City train moved past the Paddington slums, bleak walls covered with graffiti. The day was not properly dawning; the weather had turned, suddenly, from Indian summer to winter. I was sitting on my own, as was a glamourous redhead further up on the other side of the aisle. She reminded me of the redheaded student I had imagined making a pass at Charsky, outside the theatre. I wished I had had the courage to sit opposite her. She was reading a Mills & Boon romance. I watched her profile in the rainy window, and recalled Akhmatova: *Transparent profile through the carriage glass.*

Through the girl I touched a poet writing in 1940, and the friend, the beauty, she remembered sitting in a train in 1913.

Clear skies, Flaubert, insomnia, the lilac flowering late . . . That crystal world before the shattering of illusions and civilizations.

I opened *Psychological Correspondences* at the bookmark I had slipped in as the train drew in to Paddington, just over a week ago; started to read the letters of Anna Freud and Hilda Doolittle. But the fictions we had created were too close. Last night, Masha had simply been unable to draw our story to a satisfactory end, though she had gone on improvising into the early hours, beyond the point of exhaustion for all of us. For Surkov, due to go to the TV studios at an unearthly hour, there was almost no time for sleep. He lay down on his bed in his clothes.

They would, they said, try to finish the story on the flight home.

And I was to be the narrator. I wondered what parody of my voice they would create; and would it be any less 'true' to me than the voice I might have created for myself? Probably not; for after a few decades of life, wasn't everyone—driven by forces beyond his control—semi-fictional at best?

I skimmed the letters of Freud's daughter, written in Maresfield Gardens in the last year of his life. My eye chanced upon a paragraph in a letter of 30 September 1939: 'A dreadful day. All of them are, but today especially so. First came the news that the Nazis have occupied Warsaw; then, this afternoon, I had the painful duty of burning the last piece my father wrote. Every word of his is sacred to me, as you know, but this was made irrational by pain and morphia. You can imagine how I wept as the pages burned.'

I closed the book, lit a cigarette, and stared out, lulled by the sound and rhythm of the train.

The redhead had finished her romance, and she was putting headphones on. I did the same, after slotting in the tape of my Friday night impromptu. I wanted to hear how I sounded. Masha had complimented me, but Sergei and Victor had said nothing. Was it any good?

As Anna was saying good-bye to her husband, going off to work, I caught sight of a half-familiar figure stalking down the aisle behind a woman balancing a tray of snacks. He had a thick auburn beard, a barrel chest bursting out of a black waistcoat . . . Charsky! Seeing me, his fleshy lips parted in a smile. 'Good morning! May I?' He indicated the seat opposite. I stopped the recording, took off the headphones, and smiled back. 'Hello! Yes, do. This is a surprise.'

Slipping into the seat, he said, 'I saw you at Paddington; I thought you might be getting this train. I'm going to a seminar in computer viruses at Reading University.'

Hiding my relief that he was not travelling far, I asked him about the viruses and he tried to explain in layman's language; but it was still too difficult for me. 'Well, that's enough of talking shop,' he said. 'Did you watch Surkov's interview this morning? I missed it, unfortunately, but heard about it on the news—Thatcher's intervention. Extraordinary!'

I nodded. The whole interview had been extraordinary, I said, but one could hardly blame him for getting angry and emotional; he had had a terrible experience. Charsky responded with a sly smile. 'I wonder if he really has? Would it surprise you to know we've been expecting some big news story involving him all week?'

I frowned. 'How do you mean?'

'I can't go into details. I'm being indiscreet as it is. Put it this way: the piece in the *Sunday Times* is just what Gorbachev needs. You can be sure it'll be reported fully in the Soviet press. Something pretty dreadful almost happened a couple of months ago; I can't tell you what, but it seemed to show that reactionary forces in the Soviet Union would stop at nothing to destroy the reforms. Gorbachev has to put the wind up these people, but in a subtle way. Well, here's Surkov, an important writer, intimate of Raisa, hinting that Gorbachev might have to strike first—blood might have to flow, etc. The perfect medium . . .'

He smiled again; his eyes stared into mine. My brain was spinning.

'Miss Hayes-Drummond has helped the Soviets before,' he went on. 'She was quite radical at Cambridge; presumably a rebellion against her father.' As for Surkov, he had always helped the KGB; though he wasn't a bad fellow, and had probably done more good than harm. This time he was *against* the KGB.

'Are you saying there was no rape?'

He shook his head. 'He had a few uncomfortable hours with the police, and then he knew she would ring up and say she couldn't go through with it. There was no rape nor any suggestion of it. He went to her flat, they gave each other a few marks: *perhaps* they made love, to provide evidence of intercourse, but it's just as likely she went to bed with her boyfriend while Surkov composed the pieces for the *Sunday Times* and *News of the World*.'

'Jesus.' I grabbed my cigarettes, hesitated when he flinched, but went ahead when he gestured permissively. 'How do you know this?'

Charsky shrugged. 'We intercept a lot of traffic. But you only had to use your eyes in the Paddington bookstall. Why do you think his novel's suddenly appeared, in large quantities, when I haven't seen it in any bookshop for years? It's obvious Surkov tipped Penguin the wink that he was going to be in the news. This is Surkov's rake off for helping Gorbachev out—massive publicity. And the PM's contribution won't exactly hurt.'

I licked my dry lips, stared down at my hands. If Surkov had been acting, he had done so superbly; quite as well as Anna Charsky.

'Then there's rumour,' he continued. 'The French and German press have him down this morning as having tried to rape Princess Margaret. I imagine because she was mentioned in the *News of the World* story. His continental sales will soar too.'

'But why did there have to be a rape charge, from Gorbachev's standpoint?' I asked. 'He could have said those things anyway.'

'Gorbachev's enemies would have smelt a rat. It had to seem like a confidential exchange—pillow-talk, if you like—revealed by a vengeful reporter. It was cleverly done.' He glanced out at the drizzled murk. 'I knew we'd pay for that fine weather. We'll be glad to get home. We want the baby to be born in Israel.' He glanced at his watch. 'I'd better get back to my seat.' He rose, offered his hand. 'It's been good meeting you.'

I shook his hand, he eased himself out and strode off down the aisle. I stared into space for a long time, thinking of Charsky's revelations. The tired industrial wasteland of Reading arrived. I put on my headphones and restarted the Sony. A train whipped past us at high speed, heading for London. Charsky was in the bath, reflecting on his mother, as I waited for the other Charsky to walk down the platform, briefcase in hand, hunched against the blowing rain. But I didn't spot him in the seethe of activity.

The seethe of activity seemed to increase rather than diminish. Porters were running about. A rubicund guard rushed through our carriage at an asthmatic trot. The train did not move out, but lingered. I buried myself in the improvisation.

The train drew out at last, forty minutes late, and rumbled towards the West Country. Reaching the final words of my improvisations, I heard myself say I felt sick and must go to bed. Masha's compliment was less distinctly audible; there was the faint sound of footsteps and a closing door. I realised I'd neglected to switch off the recorder, and no one else had thought of doing so. I waited, with masochistic curiosity, for what they might say privately about my performance—which struck me, on hearing it, as not at all bad. I expected something negative, but was taken aback by the vehemence of Rozanov's outburst . . .

ROZANOV: What the fuck does he know about children of violence?

SURKOV: Oh, everything! He spent two weeks in our country!

MASHA: Well, I didn't think he did too badly. (*A yawn.*) I must go to bed too. Good-night.

SURKOV/ROZANOV: Good-night.

Door closing. Silence. A yawn.

ROZANOV: You've had a rough day, my friend! But thank God you're not in a police cell! Why don't you hit the sack?

SURKOV: Oh, I'm okay. At least I've been getting some sleep this week. I don't know how you've managed it, night after night. Whoever she is. It's none of my business. I just wonder how you've kept going.

ROZANOV: Thank you for not asking questions.

SURKOV: We're old friends. If you want to tell me, I'm ready to listen. If you don't—that's fine.

ROZANOV: I must have a pee.

Footsteps. A flush. Footsteps.

SURKOV: The inspector was a real bastard. He thought he had a cut-and-dried case. He wanted a confession. Women like Fiona Hayes-Drummond don't scream and weep unless they're genuinely distraught. The guy would have been a KGB interrogator under Stalin, and enjoyed every moment of it. Have another drink. You ready to get straight down to work when we get home?

ROZANOV: Can we really lick it into shape in just a couple of weeks? It's a mess.

SURKOV: No problem! Sonia can make us lots of cups of Earl Grey!

ROZANOV: If it doesn't work, they could surely bring out a volume of your poems?

Distant chimes of Big Ben.

SURKOV: Three o'clock . . . Shouldn't you be off on your assignation? . . . No, Abramsohn says it's got to be a novel if it's to be a big seller. As I haven't got one I can offer, he says a collaboration would be okay, my publishers would go for that; you know, East and West, it could be a good selling point.

ROZANOV: I wonder if we should have mentioned it when we spoke of revealing our collaboration.

SURKOV: Not till the book's in print. Which should be around New Year. He'd only bring up the fucking contract. Masha thinks he should be the narrator, by the way. It's time he got a little more involved—squirm a little.

ROZANOV: I'd go along with that.

SURKOV: If it does as well as my publishers expect, he ought to be damned pleased. . . . They'll want you in America too, Sergei. All of us.

ROZANOV: But suppose Dukakis loses?

SURKOV: He won't. But if he does, there's nothing lost; it can just come out in the usual way.

ROZANOV: Modestly. Like a silent fart.

SURKOV: We should have taken these books into our own hands long ago. It's partly my fault—I didn't want to spare the time from my own novel.

ROZANOV: How's it going?

SURKOV: Well, it's already immensely long, and I guess it won't be finished for another year. It's a pity I don't have it ready; on the other hand it would have embarrassed Dukakis. It's dynamite.

ROZANOV: You've kept it pretty close to your chest. What's the theme?

SURKOV: Religious mass-hysteria. It starts with civil war in Afghanistan, following our withdrawal; then the fighting spreads to the whole Middle East, and even into India. Muslims at war with Israelis and Hindus, Hindus with Sikhs. It's going to be enormously offensive to all religious freaks. Sikh soldiers gang-rape a Hindu girl in the holy temple at Amritsar; an ayatollah gets dropped, in little pieces, from a plane flying over Mecca. I'll still be pretty hot news, so the novel's bound to attract huge attention, and there'll be uproar. It could cost me my life. Well, we all have to die sometime.

ROZANOV: Death's not so unpleasant.

SURKOV: I was chafing to get back to it. But now I don't mind giving up a couple of weeks to this project, with you and Masha. It will be fun.

ROZANOV: (*after a pause; a sigh*): It's probably a good thing I'll be busy. It will help take my mind off—other things. I guess I'd better be open with you.

SURKOV: Only if you feel like it.

ROZANOV: Well, I could do with telling someone—

Lost in their conversation, at first I didn't feel the hand on my shoulder. Then I looked up and saw the rubicund guard, clipper at ready. I stopped the cassette and pulled off the headphones. 'Sorry!'

'There's no hurry, my 'andsome,' he said in a rich West Country accent. 'Quite a change in the weather.'

I glanced out. It was no longer a drizzle but swathes of sleet and hail, blanketing the peaceful fields. I found my ticket after a slight panic, rummaging through all my pockets and spilling out a mass of debris—credit cards, library ticket, video-shop membership card, driving licence, etc.

I asked him why we'd been delayed at Reading. He eased his bulk into the seat in front of me, his face mournful yet touched with excitement. 'We had an accident. A chap was killed. Stepped out of the wrong door and right under the 10.15 from Exeter. Poor bugger. He was some sight, you! Shook me up, I can tell 'ee!'

'Good grief! I don't wonder at it!'

'Foreign chap. Probably not used to our trains. It happens more times than you'd think. Not very old; well-built fellow; thick auburn beard.' He stroked his chin in illustration.

'My God! Charsky!' I exclaimed.

'That was the name! They found a credit card. You knew him, then?'

'Just slightly. But we were talking just before he got off the train.' My hand shook, lighting a cigarette.

He hauled himself to his feet. 'Well, that's how it do go. You're here one moment, and the next—'

He swayed off towards the redhead.

I stared into space, shocked. But quite swiftly the shock faded to a mild sympathy for the wife. The childbirth would be sad.

There was no point brooding on it. I put my headphones back on, remembering that Rozanov had seemed on the point of revealing who he had been sleeping with. I pressed the Start button.

ROZANOV:—It's embarrassing. You won't believe it. Who do you think I've been seeing?

SURKOV: Cita Lemminkaïnen?

ROZANOV: Maria Sanchez.

SURKOV: But she's ancient!

ROZANOV: I know! It doesn't seem to matter. Her eyes are young. Her spirit is young. I'm in love with her.

SURKOV: Jesus! I can see her power, I really can; but all the same . . . How did it start?

ROZANOV: It was very strange! At the reception—you remember we both went to the wrong one—she happened to say she suffered from insomnia and invariably wakes up at around four. That's when she does her writing. So I said I didn't expect to go to bed much before four, and maybe I should call on her for a nightcap. To my surprise she said, Yes, do that! Well, I had no thought of anything occurring, nor did she: she's never been unfaithful to her husband, and thought sex had gone forever. But when we were together, it just happened in the most natural way possible. And it was incredibly beautiful, Victor! She's the most amazing lover! I swear she fucks with her eyes! Yet she's recuperating from a bad illness, and has to rest every afternoon: God knows what she'd be like if she were well! She's as overcome by it as I am, but terrified there'll be a scandal. She's sworn me to absolute secrecy; so you must tell no one.

SURKOV: Of course not.

ROZANOV: I don't know how I shall cope when she leaves on Sunday. (*Sound of pacing.*) I've never felt like this about anyone, Victor. I feel we are soul-mates. But probably I shall never see her again. I find that thought unbearable. Love is worse than a *psikhushka*. I've even considered defecting and flying after her to Bolivia: finding a flat near her. But of course it's impossible.

SURKOV: It's amazing . . . You don't think . . . No, that's crazy.

ROZANOV: What?

SURKOV: Well, it's just something Márquez said. He's met her a couple of times, and he says she's entirely different on this trip; totally transformed; younger, much more animated. You might suggest it's because she's in love; yet he said it on the first evening. It's crazy, but I remembered that blonde typist you fell for in the Crimea last year; only she turned out to be Avavnuk, your spirit-wife, playing a trick on you. You don't think—?

ROZANOV: No. (*The pacing halts.*) No, I'm sure of it. In Yalta she gave herself away after a couple of days, by becoming angry, hitting me. Avavnuk can't hide her aggression for long. Maria's too gentle: oh, a few love-bites on my chin, but that's a different matter.

SURKOV: I just wondered. Has Avavnuk come to you this week?

ROZANOV: No. She's probably fucking some of her other husbands.

SURKOV: Or wives.

ROZANOV: Or wives. It won't stop her being angry and jealous—angrier even than Sonia, who's bound to find out.

SURKOV: Perhaps Maria could fly to Washington when we're there in January?

ROZANOV: That's a thought! But I doubt if—

The tape recorder clicked off.

Passing the headphoned redhead on the way to the buffet, I saw she had started on a paperback whose cover showed a tank surging through snow, a blood-covered young woman lying in its path: *Leningrad Awakes!* In a nonsmoking compartment a military-looking gentleman was also immersed in a virginal copy of it. I had never before seen anyone reading Surkov's novel. Someone else was reading the *Sun*, whose headline said MAGGIE MET RAUNCHY RED. Surkov leered up at me. I hovered for a moment, reading, 'Exclusive by Nick Smith.' I caught a few other words and phrases—'Thatcher . . . Cadogan Square . . . private messages from Gorbachev . . . Chelsea police station . . .'—but had to move on. The train was alive with the yellow-haired self-publicist. He would have a big bestseller on his hands, with a ten-year-old novel that Penguin must long ago have considered pulping.

I lurched back to my seat, spilling my coffee. A young man had a radio on, and I caught: '. . . *angry reactions from women's groups to an interview this morning on TV A.M., in which . . .*' The voice faded; emerged again to say '. . . *Mrs Mary Whitehouse called it a . . .*' Then the young man switched to a pop programme. I swayed on, doors sliding magically back.

As I neared the redhead she glanced up from her paperback and, while hearing inaudible music, gave me a look—the Russians call it *zloi*: sly, cunning, knowing.

Avavnuk!

No. Surely not. No such luck. Just a climax in the music, perhaps. She returned to her book.

The sleet and hail had turned to watery snow, flailing against the windows, and the railway embankments were coated with white. This was like Pushkin's *Devils*: like the *Eigernordwand*. Poor Kurz trying to free the rope, so near and yet so far. *'Ich cann nicht mehr!'* . . . 'Mistah Kurz—he dead!'

The snow brought a feeling of unreality. Had I only imagined I had been in the company of Sergei, Victor and Masha? Had I spent the entire week with Hauptmann and Lemminkaïnen, Legrand and Murphy, Kington Aimes and Douglas Parkin, Bromley, Brown and Davenport? Was I simply punch-drunk from spending too much time with brigands of the wood, political conspirators, and charlatans trading in elixirs and arsenic?

Sleepy from too-little sleep and the train's airless heat, I rested my head and closed my eyes. I was in an Alpine sanatorium, lying naked with Masha. She was terribly thin and pale. 'I've just heard I've got cancer,' she said in Russian.

'You're better off than I,' I responded in English. 'I'm an alcoholic and a junkie, my brain and liver are shot to pieces. Nothing can save me. Whereas you've been living a healthy, bracing life; once they remove the cancer you'll be really fit.'

She looked a little more cheerful; there was even a glow in her cheeks. 'Let's go skiing!' she suggested.

'Let's make love! Let's out-fuck Victor's fantasy!'

'I can't, I'm all bloody.'

'I don't mind.'

'I'm only your fantasy, your improvisation. We can lie together but that's all.'

My head slumping towards the aisle, I jerked awake and righted myself.

Snow whirled through semi-darkness. It reminded me of Chagall's painting of two lovers pressed close together in a snowy landscape, called *Between Darkness and Light*.

I opened my book again to Anna Freud's wartime letters. She described for her friend the siren sounding while she was in the West End; how she'd dived into an Underground shelter, and all the people there sang popular songs as the bombs were falling.

Now that London was far behind me, I could see it with affection through images of war. It is the only London I can love: the bombed-out streets; WAAFs in underground ops-rooms moving Battle of Britain squadrons around; Vera Lynn leading a theatre of servicemen in "We'll Meet Again" . . . And when the fragile victory came—young soldiers climbing the statue of Eros; girls in square-shouldered blouses and flared skirts kicking their legs in joy, arm in arm with American soldiers; Churchill and the tongue-tied king on the balcony of Buckingham Palace besieged by Londoners . . . Such images never failed to move me. I too was a child of violence.

I thought of Surkov's chilling tale of the nuclear sub that had aimed its missiles on London. The auburn-bearded, the late, Charsky had also hinted at it. There would have been no recovery from that blitz; no brave and cheerful firefighters, no singing in the shelters.

Masha had been clever in suggesting Ivan Sakulin as the crazed commander. A Russian convinced he had caught AIDS might well blame the West. Yet I was fearful for Anna. I hoped the sinister youth had hurled a lie in reprisal against Sakulin's rejection.

I was sure that was it. I closed the book and took a notebook and biro from my bag. I wanted to finish the story. The story of the living, fictional, indestructible Charskys. My version would never see the light of day, but what did that matter?

· 24 ·

Anna lay in bed, in *carezza* with Dmitri. They were half-attending to events on a small black-and-white TV, but Anna was reflecting on Sophie Stolz. A postscript to the correspondence, read while her husband had been making them some breakfast, summarized Sophie's later history. She had given birth to three daughters and six sons, some of whom had done well for themselves. Hermann Stolz, for example, had been a leading engineer with Krupps; Gottfried, an SS major, had distinguished himself on the Russian front in the Second World War; later, after a short spell of imprisonment for war crimes, he had risen high with BMW. One of his sons, a sociology professor at Princeton, had stumbled on his grandmother's correspondence with Krafft-Ebing while researching a book on Freud's precursors. He recalled his grandmother, a respectable old woman dressed in black, with a portrait of the Führer in every room. She had died peacefully in her bed on Kristallnacht.

There was a poem in it, Anna was thinking. An old German lady, who had once had masochistic fantasies, dying peacefully on Kristallnacht. It excited her. She would put aside *Yes, I remember the Stockhausen*; or abandon it even. This was a much more pregnant theme. The SS major would come into it; he had fought and killed outside Leningrad. Her mother, white-faced, spattered with blood . . .

Her thoughts broke off. The dull events on the TV screen had suddenly become interesting. In a reception hall at the Hermitage, Raisa Gorbachev was introducing Mrs Reagan to various artists: four or five men and one woman, the famous blind film director, Bella Kropotkin. Anna felt her husband—his breath warm at her nape, his thighs scissored between hers in *carezza*—become tense.

'Speak of the devil!' she said. 'She really is stunningly attractive, darling. I can't blame you.'

'She's a bitch,' Charsky hissed.

'Of course. A stunningly attractive bitch.'

'She must have known all the time I wasn't going to get the part.'

'That's true. But I don't believe you yielded to the casting couch, did you? I think you fell head-over-heels in love with her.'

She felt him swallow hard.

'Be honest,' she insisted. 'You fell for her.'

'I thought so,' he confessed.

'You're still dazzled by her. And who wouldn't be? You can see even Raisa and Nancy are dazzled. I don't mind. I think it's interesting you could tell me you were still in love with me, in the morning, and then the same night tell another woman you were in love with her. I'm sure you *did* tell her that. Didn't you?'

'Yes.' Was she a witch, this wife of his?

Charsky, in fact, had been stricken all over again by his powerful feelings for Bella. He had to blink back tears, and somehow give Anna the impression that he no longer felt anything. The tension actually produced a moment of poetic creation: a couple of rhyming lines, in which he reached out to Bella in passion, sprang into his mind with a childlike force. He wondered if they were any good. He thought perhaps they were. They moved him. Not since he had first met Anna, at a poetry reading with his brother, had he felt stirred to compose verses, trying to compete.

She ran her hand affectionately over his thigh. 'I really don't mind. I think if she clicked her fingers you'd go running to her again—wouldn't you?'

'No.'

'You're a liar, my dear. And she'll do it; she's that sort. You won't be able to resist, you'll fall again, and again I'll forgive you. Who could resist that splendid yellow mane, that opulent bust!'

'I'm sure she's padded her bra,' Charsky said in a painfully light tone. 'Her bosom actually isn't very big.'

'Well, you like looking at big breasts, but I doubt if you'd like them throttling you in bed.'

'You're right!' he said, surprised, stroking her breast gently. 'You know me so well.' The blind artist was speaking very intensely, and Mrs Reagan, her cheeks rouged, wore a fixed smile, pretending interest. 'Actually,' continued Charsky, 'Bella looks better on TV and in photos than she does in real life. Her face when you meet her is a bit gaunt and wrinkled.'

'Really? Oh, but she's marvellous!' She began to move in her husband's embrace. 'Darling, couldn't we try to get her and my toy-boy together, with us!'

His voice trembled at her ear. 'You want him—again?'

'Only if you could be there too.'

He began to move in rhythm with her. Bella and the group of Soviet artists had vanished from the screen; Raisa and Nancy were clasping hands, smiling into each other's eyes. 'Peace,' he murmured, 'and decency, our dream for so long, are going to be very hard to cope with.'

'Very hard. But the decency won't last,' she said with sudden appalled conviction. 'Our habit of suffering, our need to be abused, would have to turn inwards, and that would be unbearable.'

And do I even *want* it? she asked herself. There's a curious spiritual freedom in living under a dictatorship that wouldn't be possible in a so-called democracy. . . .

Charsky's eyes closed, he had a sudden vision of his mother's face, but noseless and hollowed into the shape of a cobra's hood. It became the Eiger's North Face, familiar to him from photographs. He saw himself trapped on that face. The nightmare vision passed.

'I hope you're wrong, Anna.'

'Well, maybe I am. Nothing's predictable. Who could have predicted this?'

For a moment she had a vision of perfect harmony; a sense that she was embracing not only Dmitri, but Freud, and Marie and Anastasia Romanov, and Sergei's father—his mother too—indeed, everything that had ever lived or would live.

She drew her husband into a kiss, and they began to move more urgently in the familiar embrace. His face buried against her hair, breathing its newly washed scent, he felt a sudden poignant desire for England. He smelt a sweet-scented wood. *Daffodils, That come before the swallow dares, and take The winds of March with beauty*. . . . England, where he had been so happy he had tried to commit suicide. There was to be a return visit to Stratford next spring, and there were hints that the leading actors might be able to take their wives. Maybe they should live there, far away from Bella. It was the one foreign country where he felt he could live. Leafy, free, beautiful England . . .

His reverie, in the rhythms of love, was shattered by the telephone's ringing. 'Leave it!' he murmured; but it went on ringing and at last she stretched to pick it up. Panting a little, she said, 'Yes?'

'Could I speak to Comrade Charsky?' It was Bella's drawling, condescending voice.

'Just a moment.'

Her heart fluttered as she handed him the phone.

'Hello.'

She felt him stiffen in her arms as the voice said, 'This is Bella Kropotkin.'

Charsky had to take a deep breath; his head was spinning. 'Oh, hello!' he said. 'Anna and I have just been watching you on TV.'

'I didn't want to leave Leningrad without speaking to you again. I was rather hard on you this morning. Well, I was put out; I thought, at the very least you could have phoned. But then, anyone could fall asleep after such an amazing performance. Truly, I was most impressed.'

She paused, waiting for Charsky to respond, but he was lost for words. She went on: 'I don't quite see you as Komarovsky. But there are other roles. I'm returning to Leningrad in about a month—I'm planning to hold some auditions—and I hope we can meet then? Perhaps have dinner?'

'I'm not sure.'

'Oh, please say yes!'

'Yes. All right.'

'Splendid! I'll be in touch.'

Anna took the phone from him and they lay quietly together. She touched him: 'You're still hard! Good! I want you in me again. . . . You see, what did I tell you, darling? "An amazing performance! I was most impressed"!' she mocked.

'How cold-blooded of her!' Charsky said, his heart full of rapture and anguish. He would see her again. 'How could she refer to it as a *performance*!' he said bitterly.

'She was referring to your theatrical performance. But of course she was being playful. She must have known I was close and could overhear her. She made it sound, for my benefit, as if she meant your Claudius, while knowing that you would take it in another way. She could hardly say, Your love-making was wonderful!'

'What did she mean, I could have phoned?'

'Did she say that?'

'Yes. I couldn't have rung her before I did—I was dead to the world. Why did she decide to go back to the hotel in the middle of the night? Well, it doesn't matter. She's a complete bitch.'

He thought, this pain—torn between them both—will be unbearable. It will be merely survival. An Icefield.

England . . . Yes, it must be England. . . .

They were silent, moving in harmony. Ripples of excitement ran through her. She murmured, panting: 'Yes, I'd like Bella, I'd like to watch you fuck her—and I know who I'd like to have in bed with us!'

'Ivan,' he groaned.

'Yes!'

'You *have* had him!'

'No, but I do find him sexy. You and I and Ivan and Bella . . . Let's try to arrange it, my dear!' As she pressed him into her more deeply than either of them would have thought possible, she recalled and murmured a phrase of the youthful Pushkin, addressed to a courtesan: *Grant me one night of rapture, of oblivion!*

It was beautiful, she thought later, as they lay at peace; but still it was not *impossible* enough. Where was the final rapture? What was the code for Vega?

· 25 ·

I slotted into my recorder a tape of Rachmaninov songs. *Do not sing to me again / Your songs of sad Georgia . . .* The lyrical, golden voice of Liubov Charents, Masha's lover and companion. I'd met her a couple of times when, performing in London, she had brought manuscripts from my collaborators. An unforgettable woman, built on gigantic proportions yet beautiful and magnetic. A lioness. She had slept with Shimon Barash as well as Masha.

The snow was falling more thickly. Though little past noon, the day was already quite dark. The lights from isolated cottages glimmered. I watched the whirling flakes and also the faint reflection of the redhead. She had removed her headphones and was knitting. She seemed aware of my glance. Those eyes, *zloi*, cunning, knowing. What had before seemed a wild surmise now struck me as more and more likely.

I stopped the music and took the headphones off. I would approach her. I would take my courage in my hands. I'd been cautious the whole fucking week, while my friends had engaged in passionate affairs, got arrested for rape, acted as mediums, resurrected the dead.

I slid into the seat opposite her. She glanced up from her knitting.

'Are you Avavnuk?' I asked.

Her dark, rather slanting eyes widened. For a moment she looked shaken. Then she smiled. 'I don't know how you found that out,' she said in pleasant standard English; 'but yes, I am.'

I took out my cigarettes and offered her one. Laying her knitting aside, she accepted.

'The snow must remind you of home.'

'Yes.'

'You've had an interesting week.'

She breathed out smoke. Her eyes danced. 'It's been immense fun. Death can be immense fun.'

I said, 'I've always thought they were Cold War enemies—death and life.'

'Yes, and there are things to be said for both sides. And against both sides. I can't quite get the sheer physical pleasure anymore. It makes me angry sometimes when I'm fucking.'

I asked her if that was why she became violent. As with Masha.

'Ah, so you know about that!' Partly, that was so, she replied. But also I must know that violence was in-built. The universe had begun with a massive explosion. But she, Avavnuk, had never harmed anyone.

'Tell me more about death.'

'Death is life's lover. They lie together.'

Though I pressed her, she would say no more.

'Why are you here—on this train?'

'An impulse. I follow my impulses.'

'Will you confess to Sergei—about Maria?'

'Oh, of course! I shall tease him!'

'Wasn't it rather cruel?'

'No, no!' She gave her red curls a vehement shake. 'I'm good for him, and good for his marriage. When he was married to Nina, you know how he was torn between her and Sonia. The struggle exhausted him. If he had a normal affair now, for any length of time, he would be destroyed. But on the other hand, without passion he would wither away. He can do nothing about me, I come and go like the wind; I give him what he needs, without guilt.'

I asked, 'How will Maria Sanchez remember the Festival?'

'Oh, as after a fever; something between amnesia and a dream. Just like this girl'—she put her hands to her breasts—'who's visiting her mother in Penzance. I gave the old lady a good time. She'll think she went slightly crazy. She will have a lot to confess.'

I said on impulse: 'And were you Thatcher in Cadogan Square?'

She smiled, and murmured, 'Believe me, Victor does not write his best signature in white ink! He's okay, though. He gives almost all his earnings to the summer camps, where children learn the truth about Stalinism.'

'I didn't know that.'

'No one does.' She picked up her knitting and restarted. It looked like a baby's jacket, blue.

'I would like a spirit-wife,' I said. 'Will you come to me sometimes?'

'How do you know I haven't come already?' Her lips curled joyously. 'It was a pretty boring film.'

'Jesus!'

There had been an incident in a cinema. A momentary yielding to temptation, under encouragement as I had thought; a brushed shoulder, parted knees, a skirt ridden high; a slapped face. Nothing of any relevance to this story.

'But that was just a diversion. I really can't say if I'll come to you properly, or if we can meet in the next few days. I don't see my mother very often.'

She turned the conversation back to the Festival and my Russian friends. She confirmed what the tape had already hinted: they planned to publish our novel in time for the Dukakis Inaugural. Absurd! I said; and, though their energy was admirable, they would find that a novel based on our improvisations would take at least as long as a pregnancy.

This girl is pregnant, she said. Just a few weeks. She is disturbed, and wants to talk to her mother about it. She would like to bear the child, but only if her mother will look after it. There is a spirit here (her hand going to her stomach) who hovers between life and death.

A blurred voice told us the buffet would close at Plymouth. I asked her if she would like a coffee and a sandwich. That would be nice, she said.

I went down the train. A long queue had formed. I was still waiting to be served as Plymouth's urban sprawl, with house lights gleaming, appeared in the gloom. The train was drawing into the station as I struggled back, swaying away from passengers and cases, my plastic tray awash.

Drawing close to Avavnuk, I saw it was not she anymore. Knitting, she glanced at me with dull, blank, uninterested eyes. I paused near her; but very clearly she was just a girl, a pregnant girl, visiting her mother in Penzance. She glanced down at Surkov's book with a distant, slightly puzzled, air. I stumbled on to my seat, put down the awash tray, and gazed out at the rushing travellers, the swirling flakes. I plucked the lid off a coffee, and picked up *Psychological Correspondences*, but my mind was still on Avavnuk. I imagined her appearing, at this instant, to Rozanov; perhaps as he rested after his journey; while Sonia moved around downstairs preparing a meal, with a faint rattling of dishes.

But no—impossible—they had not yet landed. They would be somewhere over White Russia or Lithuania; I saw them huddled together, they just couldn't think how to end the novel; Rozanov was saying, 'This is absurd; there must be a very simple resolution. Let's imagine . . . Let's imagine . . .'

Bella Kropotkin, approaching wearily her seventh audition of the day, found herself being tightly embraced by the actor Charsky, and devoured with kisses. After the initial shock she warmed to his unorthodox technique, this playing of a role to impress her with his dramatic prowess—the role of someone resuming an intimate acquaintance; and she entered into the spirit of it, confessing the sleepless nights she had spent in the fires of longing . . .

FOR THE BEST IN PAPERBACKS, LOOK FOR THE

In every corner of the world, on every subject under the sun, Penguin represents quality and variety—the very best in publishing today.

For complete information about books available from Penguin—including Pelicans, Puffins, Peregrines, and Penguin Classics—and how to order them, write to us at the appropriate address below. Please note that for copyright reasons the selection of books varies from country to country.

In the United Kingdom: For a complete list of books available from Penguin in the U.K., please write to *Dept E.P., Penguin Books Ltd, Harmondsworth, Middlesex, UB7 0DA*.

In the United States: For a complete list of books available from Penguin in the U.S., please write to *Dept BA, Penguin*, Box 120, Bergenfield, New Jersey 07621-0120.

In Canada: For a complete list of books available from Penguin in Canada, please write to *Penguin Books Ltd, 2801 John Street, Markham, Ontario L3R 1B4*.

In Australia: For a complete list of books available from Penguin in Australia, please write to the *Marketing Department, Penguin Books Ltd, P.O. Box 257, Ringwood, Victoria 3134*.

In New Zealand: For a complete list of books available from Penguin in New Zealand, please write to the *Marketing Department, Penguin Books (NZ) Ltd, Private Bag, Takapuna, Auckland 9*.

In India: For a complete list of books available from Penguin, please write to *Penguin Overseas Ltd, 706 Eros Apartments, 56 Nehru Place, New Delhi, 110019*.

In Holland: For a complete list of books available from Penguin in Holland, please write to *Penguin Books Nederland B.V., Postbus 195, NL-1380AD Weesp, Netherlands*.

In Germany: For a complete list of books available from Penguin, please write to *Penguin Books Ltd, Friedrichstrasse 10-12, D-6000 Frankfurt Main 1, Federal Republic of Germany*.

In Spain: For a complete list of books available from Penguin in Spain, please write to *Longman, Penguin España, Calle San Nicolas 15, E-28013 Madrid, Spain*.

In Japan: For a complete list of books available from Penguin in Japan, please write to *Longman Penguin Japan Co Ltd, Yamaguchi Building, 2-12-9 Kanda Jimbocho, Chiyoda-Ku, Tokyo 101, Japan*.